RECURSION

DAVID J HARRISON

The Book Guild Ltd

First published in Great Britain in 2021 by
The Book Guild Ltd
9 Priory Business Park
Wistow Road, Kibworth
Leicestershire, LE8 0RX
Freephone: 0800 999 2982
www.bookguild.co.uk
Email: info@bookguild.co.uk
Twitter: @bookguild

Typeset in 10.5pt Minion Pro

Printed on FSC accredited paper
Printed and bound in Great Britain by 4edge Limited

ISBN 978 1913913 489

British Library Cataloguing in Publication Data.
A catalogue record for this book is available from the British Library.

For Vicki

PRELUDE

RITUAL

As far as Haruki Kensagi was concerned, the Captain didn't need to say anything twice. His words were precious. And the congregation cherished every one of them.

'With my voice I am calling to you.' The Captain's words hung over the crowd, they drifted slowly along the hillside and ambled through the valley. The atmosphere was still and bated.

Haruki shuffled uncomfortably where he stood. He had been there a while now and was feeling the tension in his body. He would have liked to have put his hands on the small of his back and push out his hips. He would have liked to stretch out the growing pain at his lumbar region. But he dared not move. He didn't want to draw attention to himself any more than was necessary. He still felt like an outsider, even though he knew that this was the inner circle.

He'd been chosen for this. That's how the Captain had put it. And that's how the other villagers saw it too. They looked annoyed when Haruki took centre stage in his attentions. They were clearly jealous. They muttered darkly to each other as he passed them.

But to his face they were open and welcoming. In fact each of those he'd met so far had intimated that something momentous was going to happen tonight. Haruki didn't see that he had any choice but to wait and see. Besides, there was no denying that the Captain had captured his attention.

Behind him was the dramatic slope of the hill the locals knew as 'Noonday Sun'. Haruki and the others were gathered on its sister, 'Midnight Moon'. From the position and colour of the sun, Haruki guessed the time to be six in the evening. The grasses that furred the slopes shone bright amber as the light raged hard against the oncoming evening.

The sunset echoed the colour of the Captain's skin. He was one of those men whom time didn't seem to touch. He'd been around a bit, Haruki had heard. Maggie said that he'd fought the Argentinians at Goose Green. But that was forty years ago and now he didn't look a day over forty. His skin still held the taut elasticity of youth and his eyes were wide, bright and strangely symmetrical.

That was one of the first things Haruki had noticed. Most faces he painted were flawed in one way or another. He was an artist; he understood the inconsistencies of the human form, which was inherently asymmetrical. Some faces were born like that and others became this way through use, wear and tear. Muscles on one side didn't perfectly translate to the other. They were tightened by expression. Loosened by sleep.

But the Captain didn't seem to have the same flaws. It was as if he came out of a different mould. A perfect mould.

His golden hair was loosely tied at the back of his head into a bun with a bright blue ribbon. Haruki paid attention to his colours. It was the same blue as the colour of the tarpaulin he'd found at the bottom of his pit.

And the Captain's eyes were the colour of the pit itself. Dark and deep, but looking more closely he saw they were ringed with silver.

Haruki had eventually climbed out of the pit, but it seemed to him that it was harder to escape the Captain's dark and bottomless stare.

He wore jeans that accentuated his slim frame and his denim shirt was open almost to the naval. A rosary hung around his neck. Christ dangled between his pectorals.

'I call each and every one of you. But only one will answer.'

One did answer. A lovely young woman stepped forward. She had braided blonde hair and wore a white cotton dress. 'I answer you with my voice,' the girl said. It was Judy. Haruki recognised her from the day before.

'Why have you come?' the Captain said.

'I seek the truth,' Judy said, 'and to put an end to the lie.'

'Which lie?' His voice was loud and theatrical. It had that resonant quality you only hear from trained performers. There was something distinctly Shakespearean about this performance.

'The beautiful lie. The falsehood of living.'

'You want the painful truth? The sincerity of death?' His voice rose into an irresistible crescendo as he chanted these words. He could have been in church, reading from the gospel.

'I do,' Judy said. Then she faced the congregation. They were almost licking their lips in anticipation. 'Who will bear me into the honesty of the dark?' Her voice rang out like a dropped bell.

Another stepped forward. Haruki recognised her too. It was Maggie, Judy's sister. She stepped forward and as she walked by, she said, 'It's all right, she has something inside her that needs to come out.' Maggie walked out to them and faced Judy. She acted with the confidence of someone who had done this before. Like it was a well-worn ritual. 'I will take you home,' she said.

Was that it? Would Maggie now lead Judy away, back down the hill into the village and home to the little cottage they shared? But then Maggie stepped around the back of Judy and grasped her arms at her elbows. She held them back behind her body. Then the Captain stepped forward and hugged Judy. He kissed her on the lips.

Judy gasped. Her eyes fixed on something in the distance.

Haruki didn't see the knife until the Captain stepped back. Judy's front was red and wet and it was spreading across her white dress. Her face was frozen in surprise, her mouth open and her eyes wide.

Blood poured down her front like water from a tap, and though she tried her best to stand straight, she staggered and rolled like a new-born calf. At the point her legs gave way Maggie caught her before she hit the ground.

Dragging her away by her shoulders, Maggie took her down the hill towards the village and the Captain resumed his sermon as if nothing had happened. Haruki wanted to move. He wanted to go to Maggie but couldn't. Instead he listened to him speak about 'God's' work, or the 'good' work. His mind was doing somersaults. It was looping too fast to concentrate. It was everywhere at once, but his body remained rooted with fear, and curiosity.

'I have called you here with my voice,' the Captain said.

'With your voice you have called us,' the congregation repeated.

'But we also call Him. He comes tonight,' the Captain said.

'We cannot let Him,' the others chanted.

'So, will you dig for me, my brothers and sisters? Will you dig for Him?'

'We will. We will dig.'

Shovels appeared in the Captain's hands and he distributed them as he walked among the gathering. When it was Haruki's turn to accept, the Captain pierced him with his gaze. 'Haruki. Will you dig for me?' Haruki nodded but he didn't know why.

The Captain thrust the spade into his hands. He hefted the implement before thrusting it hard into the softly yielding earth. He felt the brush of a hand at his shoulder. From close behind him came the Captain's whispered words. The whiff of vanilla came to him. It was the Captain's scent.

'It was this way with Judy. You have to make the cut,' the Captain said, his hand suddenly at Haruki's middle. His hard body pressed firmly at Haruki's back. He could feel the man's fingers explore his stomach through his thin shirt. 'You have to thrust it deep. Use your diaphragm. Put your foot on it.' Haruki nodded, and his discomfort at being singled out was matched only by his sense of disappointment when the Captain moved on to the next person.

He pressed his body weight down through his foot and into the spade. He was transported back to his home in London. To the little garden that he'd once shared with his wife Jane. He'd put on boots and a waxed raincoat that night and headed out into the field. Past the tall willow herb that had overgrown around the fringes and into the centre where he'd found her digging. She was already four feet down when he joined her in the pit. Together they wordlessly heaved their spades, shoulders rounded, backs to the moon.

Today Haruki dug for the Captain. He was always digging in some way and perhaps this was why he had been chosen. He dug with his brushes.

But the Captain required no such finesse. No such artistry. No such search for truth and beauty, or whatever else Haruki like to pretend was behind his calling. Today the Captain simply required him to dig.

So, he dug.

Haruki stood, spade in hand. He'd finished a little after the others but that was okay. His pit was the largest, and the deepest. And the edges were straight, almost as if a dozer had come up the hill and gouged the deep channel into the hillside. He looked around at the others; there was no pattern to where the other pits lay dotted around. None that he could see anyway. His was a six-by-six square, neat sides patted smooth by his spade and smothered with his hands. The others' pits were jagged, haphazard or if neater, then thinner. Like graves.

He shivered as a line of sweat ran down his back. Without the energy of the digging to sustain him, he was suddenly cold. He felt like shivering but doubted he had the stamina left even for that.

The Captain was among them again. He hugged and kissed his way through the congregation until he came to Haruki. There were seven pits in total. The Captain needed seven pits, though for what, Haruki could only guess.

'You've done good work,' the Captain said, taking Haruki's hand in his. 'Very good work. I knew you wouldn't disappoint me.'

Haruki beamed, suddenly warm again. He wanted to be closer to the Captain; he wanted the same embrace he'd given the others. The damp, turned earth filled Haruki's nostrils, but underneath all that, the Captain's vanilla scent stood out. He held Haruki's hands firmly in his. 'You want to say something, Haruki?'

'What are they for?'

'For Him,' the Captain said, 'and for you.'

He took both hands from Haruki's and used them to indicate for Haruki to descend into his own pit. Haruki watched the others dutifully obey. Some jumped right in with both feet; others, who might have had deeper pits, lowered themselves more gingerly until they could no longer be seen from the grassy surface of the hill. The sunlight on Noonday Sun had faded and the moon began to spill its light onto Midnight Moon. Haruki lowered himself into the pit and lay down on his back diagonally across his square in the earth. He saw the Captain look down on him, smile and turn away.

Above him, the moon wasn't directly visible, but its light reached a little way into the pit. On one wall he watched the moon shadow shorten and recede. Then it faded away completely, leaving only the light of the stars.

The more he stared at the stars, the more he saw. He found

that he wasn't just looking at them; he watched them. But the ones he isolated for direct scrutiny were the ones that eluded his sight. Once he looked directly at a star, it faded from view and only came back when he shifted his gaze. The stars wanted to be seen in unison. They were a collective, refusing to be singled out and divided. Haruki's brushes would have difficulty with these. But given such a background, what a portrait he would be able to paint. At first the stars were white pinpricks set into a midnight blue backcloth. But then his eye began to pick out colours from the space between. A purple wash streaked across the night sky. Reds and greens presented themselves in and around the planets. For the nebula and gas clouds, a swirl of pink and white that adjusted itself growing deeper and lighter, pulsating with each breath Haruki took.

He was aware that his breathing had slowed. He felt weaker than before, his eyes hooded over with tiredness. And at the edges of his sight, a creeping kaleidoscope of colour, crawling across the night sky.

Haruki woke to see the Captain and many others looming over him. He stood and brushed himself down, feeling abashed at the attention. How long had he slept? Two, three hours? The sky was brightening, so perhaps all night. The Captain helped him out of the pit and took him into a tight hug. 'You did it,' he whispered. 'We did it.'

Haruki recognised Maggie behind the Captain and, incredibly, her sister Judy. Judy held on tight to the shovel and almost seemed to be leaning on it for support. She smiled at Haruki, her white blouse unsullied by the digging, unblemished by the Captain's knife. Then others passed in front of him and he lost sight of her.

Spades in hand, wordlessly, they trudged down the hill towards the village. Closer to the settlement, people lined the path. The villagers had turned out for them and nodded their gratitude. Some held chains of flowers, daisies and primroses.

Some scattered flowers or scented wood shavings at their feet. And at the end of the line, closest to the village, Judy sat on a stool, supported by Maggie. They smiled at him.

'Thank you,' Judy said, her voice thin and weak.

'I didn't do anything,' Haruki said.

'Yes, you did.' Maggie laid a hand on his shoulder. 'We all did. And you are one of us now.'

PART ONE

HARUKI

BEFORE?

KIREJI

The palette wasn't working for him, so he washed it out and started again from scratch. Globs of oil paint splattered on the metal bottom of the sink. The oil was unable to mix with the water, so as the liquid drained, the lumps of colour lay beached. He wiped the sink with the flat of his palm, hoping to push the paint towards the plug hole, but he succeeded only in covering his hand with wet viscous stains. It was a surprisingly pleasant mix of colour that looked better on his fingers than it had on the artist's palette. He twisted his hand around and around, admiring it in the morning sunshine that fell through the kitchen window. This hand was the only decent thing that Haruki Kensagi had been able to paint for a while.

Jane had left him at the beginning of the year and since then his only solace was the fact that he could make as much mess as he liked. She wasn't there to admonish him for leaving paint splatters around the sides of the sink. And she wasn't on hand to chide him for playing the wasted colours through his hands, as he did now, letting the best part of a whole tube slip through his fingers. He could even leave the sink unwashed if he wanted to.

He had often imagined Jane coming back to him. From time to time he still found himself glancing towards the doorway imagining he saw her lovely face illuminated by the daylight, her rich, dark skin made more luminous, honeyed by the sunshine.

Regularly, he heard the scraping of her shoes on the front path, or the quiet roll of her electric car on the driveway. Only to find it was a neighbour, or delivery driver. Other times he would mistake his own coat draped on the balustrade, for hers. He would run like an excited child into living room and expect to see her watching television or reading a book. He found himself having to remember time and time again that she wasn't with him any longer and that this time, she wouldn't be coming back.

He still hadn't got used to the silence and stillness of the house. Though it had been several months now. He had accepted for a long time that she no longer loved him. He only had himself to blame, having spent too much time with his brushes. She had said that over the years that he'd become distracted and withdrawn. That was probably true. And if Jane thought so, then it must have been true. She was always right about everything. She was one of those people whose instincts could be trusted. So, if she stayed away, it was probably for the best.

But what he couldn't accept yet was the small details of her absence. Her old armchair retained her shape. It sagged in the middle just in the right place. It looked as if it missed her as much as Haruki did. And if he didn't look directly at the chair, he could almost see her sat there. Hers was a nagging absence. Their house was imbued with her presence. Every part of it reminded him of her. If he opened the bedroom door, he would expect to see her lying on the bed. Her perfume still lingered too keenly on the pillow at her side of the bed. He really should throw it away. He had already removed all of her bottles and tubes and bars of soap, but still her scent persisted, no matter how much he cleaned and scrubbed.

Undoubtedly, this was why he was having trouble painting. His art was a reflection of himself. But he no longer knew who he was. Without Jane, he didn't know what he was.

Haruki tried to scrape the dried layers of remaining colour off his palette using an old brush that had grown stiff with disuse. As he pried open the skin of old dried paint, it came away peeling like a scab from a re-opened wound. Behind it the raw glisten of new colour.

It should have been long since replaced but he couldn't consider getting a new palette board. If he replaced that, there would be no continuity, no link between those paintings he'd had accepted for display at the Tate and the Scottish National and these new pieces. Brushes, paint, pencil, canvas. All these would be replaced in the course of time and activity. But not his old palette board. It had been with him since the beginning. It was as important to his process as Haruki was himself. Without his old board, whatever he painted wouldn't be any good. It wouldn't be art.

For him, art was about relationships. The relationship between Haruki and his materials. Between his brush and the canvas. And most importantly between the subject of the portrait and himself, the artist. When he painted, something had to pass through those things. Something had to fill the space in between them. Haruki didn't know what that something was, except that he felt always that there was some kind of tension that needed to be resolved. A question needing an answer. Whatever it was, he recognised it when it was there. And he felt its absence when it wasn't.

He no longer painted portraits. This was a promise to Jane. The process was too intimate. It was unsettling how close Haruki came to his subjects. He revealed too much about himself in the process. He left himself too vulnerable. He opened up too wide; it felt like he was merging a part of his mind to theirs. These were not affairs in the classical sense and rarely involved sex. They were far more intimate than that.

When the palette board was relatively clean, he left it in the airing cupboard to dry. A third of a kilo of seasoned and oiled beech wood would take a while to dry out before it could be used. So, he started to prepare lunch.

In the kitchen Haruki took his chef's knife from a bamboo box that he kept on the windowsill. Years ago he'd invested in a Shun Premier. Eight inches of super-hard steel, sandwiched between thirty-two layers of softer steel to create a patterned Damascus blade. The sixteen layers of softer steel on each side protected the hard but brittle core and allowed the knife to flex whilst also retaining its sharpness. He rotated the knife in his hands as he was accustomed to doing before using it. He hefted its weight. He held it up to the light and traced the waves of folded steel as the light caught it on the broad side of the blade. He thought about the photons that bounced off the steel and into his retina. In that sense he could feel this knife, even without touching it.

It would slice through just about anything. It would separate one thing from another with cold indifference. It didn't care what or why. It just cut. That was its single, uncomplicated purpose and it did it very well. The knife was like how Haruki himself wanted to be. He wanted one single purpose. To paint. He did not want distractions.

Haruki unwrapped a block of tofu and placed it carefully on the chopping board. Then he dabbed it with a square of kitchen towel to remove the excess moisture. He took care that the silky, delicate substance didn't break apart. The knife hovered. He allowed it to feel where to cut. He trusted it to make that decision for itself.

After a moment's hesitation, the blade plunged down. Haruki was a bystander and he watched it part the milky-white substance. He felt no resistance from the tofu. The blade was too sharp and the tofu soft. The knife separated the block with clean geometric lines. Two perfect cuts one way, then two the other way until he had nine smaller blocks of identical size and shape. Each was separated from the other by only a hairline crack. A distance so small, yet irreparable.

From the cupboard Haruki took a jar of white miso paste and spooned some of it into a mixing bowl. To that he added a dash of mirin; the honeyed liquid oozed over the lump of paste. He then used a small dessert fork to stir vigorously until the mixture was a smooth gloss. With the Shun Premier he scooped up the divided block of tofu and placed it in the centre of an earthenware plate that he'd specially selected. Then he upended the mixing bowl to drizzle the contents over the tofu.

He rinsed the knife before slicing a lemon on the cutting board. Haruki could no more feel the blade cut into the lemon's rind as he could the tofu. A squeeze of lemon and his meal was complete. He placed in on a white lacquered tray together with a glass of chilled Chinese yellow rice wine. Lastly, he added a fine pair of aluminium chopsticks on the side. But instead of eating it, Haruki took the tray into his studio and placed it under the window. Light streamed down and made the mirin sauce glisten.

Haruki squeezed out a tube of titanium white and placed dollops all over the palette. He added some yellow and the subtlest a hint of green and then he mixed them to form several shades and hues that he thought reflected the still life in front of him. Now his palette was complete, he could begin to paint.

The phrase 'still life' had never agreed with Haruki. Nothing was ever truly still. It was his role as the artist to bring out the life and the movement in a piece. For Haruki, all things were imbued with potential energy. If the chopsticks fell from the plate, they would explode in a clatter of sounds and movement. If the tofu was not handled just right or if the knife was not super sharp, it would break apart, perhaps even fall from the plate or cutting block and land on the floor. If this happened it would splatter against the carpet and require some considerable effort to clean up. When ingested, the mirin sauce would provoke chemical reactions within the human body. It would elicit a taste response that would send neurons spiralling in a kaleidoscopic pattern of electricity around his brain. Everything had a cause and a consequence. Everything contained both of these within it. Everything in the universe had this future potential and it was this that Haruki had to capture when he painted. If he failed to represent these things, then Haruki had no business taking up the brush.

He held the brush over the palette and waited for it to find how and where to start. He stared at the canvas and at the tofu. His mouth watered but he found no inspiration. After time, Haruki selected a colour, titanium white mixed with Naples yellow. He allowed the brush to hover over the canvas. But there it remained. He thought of Jane. If she were watching, she'd have no cause for complaint that instead of establishing a close relationship with the subject of his portrait, he was instead attempting to paint his lunch.

Another thought came to Haruki.

Unable to paint,
Brush hovers over canvas.
The pit of despair.

A good haiku cuts as well as any Shun Premier. The poem's *kireji*, the cutting word, separates the three phrases perfectly. Often the *kireji* is an exclamation or is simply silent, left unsaid but observed all the same. If placed at the end of the haiku a good *kireji* can bring the reader back to the beginning in a circular pattern, but if placed elsewhere in the verse it performs the dual act of both cutting and joining. The *kireji* becomes a paradox.

What was the *kireji* in his haiku?

Haruki didn't know. He'd had enough for one day. He went for a walk.

Outside, the garden was raging with life. Furtive blackbirds hopped in and out of the bushes, chasing bugs that fluttered amongst the undergrowth or tracking down lone seeds that lay shining like jewels on the lawn. The gardener came once a week to cut the grass, but Haruki wouldn't let him touch the bushes until late summer, when the birds had finished with their nests. A baby blue tit shivered and shrieked with insistence as its parent fed it beak-to-beak. It looked like it had just fledged, with its cotton-wool head and soft body.

Dandelion seeds drifted across his path as Haruki headed out the bottom of his garden and into the wide field beyond. It was a fallow year. Before that it was barley and before that wheat. Haruki and Jane used to count the years by what crop was growing, and what wildlife made their homes amongst the growth. With the cereals came yellow wagtails and harvest mice. They in turn enticed stoats and weasels out of the woods on raiding parties, searching for nests and holes. They used to sit at the bottom of the garden with binoculars and they'd watch the little bandits return home, wet-mouthed from the eggs at springtime. During the summer months they would catch fledglings and break them between their sharp teeth before trotting back to their own young.

The two chairs were still there but were now overgrown with detritus. Leaf litter and bird mess covered them.

The field was fast becoming a meadow as he wandered to its middle through high stalks of grass already going to seed, and amongst cornflower, and oxeyes, and the many other flowers that Haruki had no names for. He ambled between the high willow herb with their violet heads and distinctive paradoxical smell. In equal measures of sweet perfume and earthy decay.

The willow herb obscured much from sight, which was why Haruki didn't notice the pit until he almost fell into it. It gaped, right in the centre of the fallow field. A twelve-by-twelve-metre excavation of dank earth. Freshly gouged from its verdant surroundings. The sides were smooth but precise, as if mechanically dug with heavy machinery. Though there were no tracks, no flattened grass except the little narrow path that he had made getting here. And he hadn't heard any diggers operating recently. The bottom seemed deeper because of the rich dark loam that it was cut into. The black soil made it difficult to see the bottom, though Haruki guessed it was only six feet or so below the surface.

The pit could have been a paradox, or a metaphor, or a *kireji*. Haruki didn't know which, or he didn't care. He just knew that he wanted to paint it. He wanted to explore it because he was drawn to its severe incongruity amongst all these wildflowers.

Haruki hurried back to the house and by the time he made it into the studio, he was dripping with sweat. He grabbed his easel, the blank canvas, his box of paints and, of course, his old palette, which he wiped with a roll of tissue paper until it was clean of all the whites and beiges he'd wasted on it earlier. The long grass swished behind him as he scythed through with his paraphernalia. The trailing leg of his easel took off the heads of several flowers. Heads that would grow back.

Haruki's arms ached from carrying his gear, the easel in particular. And the heavy paint box had dug into his hands to the extent that the depressions of the handle lingered on the inside of his fingers long after he had set it down. It made his fingers an odd shape. Flat and white, like they didn't belong to him. He erected the easel and placed his canvas on it. He squeezed the colours out of the palette. Mostly greens and browns this time, and black. But he also selected crimson for the field poppies, yellow for the St John's wort, violet for the willow herb. He immediately felt a sense of assured calm and confidence. He took as a very good sign of things to come the fact that he was able to use so many colours. His eye was in.

Haruki allowed the paintbrush to hover over the palette.

He felt nothing, but he didn't panic. It was often this way. Sometimes it took a while. It would come. He closed his eyes. Then it was as if the hand holding the brush felt heavier. It was almost imperceptible, but he immediately recognised the familiar feeling. The brush was divining its purpose. Just like his knife had known how to cut the tofu, the brush knew where to apply the paint. And though Haruki had revelled in all of the bright colours that he thought he might need, he wasn't surprised when his hand went directly for the darks.

The brush scooped up brown madder and smeared it across an inch of bare palette, then the tip picked up some raw sienna, the burnt sienna, and then he really surprised himself by selecting a flash of cadmium green pale. He used a figure of eight to half-mix the paints, leaving streaks abundant on the head of the brush. Then he started to apply the paint onto the blank canvas.

His style was confident, sweeping brushstrokes. It was his hallmark. But instead, he stabbed at the canvas, thrusting more and more paint on top, later after layer. He used the brush like it was a palette knife, pressing with a short, staccato motions. First one way, then another. Then on the bias, so that the canvas was a checkerboard of texture and rich, dark colour. This built up over the course of a half hour's furious activity. He thought it the most exhilarating session he'd ever had. He simply had to lean back and allow his hands free motion over the canvas. Free will over the colour and texture.

After a while something made him stop. Dripping with sweat and heaving from exertion, he set down his brush and shook the cramp from his arms. Stepping away from the painting, he could see immediately that it was a masterpiece.

He could feel the connection between himself and the pit. It was a hole, a void. It was an empty space full of nothing. And yet right then it was everything to him. And he recognised the irony in this. Recently, he'd succeeded in painting nothing. But now in painting 'nothing', he had filled the canvas with paint. He'd just filled the last half hour with enjoyment. And because of this he'd filled himself with happiness, and relief. He'd painted an empty space, but he'd filled it. He'd filled it with colour. He'd filled it with texture. He'd put everything he had into it.

And when Haruki stepped back to look at the painting, it became imbued with a life all of its own. When he was in the act of painting, he felt intimately connected with the artwork. He felt every squash and squelch of the oil, the coarse texture of the canvas, and the round stiffness of the brush. But now he'd stepped away, the distance between himself and the painting, though small, felt irreparable. Once he had separated himself from the painting. Once he looked at it from a distance. It was as if he hadn't had anything to do with it at all. It was thing, in and of itself.

His mind switched to practical matters. He wondered how he was going to get it back to the house without smearing the wet paint. Oil paints can take hours to dry, but because he'd used so much and applied it so thickly, this one might take days before it could be handled safely.

A dandelion seed drifted across him and landed on the sticky canvas, just to the right of centre. It struggled there a while, stuck by its seed head. The slightest of contact with the paint. He waited for a breeze to lift it once more on its fecund journey. Its feathery head fluttered minutely, but instead of lifting itself off the paint, it fell flat and stuck completely. The little dab of white pulled the observers' eye away from the depth of the image and spoilt everything. Whatever spell he'd managed to conjure and capture within the artwork was compromised by this tiny speck of nature.

Haruki looked closely at the image. He reached into his paint box and took out a scalpel. He held it over the little seed and as was his custom, he allowed the blade to decide when and where to make the incision that would return the painting to its former state of perfection. It dipped its head and inserted its sharp point under the seed.

But it went too far. The scalpel lifted off more of the slick brown madder than it should have done. And the curious thing was that under that earthy layer of paint was a shock of bright blue. A blue that he hadn't selected on his palette. A blue that he didn't even have in his inventory. He rummaged in his paint box and found several other blues, Prussian, Windsor and cobalt deep, but nothing that matched the light blue smear he could now see.

However, it had got there; it had to go. He reached for a tissue to wipe the colour out, but then something caught his eye. Not in the painting, but in the pit, at the bottom. A bright blue streak that was not present earlier.

Haruki went closer to the edge and looked down. Six feet below him rustled a blue plastic sheet. It looked like it was covering something up. Something was wrapped up in it. A breeze rippled the surface of the blue plastic and a very faint sound carried from it. A burr on the wind, a whisper in the shadows. He sat on the edge and levered himself off. He jumped into the pit.

The bottom was soft, so he hardly felt the jolt of landing. The earth had a pleasant smell, a musty, rich scent like a delicious mushroom or a heady truffle. And it was refreshingly cool down there. He was still hot after his exertions and so he felt drawn to lie there on his back a while and enjoy the cool dark. But the blue plastic sheet flapped at his attention. He could not think how he had not noticed it earlier.

Whatever the plastic sheet covered, it was large and square. Haruki reached out to touch it. The plastic was cool to the touch, like the pit itself. He pulled gently at a loose flap and drew it back to see what was underneath.

It was a painting. With a handful of others stacked underneath. His stomach lurched in recognition as he saw the thickly daubed canvas. Dollops of browns, stacked on top of each other, layer after layer. Swirls of yellows, specks of red. But mostly daubs of brown madder and burnt sienna. It was almost identical to the one he'd just painted. The one that was at the top of the pit drying in the breeze. He rifled through the paintings, desperate to see the other. Each was almost a facsimile of the other and all of them contained a little smear of blue just off from the centre.

> *Unable to paint,*
> *Brush hovers over canvas.*
> *The pit of despair.*

Haruki arranged the paintings next to each other and stood them up, leaning them against one side of the earthy pit. Behind his confusion, he felt a certain satisfaction that he'd maintained a consistency of style over the course of these paintings. If he'd applied this same way of layering colour upon colour to his other work, it might be distinctive enough to get him back into the Tate. He saw this working best with a tight colour palette like the browns in the pit. Or the blues in the sky. Yes, why not?

Haruki felt drained, exhausted. More than anything, he wanted to lie down. He flopped onto his back next to the paintings and felt the cool of the musty earth seep into him. He looked up to the sky, allowing his mind to hover above. He gave himself the freedom to relax. He slowed his breath and stilled his racing pulse. He listened to the flutter of the plastic wrap and realised that he was lying relative to where the blue smear had been in his paintings. If he could have been bothered to climb back up and examine the painting he'd just completed, it wouldn't have surprised him if instead of the streak of blue, he'd found the outline of a body.

But should he climb out of the pit at all? It felt so peaceful down there. He felt at home in the earth. He rather wanted to stay, for a little longer at least.

If he did find the outline of a body in the painting he had just completed, what would he do about it? Would he pick up the brush again and try to paint over it? Would he get out the scalpel and cut himself out of the scene? Or would he just leave things as they were?

Haruki allowed his mind to rise and drift. It hovered over and above him. He saw himself from above. He opened his eyes and for a moment he saw himself from below.

Clouds hung above him. Both massive and weightless. A magpie streamed past.

It was bright blue in the sunlight, but black in the shade.

BARROWTHWAITE

After waking up in the pit for who knew how many mornings in succession, Haruki realised he had to get help. Instead, he got a holiday.

He'd telephoned his agent, Thomas Peters, and although it was, in Haruki's eyes at least, a cry for help, Peters hadn't arranged for him to seek professional help. 'You'll feel better after a rest,' he'd said. 'I know of an old cottage in the Lakes. Out of the way. Space to think. You'll be right as rain up there, there's a good chap.'

Haruki had taken a train from Kings Cross to Peterborough, where he changed for one going further north, past the midlands and through several post-industrial Lancashire villages. He had passed by the hulks of dark mills. Once splendid jewels in the rich crown of the textile trade, now the buildings stood empty, gutted and abandoned. Or forlornly re-purposed as child play centres, or hand car washes.

Eventually he was spat out at Preston, where he had an hour to stalk the bitterly cold streets of a rough industrial northern town. Only later did his painter's eye appreciate that the dull, damp streets held as much character as the gently dramatic fells and tors that he saw when his connecting train reached the fringes of the Lake District.

The car that awaited him at Oxenholme spirited him away further north. Soon all semblance of civilisation fell away. Yet the sun made a welcome reappearance and he enjoyed the journey, eagerly looking out of the window and drinking in the sight of towering ridges casting sharp shadows on the valley below. But then it grew dull again. The autumn sunshine was losing its battle against the encroaching gloom. There was still daylight in the air, but it was fading fast, and the previous downpour had turned the sky steel grey, dark and brooding.

As he entered the village it started to rain again. This time more heavily than he had thought it was possible to do so. A woman was running in the opposite direction. The car windows were drenched, so he couldn't see her face clearly, but he felt that there was something familiar about her. She moved like Jane did. Jane was graceful from the waist up, her long sweeping arms articulate and refined, but she ran like a duck. Haruki turned around and looked out of the back window. The woman had stopped. She turned around and followed the movement of his car as it rushed past. Haruki felt unsettled. He experienced a nagging doubt, as if he needed to be somewhere else right at that moment. As if leaving the woman behind in his wake was a loss that he would come to rue. But Haruki didn't stop the car; he slumped back in his seat and tried to shrug off the feeling.

Jane was three hundred miles away with her orchestra in London and this wet woman on the roadside represented nothing more than a mere smudge of colour in an otherwise drab day. So, he put both women out of his mind.

Ahead was a red telephone box. It stood next to an old building made from the local grey-green slate. Possibly a post office. Haruki could just about make out the red and yellow sign above the door. The taxi slowed and stopped. 'Driver, this isn't the place. I can give you directions when you're further into the village.'

'This is the place,' the driver said. 'This is always the place.' These were the first words the driver had said to Haruki the entire journey and they were uttered with such finality that he was sure they would be his last. Haruki had little choice but to get out from the back seat and collect his luggage from the back. The instant the boot closed, the engine revved and the taxi moved off. It performed a brisk three-point turn in the road and tore away in the direction it had come. Haruki was left standing in the rain.

Water lay in a deep puddle across the surface of the road. There was no pavement and, short of stepping into a muddy verge, there was no skirting around the puddle. He had no choice but to wade through it. He began to wish that he'd dressed more appropriately. Boots would have been good, instead of the polished brown ombre brogues he was wearing. He'd have to get them cleaned and probably re-stretched at this rate.

From the direction of the village he saw a figure trudging towards him. It was joined by another and then more, until a whole troupe was making their way towards him. Was it a greeting party, or an exodus? Then the people stopped and parted, lining the road on either side. There were two dozen or so, of all ages.

As he walked closer he saw that they were all dressed in outdoor gear, coats and hats being some proof against the driving rain, and they seemed in absolutely no hurry to get out of the nasty weather. Haruki supposed that northerners took a different attitude towards getting cold and wet than they did in the south. But what were they all doing here out in this filthy weather?

He heard the sound of bells and, as if in response to that, the sky brightened and the sun came out from behind a slate grey cloud. It sparkled off the rain-slick road.

The bells rose to a crescendo as a half-dozen men stomped towards him down the centre of the road. They were dressed in white, with black socks and thick black leather clogs that were laced high above their ankles. The bells were attached to their footwear and were worn at their elbows and knees. Every movement of these men sent shards of sound flying in every direction. The morris men pulled at something. They dragged behind them a small wooden cart that was piled high with what looked to be sheaves of straw or wheat. The pile was some twelve feet high and it was stacked neatly but not tied. It looked ready to spill over and collapse at any pitch or roll as it trundled along the road.

A man broke free from the crowd and numbly scampered up the pile of wheat. To great cheers he made it to the top and sat astride. Reaching into his open blue shirt, he threw sweets into the crowd. Children rushed forward out from under the feet of the adults and snatched them up. Amongst them a fat old man dressed flamboyantly in red velvet fought for his fair share. When he had enough, he sat down on the wet road and immediately started to eat them.

The cart trundled past the velvet stranger and the crowd fell into line behind it. Now drums began to bang and the following crowd shifted their feet in time with the drumbeats. Haruki shuffled to the side and let the procession pass. When the cart was level with him, the man on the top leaned over towards him. He was around Haruki's age, with bright eyes and light blond hair tied back into a ponytail. He grasped a handful of sweets, but instead of tossing them at Haruki, he leant down and said something. Although the bells and the drumbeats were loud, and the man spoke quietly; Haruki could hear him perfectly.

'Opposite the post office,' he said, 'take the path up the hill. Ask for Maggie at the farmhouse.'

Haruki had no chance to reply because the cart trundled off, bringing with it a tide of procession-goers who filed past him in tune to the drumbeats. Morris men danced in the cart's wake. Some wore horses' heads and pranced up and down, mimicking the beast. Others wore blackened faces and hit out at each other with sticks

'It's the coal,' a man said to him on his way past. 'Dark faces come out of a mine.' Haruki supposed the man had seen the ethnicity in Haruki's features and must have felt that he was owed an explanation.

Many of the other villagers nodded and smiled at him, but none engaged him further in conversation. They were too taken with the joy of following the cart around. When it had thumped and jangled itself well out of the village, he picked up his case and walked on. Almost immediately he saw the footpath opposite the post office. It led up the hill and was signposted 'Hilltops'. That was the rental property. The man on the cart must have known he was due to stay there. Perhaps they didn't get too many visitors to the village.

The path was tacky with mud and sheep droppings, and he had to work overtime to keep it off his shoes. After five or ten minutes, a whitewashed building came into sight at the top of the hill about a hundred metres away. It was a small farmhouse cottage with a warm orange light glowing from a downstairs window. It looked inviting.

He shifted his weekender holdall more firmly onto his shoulder and started to walk. Shortly after the passing of the cart, the sun had begun to creep back behind a cloud and the sky grew dark again. It was so dark now that he had to use his phone to light the way and avoid obstacles.

He saw movement in the upstairs window of the white cottage. A waft of white as lace curtains pulled back from the upstairs window directly above him. He saw two young girls staring down at him. Both were dressed in white nightgowns, both with alabaster skin and dark hair mussed and ruffled with sleep. Haruki raised a hand in greeting, but the girls did not reciprocate his gesture.

A raised voice from within captured his attention. A shriek of laughter from the downstairs room with the warm glow. When Haruki looked up again at the window a second later, the girls were gone.

The front door opened immediately. 'Yes? Who's there?' A woman stood with her back to the yellow-orange light escaping the downstairs room. She was younger than Haruki, early thirties or late twenties, and she was dressed in jeans and a white vest. A thick grey cardigan covered her arms but hung loosely off one shoulder, revealing thin bones behind pale skin. Her dark hair was a bird's nest. 'You're a man,' the woman said.

This was not the greeting he'd expected. 'I've come about Hilltops,' he said.

'Do I scare you?'

'I beg your pardon?'

'Do I scare you?'

'No,' Haruki said. 'Not yet,' he added.

'Hear that, Judy? He's a man and I don't scare him. So, you're wrong, I don't scare away every man who comes knocking.'

A peal of laughter came from inside. The woman turned back to Haruki. 'You'd better come in whilst I find out what I've done with the keys. Although I can't imagine how you're going to find the place in this weather.' The woman touched Haruki's arm in a friendly gesture. 'I had better come with you. I would never leave a man stranded and defenceless.'

'That's really not necessary,' Haruki said, dripping onto her door mat. 'Just point me onto the right road.'

'Oh, there isn't a road.' A younger woman who lounged on the sofa inside laughed. She looked very comfortable in front of a welcoming, roaring fire. 'There's a track. But it doubles up as a stream most of the time.'

'This is Judy. And I'm Maggie.'

Haruki initially made to shake Maggie's hand but decided that was too formal. Instead he turned the motion into a weak wave. 'I'm Haruki. Sorry to disturb you all. I'm afraid I might have woken the children upstairs.'

'It's just the two of us here,' Maggie said. 'There's no one upstairs.'

'But I just saw—'

'You saw us,' Judy said. 'It was us you waved at.' The sides of her mouth curled up into a feline smile.

'But you answered the door too quickly, you wouldn't have had time to—'

'You're not in London now. We have all the time we need here. Life is lived at a different pace than you're used to, no doubt.'

The orange firelight cast queer shadows onto Maggie's attractive face. Her brown hair was loosely tied back with a turquoise ribbon, but that didn't prevent it from sticking up every which way. Her face was round and her eyes large and hazel. Her small nose had an ever-so-slight upturn at its tip. Haruki imagined the sweep of the brush that would capture her profile. In that sense he could almost feel the woman's face. Judy was a younger version of Maggie. She was in her pyjamas. Her round face was rosy, flushed by the fire.

Haruki was conscious that he was stood dripping over the threshold. 'I don't wish to be any trouble – just give me the keys and point me in the right direction.'

Both the women snorted with laughter. Maggie sized Haruki up, her eyes resting on his brown brogues and flannel trousers. 'It's filthy outside; I can't let you go traipsing around the fells alone on an evening like this. You'll catch your death most likely and even if not, you'll be a burden to the mountain rescue.' But then her words fell flat as her gaze fell on the window. It was distinctly brighter outside than it had been a minute ago. 'Westmoreland weather,' Maggie said with a shrug.

'The Captain has the keys,' Judy called from her cat-like pose, coiled on the sofa. 'You'll have to take him there.'

'I suppose. Come on then, let's head out.' Maggie shoved past Haruki, who danced out of the way as she reached behind him for her old Barbour coat that was hung on a row of hooks by the door. She stepped into a pair of old boots but didn't bother doing the laces because there apparently weren't any to do up. 'Well, what are you waiting for?' Maggie held the door open for Haruki, who walked out into the rapidly improving evening. The sun had made a reappearance, as strong as it ever had been that day, and even a streak of blue could be seen behind the evaporating clouds.

The dirt track hadn't dried any in the last few minutes, so Haruki had to tread carefully, but Maggie trudged directly down the centre, heedless of puddle or impediment. 'Who's the Captain?' he asked.

But Maggie ignored the question. She had one of her own. 'What brings you to the village? You don't look like the type we usually get here.'

'I'm an artist. A painter.'

'Ah, I see. Do you paint people?'

'I used to.'

'Maybe you'll paint me sometime.' Maggie's smile was warm and inviting.

Haruki grew suddenly embarrassed. 'I'm concentrating on landscapes these days. Maybe still life.' His face burned hot and he was glad Maggie wasn't looking at him.

'Suit yourself.' Maggie nodded, then she fell silent. The truth was that he found himself wanting very much to paint her likeness.

They reached the end of the track, turned onto the main road and started down the hill towards the village. Twenty yards later, Maggie veered off the road and hopped nimbly over a stile. 'Short cut,' she said. 'Throw over your bag.' Haruki handed her his holdall and she hefted it appraisingly. 'It's heavy. You're stronger than you look.'

Haruki thought the same thing about Maggie.

Once Haruki was safely over the stile, she gave him his bag back. 'Listen, I'm really sorry, but I daren't leave Judy on her own for long.' Maggie pointed down the hill. 'There's another stile on your left. That'll take you to the Captain. So long, Ken.'

'It's Haruki.'

'Sure,' said Maggie as she skipped lightly back up the path.

The Captain's house was a similar design to Maggie's white cottage but on a much larger scale, to the extent that Haruki wondered why hers was the 'old schoolhouse' and not this building. The house was a two-storey affair, except that a light shone out of a small attic window, set into a dark roof covered in the characteristic blue-green slate of the region. It was the stuff that all of the drystone walls were made of. Haruki trod the stone path that led from the stile and up to the front of the house. There was no driveway and no road to connect the house with the rest of the village.

A square porch jutted from the flat expanse of the front elevation. It was topped with its own pyramidal slate roof and a bell with a rope served as a knocker. A ship's bell, most likely. *Fits with the 'Captain' thing*, Haruki thought. He waggled the rope and set off the bell's clapper. It emitted a dull but sonorous sound that seemed to end too abruptly compared with the long finish that bells usually have. *Must be cracked*, he thought.

There was no answer, so he tugged at the rope again, louder this time. Still no one came to the door and as Haruki considered walking around the side of the house to see if there was any other way of attracting the attention of whoever might be inside, the heavens opened again and the torrent of rain resumed. Haruki knocked on the wooden door. It swung open at his lightest touch, inviting him inside. He didn't question this stroke of luck and was just grateful to get out of the rain.

Most front porches were used to store boots and coats, but the Captain's porch was a haven of light and dry warmth. Thick rope nets decorated the walls and low ceilings, and various other paraphernalia of the ocean was strewn about, much of it caught up in the nets themselves. A dried-out bloated spiny puffer here, a glass wicker-wrapped fisherman's float there. On a table near the door was a great wax candle with three lit and burning wicks sharing the same source of fuel. The yellow flames flickered and danced together in easy syncopation. Someone must be at home then.

The flames must have sensed the damp breeze from outside because they fluttered angrily. Haruki stepped further into the porch and shut the door against the weather. The flames fell back into their comfortable sway. He knocked loudly on the inside door, confident he'd now be heard. Initially, there was no sign of any inhabitants and on the second attempt, as before, the door swung effortlessly open. 'Hello!' Haruki called, sticking his head inside. 'Anyone home?'

He heard the sound of water bubbling and smelled something cooking. It was a sweet and heady spice, like vanilla. There was a loud thump from the room beyond and he felt the impact through the floor of whatever had cause the sound.

'Hello!' he shouted.

As the seconds passed without answer, he inched further forward into the house. Inside, a low ceiling supported by dark oak beams was suspended a foot or two above his head, and though Haruki wasn't a tall man, his shoulders hunched as his natural inclination was to duck low whilst in this room. The sailing paraphernalia bled from the porch out into the room, but only half-way, then the ropes and netting grew thinner. The fanciful sea theme gave way to green wallpaper, dark oak wainscoting and a large polished staircase of dark wood swept up into the upper floor. A more typical interior design for a large, old house in the hills.

A sturdy oak door stood opposite the staircase and beside that a dark mahogany console table with serpentine feet. Its polished mirror surface was bare except for a golden envelope that bore his name in recursive handwriting written in burgundy ink. Haruki opened the envelope, and in doing so he suffered a small papercut across the tip of his index finger. Swearing, he put the finger to his mouth and sucked on it. There was no blood in the cut, but it stung. He opened the envelope and found inside a deadbolt key. It was attached to a turquoise plastic fob on which the word 'Hilltops' was written.

He felt it rude to just take the key and leave without announcing himself, so he waited and listened for signs of life, and behind the oak door he heard the soft bubble of boiling water. Then a telephone rang, making him start.

It was a harsh bell, like the one from an old baker-light telephone from his childhood. From behind the door he heard a man's voice answer. The tone was low and hushed, and after only a few words, he heard the receiver click back into place.

Haruki lightly knocked on the kitchen door and slowly pushed it open.

It wasn't a kitchen but a bare room that had been whitewashed, with smooth plaster walls, ceiling and floor. There was no furniture as far as he could see, though he was initially snow-blinded by the startling all-white interior. He blinked away the disorientating brightness and after time his pupils narrowed enough for him to become accustomed to the light. Then he began to see that the room was not completely empty. Strong sunlight poured in through a skylight in the high roof and in the centre of the ceiling was attached a small white plastic chair. Below this was a plastic foam crash mat of the same colour. White, everything was white, even the sky he could see through the window. Even the wire work of a metal drain situated in the middle of the plastic mat that had been cut and fashioned around it with a slight camber on each side leading into the drain. The floor glistened wet.

A wet room then, but there was no evidence of a shower. Nothing in fact that could have produced the water he saw slowly oozing down the drain. If it was water, because it ran slowly, and the room was filled with the strong smell of sweet spice.

He bent and put his fingertip to the liquid. It was body-warm to the touch. And when he retracted his finger, the clear substance stuck to his finger like sticky jam or molten toffee. Whatever the substance was, it wasn't water.

Haruki put his finger to his nostrils and his eyes immediately watered. The scent was so powerful it was almost intoxicating. Behind the sweet vanilla there was a clean odour, like eucalyptus or menthol. It cleared his sinuses and nasal passageways, which allowed more of the vanilla to enter his lungs. It cooled him as the air raced down into him, but it also made him feel light-headed.

And then something slithered in the corner of the room. He couldn't see it when looking directly, but when he looked to the side, he saw a mass of white or translucent substance quiver and pulsate. When he looked once more directly, it stopped, then faded from view. It was as if only the movement could be detected by Haruki and not the thing itself.

His hackles raised. This didn't feel right. It was unnatural. He inched forward to where the thing was, scanning the floor and ceiling with hyper-vigilance. Suddenly, something bolted from under his feet and shot out into the centre of the room to where the big white metal mesh covered the drain. Looking obliquely, he saw a large mass of viscous liquid pour through the mesh and down the drain. The last of the liquid to go down lingering for a moment at the edge. He was quite sure that the thing had looked directly at him before leaving.

Haruki had never felt so eager before to leave a place, and he was desperate to wash his hands after touching that unnatural substance. He rushed out of the room and slammed the door behind him, but in doing so he bumped into a man on the other side who was preparing to enter. Haruki yelped in fright but was calmed by the man's kindly smile.

'Hello there.' The man was tall and sported loose sandy blond hair and had eyes of the brightest silver grey, like a full moon. His face was smooth, his skin perfect. He gave Haruki another warm smile and held out a wet cloth that he took with eager thanks, using it to wipe his hands free of the weird sticky stuff. His desire to be rid of the strange substance was greater than his need to introduce himself. The man asked, 'Are you all right?'

Haruki pointed a finger back into the room he'd just left. He wanted to ask what it was that he'd just seen. He wanted to know what the room was used for, with the chair stuck upside down on the ceiling and the large grating in the centre of a sloping plastic mat. But Haruki didn't know how to articulate the question. He didn't know where to start to describe what he saw in there.

As Haruki struggled for words, the man said, 'It's a pleasure to meet you again, Haruki. I'm the Captain.' Haruki couldn't help but admire the Captain's lean, willowy frame as he fought hard to recall whether they had indeed met before. 'On the rushcart? Down in the valley?'

Haruki remembered. 'The man with the sweets,' he said.

It was immediately apparent to Haruki that the Captain exuded a powerful vitality. He wore double denim, jeans and a shirt. The first four or five buttons of his shirt were undone, revealing a smooth, hairless chest that writhed with conditioned muscle. The first two of a six pack of abdominal muscles peeked over the first button that strained with the tightness of his shirt. The Captain wore matt black aviators on the top of his head, and these served to keep his bright mop of hair somewhat in check. The Captain smelled strongly of vanilla.

'Sorry,' Haruki said, 'I thought you might have been in the, er, kitchen.'

'We both know that's not a kitchen.' The Captain looked Haruki up and down, in obvious appraisal, and his gaze turned to Haruki's muddy boots and wet flannel turn-ups. Haruki squirmed as the Captain's eyes worked their way slowly up Haruki's legs to rest at his crotch. He felt exposed. He wanted to close his coat and button it. But he just stood still and hoped the scrutiny would end soon.

'You have Japanese heritage. And what other?'

Haruki said, 'My mother was from Ulsan.'

'Ah, beautiful.' He reached out and took Haruki's chin between his thumb and forefinger. He moved Haruki's head around in the light, looking carefully at his features. Haruki stood stock still, his arms useless by his sides. 'Absolutely beautiful. The whales there are quite something.'

'I never went,' Haruki admitted. He felt foolish; why was he telling this to the Captain? He felt as if he were in the confession box.

'Haruki, I would ask what you have come here for. Did someone call you here?'

'I needed a break from London,' Haruki said. 'My agent fixed me up with the Hilltops property.'

The Captain stared intently at Haruki. 'Property? No one owns Hilltops, or any of these buildings. We are all just custodians for what will follow.' He looked at Haruki like no one else had looked at him before. His eyes seemed to devour Haruki's appearance with a hunger that made him think of Jane on their wedding night. The Captain seemed not to be able to take his eyes off him. It made Haruki uncomfortable, and even more so when the Captain came closer to him. The man's breath was suddenly in Haruki's nostrils. His smile flashed inches from Haruki's face. His chest heaved close to Haruki's own. His hands within reach of Haruki's. All Haruki had to do was reach out and touch him.

'Do something for me, will you?' the Captain said, his breath hot and fragrant.

'Anything.' Haruki didn't know why he said that.

The Captain was surely about to touch him. It was only a matter of time. It would happen soon. Then the waiting would be over. He didn't care where the man touched him, as long as it happened.

'There's an event tomorrow. I need you. Maggie will be there.'

Haruki swallowed hard. He dared not back away from the Captain and he surely didn't want to. He nodded.

'Good man, see you up the hill at five.' The Captain skipped past him into the room beyond the oak door.

Haruki took in a gulp of air. He wasn't aware until then that he'd been holding his breath. He felt a sense of disappointment, but it wasn't overwhelming because he knew he would be seeing the Captain again soon.

HILLTOPS

Maggie was waiting for him outside the Captain's house. The weather had changed to a bright sunshine, although it looked like it was on the cusp of switching yet again. A cold crosswind was whipping in from the side of the fell.

'Judy's fine now,' Maggie said, 'so, let's get you settled before it starts to get nasty.'

'How can you tell what it's going to do?' Haruki asked.

'I can't,' Maggie said. 'No one can. But it always gets nasty, sooner or later.'

Hilltops was a half-hour walk from Maggie's house. The same track that ran down to the Captain's place ran up the hill and over the rise. A cold, green-grey house was nestled just behind a drystone wall, in the crook of a shallow dip. It was totally secluded, being the only building on the other side of the fell. The path ran right up to the front door, but it was so wet by the time they arrived that it was practically a stream. Judy had been right about that.

One of the first things Maggie did was to light the oil burner in the kitchen. This provided heat to the rest of the rooms, though Haruki had also managed to get the open fire in the lounge burning and it was closely in front of this that Maggie was standing, trying to dry her socks holding them out to the flames.

'I don't know why I'm bothering; they'll only get more wet when I go outside again,' Maggie said, unfastening her belt. 'But I do enjoy the feeling of putting on warm dry socks.'

'It was kind of you coming all the way up here at this time. Can I offer you a drink?'

Maggie raised an eyebrow. 'I *would* like to prove my sister wrong, but I can't leave her alone for long. She's not been too well.'

'Prove her wrong?'

'About scaring men off.' She laughed. 'Don't look so worried, there's no strings attached. Not yet. Just get me a mug of tea, will you? You'll find tea in the pantry and the kettle's the kind that you put on the hot plate. It should be warm enough by now.'

Haruki blushed. He felt somehow that he was making a mess of this, whatever *this* was. He'd come here for peace and tranquillity, but perhaps he'd better settle for solitude too. His interactions with the locals were confusing at best.

He hadn't brought any of his painting gear with him. This was a purposeful attempt to break the cycle of repetitive and obsessive behaviour that he'd developed. He had to learn to become a normal person again. No more obsessing about his art or his subjects. As a painter, he saw things that others didn't. As an artist, he thought differently. To others, that probably made him seem weird and detached.

It took Haruki a considerable amount of time to find the things he needed. The kitchen itself was a simple affair with nothing more than a large and complicated oil-fired contraption that doubled as both central heating and a range oven. Two large chrome hoods protected round hot plates and on one of these, Haruki placed an old iron kettle. He wondered whether it was proofed against heavy metal poisoning, but a call from Maggie asking if he 'needed help in there' spurred him to use it anyway. Whilst it was on the heat he looked around for tea bags but the kitchen had no units to speak of, just a large walk-in pantry with floor to ceiling shelves of tins, bottles and packets. It was as if someone lived here full-time.

Haruki found some Jamaica ginger cake and after time he presented it on a little platter together with a hot mug of tea and a little jug of milk. Maggie was stretched out on a small leather Chesterfield that she'd dragged closer to the fire. On the mantel, pinned in place by a heavy ornamental slate clock, were her jeans. 'I wasn't sure whether you took milk,' Haruki said, trying not to look at her bare legs stretching into her soft thighs.

'You could have simply asked me,' Maggie said, sitting up and patting the empty seat next to her. 'Will you be mother?'

Haruki put the platter of cake on a side table. 'Will I be what?'

'Will you pour the tea?'

'Ah yes, of course.'

He felt Maggie's eyes burning on him as he reached over her bare legs to put milk into her mug. They sat back cradling their tea and waiting for the warmth to radiate from their hands to the rest of their bodies. 'I think it's colder in here than it is outside,' Haruki said.

'You know what they say, cold hands, warm heart.' But then Maggie was suddenly done with the small talk. A dark cloud passed over her face. 'Why are you here?' she asked very quietly, almost timidly.

'I needed a holiday,' Haruki said. 'Some peace and quiet.'

Maggie sat up and leaned forward; she was almost as close to his face as the Captain had been. Maggie smelled of cloves and menthol, refreshing. Haruki mentally swept his brush across the contours of her face. This time he started at the slight upturn in her nose and moved down. Past her jawline, her delicate neck. His brush lingered at her throat, as if considering whether to move further down.

'Haruki, where did you go just then? You fazed out for a while. Are you all right?'

'Sorry. What did you ask?'

'I didn't, not yet. But I was going to ask how you came here. I want to know everything.'

'Everything?'

'Yes. I can't help you if I don't know everything.'

Haruki raised his eyebrows. *Help me?* What was she talking about? 'Where do you want me to start?'

'Who sent you here?'

'No one,' Haruki said. 'I was just short of inspiration, I suppose. I'm a painter, you see, and I fell into a pit.'

'A metaphorical one?'

'Both, but the trouble was that I liked it down there. Things made sense to me in a way that they didn't outside of it. And then I'd always forget about the pit until I discovered it again the following day. I suppose that sounds crazy to you?'

'That's not a word we use around here, Haruki. But go on. I want to hear more about this pit, much more.'

He caught a flash of Maggie's filigree collar bones underneath her shirt and that was enough to keep him talking. 'Sure, how much time do you have?'

'I have until my trousers dry,' Maggie said. 'I think Judy will be secure until then.' *That's a strange word to use*, Haruki thought. But he didn't pick her up on it. He had some talking of his own to do.

He lost track of time as he and Maggie talked. He enjoyed the way she really seemed to be listening to him. She watched him intently, following his gestures and scrutinising his facial features. This made him uncomfortable at first but then he grew to like the attention. He talked about his painting, his separation from Jane and, of course, about the episode with the pit. And as he talked, he was more and more convinced that all these things were connected.

Maggie reached a point in the conversation where she unfolded and stretched out her legs. 'That's a lot of detail you paint.' She stood and stretched again.

'I'm sorry, did I talk too much?'

'I asked for it, and I enjoyed talking to you, Haruki Kensagi.' She made a mock bow to him and tested her jeans. 'Well, they're dry now, best get going.' As she stretched her calves into the tight jean fabric, he tried not to look.

'What about your story?' Haruki said. 'It's your turn next.'

'Tomorrow,' Maggie said, and surprised him by planting a kiss on his cheek. 'I'll bring a jigsaw. Do you like jigsaws? Of course you do, who doesn't?'

As Maggie let herself out, Haruki was thinking about her kiss. He found interpersonal relationships difficult. The actions and words of others often left him confused and sometimes even anxious. But when he painted a person, that's when he started to understand. Everything he needed to know about someone was all there, in their faces. He needed his brushes and paint to access and interpret that information and for the first time felt pangs of unease at leaving them behind.

He wanted nothing more than to paint Maggie, but despite the thrill he felt at the thought of it, Haruki didn't dream of Maggie that night. He dreamed of the Captain.

He dreamed he was standing on a hill in the evening sunlight. He was alone except for the Captain at his back, breathing hot whispers into his ear. Before him was a pit. It stretched from his feet out into the distance and covered a vast area. It looked deep, perhaps bottomless. 'Go in, it won't hurt you,' urged the Captain. Haruki's senses were assailed by the strong scent of vanilla. He knew he was always going to step forward and fall in. He knew this was a fait accompli. He didn't want to, but he did it anyway.

MAGGIE

Haruki pottered around the cottage. It had stopped raining, but the sun had so far refused to break through the cloud cover. He found some eggs in the pantry and when he shook them, they felt fresh enough. He made himself an omelette and sat at the small dining table underneath the bay window at the front of the cottage. He looked outside at the tops of the trees that fringed the grounds. He decided he would like to get out and about. When he'd arrived yesterday there wasn't much opportunity to become acquainted with the village. He also wanted to go up further into the fells. And for that he'd need to buy some hiking boots and some waterproofs. He didn't think that the rain would hold off for long.

Down in the village, there were no retail outlets. Nothing except a church, a small village hall with a red telephone box outside and a tiny post office selling papers, and not much else except for a large range of confectionary. The kind that one can find everywhere around the country. Mars, Cadbury's and the rest. The fat old man behind the counter wasn't much help. He just pointed him in the direction of a local farm. 'Perhaps it can borrow what it needs?' he'd said. 'Frank knows there's plenty of folk willing to lend a hand.' Haruki wondered how he could travel to the nearest town. It was one thing to pre-book a taxi from his home in London to meet him in Oxenholme, but it was quite another to find public transport out here. There simply wasn't any. There were no taxicabs, no Uber and no data service even for his mobile phone. Not even the slightest hint of mobile telephone signal either.

'Phone box is out of order,' the man said as if in answer to Haruki's thoughts. The postmaster stared down at his chocolates, surveying them with quick darting glances from one to the next. 'Would it like a chocolate bar?' The man smiled excitedly from behind his counter. His dark corpulent skin rolled back behind his grin. 'Frank has almost every one it can think of. Except caramel Wispas. Frank doesn't like caramel Wispas. It's not that Frank doesn't enjoy the taste. Frank just doesn't see the point. They are neither one thing nor the other, and Frank always says that no matter what, he should always try to be himself. Frank says that if he can't be himself, then someone else will.' The man's eyes were hooded and downcast yet he grinned the grin of a schoolboy. 'What does it think about that? Not bad, eh? Frank has many more pearls of wisdom for those with an ear to hear.'

'Who's Frank?' Haruki said.

'Ah, now that is a question. And Frank is very grateful for it. It has entered into the spirit of things, I see. I commend it. Who is Frank? Frank is everything and he is nothing. Frank is large and he is small. The merest breeze carries him through the hills yet he dances on the fells with heavy feet. Frank digs with the rest yet he doesn't have to. Frank beats about the bush whilst getting to the point. In short, Frank is frank. And Frank is Frank. If it gets Frank's double meaning. And Frank likes chocolate, if it hasn't guessed already.'

'So, *you* are Frank?'

'An educated guess, from an erudite mind. Much like old Frank's. Go on, Haruki, have this one on me.' Frank held out a Crunchie bar but still didn't make eye contact. Then Haruki saw why. Behind the man's hooded eyes, his pupils oscillated wildly back and forth, maintaining no set focus at all. Frank was blind.

'How do you know my name?'

'Everyone knows, it's the fellow in Hilltops,' the old man said, putting down the Crunchie that Haruki had failed to accept. Without looking, he knew exactly where it should go and expertly laid it to rest back in its proper place on the counter. 'It'll be on the hill tonight. It'll say hello to Maggie for me.' He nodded and left Haruki puzzled as to what he meant exactly. To his back he heard the words muttered, 'There's one it'll let in, when it comes knocking.'

Back at the house, Haruki found his door unlocked. Pushing it open and peering inside, he was greeted by Maggie. She sat at the dining table in the window, a roaring fire at her back and the daylight streaming onto her face. She was in the process of arranging the pieces of a giant jigsaw. She flipped each onto its correct picture side and was sorting the straight edges into one pile and the middle pieces into another. Also, on the table was a decanter of what looked like whiskey and two cut glass tumblers. 'Hey,' she said, and waved a hand, though she didn't look up from what she was doing.

'How did you get in?' Haruki asked, but Maggie waved his question away. Without looking at him she pushed out the seat opposite her with her stockinged feet. She'd taken off her shoes and left them by the fire. Maggie poured two fingers of whiskey into each tumbler and pushed one of them towards the empty place. She took the other for herself. Haruki took the offered seat and the whiskey.

Maggie took a large gulp and refilled her glass. She didn't take her eyes off the jigsaw puzzle in front of her. Haruki realised that she'd been crying. Before he could say something, she said, 'It's the Captain. I don't know what he wants from me.'

'The Captain? Why? What's he done?'

A tear stroked her face. 'Everything, he's done everything, to all of us. He'll do it to you too. He keeps the thing away.' She paused and then her tone changed. 'Haruki, you remember me, don't you?'

'Is this something to do with what's happening tonight?'

'You wouldn't believe me if I told you. You'll need to see for yourself. Then you'll understand. It took me a while. But when I saw it, I understood. The Captain is necessary. Haruki, do you understand what that means? It means he can do what he wants. With whoever he wants.'

'Judy, you mean? Is this about Judy?'

Maggie looked up from the jigsaw and let the piece in her hand fall to the table. Her face was wet. 'I can't say. This is wrong. I'm sorry, Haruki, I really am. You should see for yourself. You should make your own mind up.' Maggie rose and went to collect her boots.

Haruki jumped up and blocked her exit. 'Maggie, what is it? What has he done to Judy?' Maggie brushed hard past Haruki, shoving him out of the way.

He couldn't say how it happened, but he and Maggie then started to tussle. He grabbed Maggie's elbow, or it might have been that she grabbed his. Maggie grunted with effort and had a wild, scared look on her face. Haruki couldn't imagine she was afraid of him, but then why was he gripping her elbows? 'Tell me what you need me to do,' he shouted. 'Just tell me what I should do. I'll go and see him!' He was lit by a flash of excitement at the thought of seeing the Captain again. 'Whatever he's doing, I'll get him to stop.'

Maggie tried to wrench free of him, but he had her firmly by the elbow. She had both fists full of Haruki's shirt as she tried to manoeuvre him away from the door. Or was it towards the door? In the heat of the moment, Haruki couldn't keep track of who was doing what. He tried to release Maggie, but somehow he couldn't. Maggie was shaking violently, or was Haruki shaking her? 'Maggie, don't worry, I'll help you.'

Maggie kicked out at Haruki and that frightened him. How had this suddenly got so rough? Again he tried to disengage, but Maggie pulled him closer to her. She twisted from side to side as if he had hold of her, but he now knew that it was the other way around. 'You can't help. No one can,' Maggie screamed. She wrenched herself from side to side, but Haruki held on to her, pushing her or being pulled against the wall in the struggle. 'Judy needs him. We need him. There's no choice.'

'Of course there's a choice. There always is. Even if you don't see it yet.' Maggie had stopped struggling. Haruki sighed with relief as they released each other.

'You'll do it?' Maggie said.

He nodded. He was about to say something, but then Maggie grabbed him again and pulled him close. This time she didn't struggle. She kissed him. Then she pushed him hard against the wall, pinning his hands with hers as she pressed her lips to his once more. Her raw strength was surprising. As was her dexterity. She began to pluck expertly at his belt buckle. He couldn't tell who undressed whom, and who instigated what, but as they lowered each other gently to the floor it had long since ceased to matter.

Afterwards, Maggie walked her fingers lightly over Haruki's bare stomach. Her breasts brushed tantalisingly against his chest. They lay on the sheepskin next to the fire, though it had long since died down, untended. Maggie teased at the edges of a smooth patch of scar tissue on the right of Haruki's stomach. It was two inches in length and discoloured to a darker shade than the rest of him. 'It's an old injury,' Haruki said, 'a stab wound. I'll tell you about it sometime.'

'You'd better,' Maggie laughed, 'because I have one just like it.' She leaned away from Haruki's body to show him her own scar. It was very similar, a two-inch line of scarring, yet where

Haruki's was dark, hers was silver against her pale skin. It was directly analogous to the positioning of Haruki's scar. If they were to lie again, one on top of another...

Haruki noticed a shadow at the window. He watched it come up to the glass and resolve itself into the shape of a dark face that peered in, watching. It lingered a few moments, before withdrawing. He couldn't say why, but he let this go.

'Promise me something,' Maggie said. She rolled off Haruki and hopped around to gather up her clothes from the floor. Haruki lay back and felt the cool air sweep over his naked body. Its icy touch tugged at his extremities. 'Promise me you won't go to the Captain.'

'I thought you wanted me to talk to him.'

'Not until after tonight. Please, promise me that. Whatever happens tonight, you won't interfere.'

'I promise,' Haruki said.

'But after tonight. Afterwards, you will, won't you? Whatever it takes, right?'

PART TWO

JANE

HARUKI

There he went again. Jane Kensagi watched her husband at the sink, washing his precious brushes. He seemed to be in another of his meditative states. He'd been in it for close to two days now. Where did he go when he was like this? Into what recesses of his mind did he retreat? Did she even exist to him, when he was like this? She didn't think so. He concentrated too hard on his 'art' and nothing else mattered during these periods. She would have been more tolerant of him if his painting was any good, but these days his work was shockingly limp and lifeless. It wasn't always like this. The Haruki she'd first been attracted to was a vibrant young talent who'd had several pieces accepted by national galleries. But that was some time ago. Lately he hadn't come up with anything nearly as good as those early paintings. And in her view he was unlikely to ever again.

When Haruki went into these fugue states of his, Jane worried that he found it increasingly harder for him to find his way back to reality. Wasn't art a reflection of reality? Sure, the artist applied licence to their own view of the world. They could twist and turn, and in many cases subvert real life, but art always needed a grounding, a refrain to which the music always returned. Haruki was losing his grounding. He was losing his sense of perspective. He hadn't talked to her for two days, and when he noticed her at all, he didn't look *at* her; he looked *through* her.

This was a perfect example of how her husband was losing it. She'd come home just now with fresh meat and eggs for breakfast, but when she'd opened the front door and entered the house, he was stood in the hallway staring at her. She'd smiled at him, but he'd just walked off, scratching his head as if trying to figure something out. He was becoming quite a strange man. She should get him some professional help one of these days. Perhaps when she wasn't quite so busy with her own work. But for the moment there was nothing else to do but leave him alone. He'd come around eventually. When he finished his painting.

At least he'd given up portraits. She'd grown tired of the complaints from those sitting for him. 'He was odd,' they said. 'Too familiar.' 'Too intense.' It was true: he liked to get into their personal space, into their heads. He liked to think that what made him 'unusual' made him an 'unusually good artist'. Those were his words, but he was wrong. He was just very odd.

She went out into the garden. Haruki had moved into the kitchen and she didn't want to be around whilst he was there. He was even weirder with his knives than with his brushes. Forgoing brunch, she took her book and a small bowl of sunflower seeds and went to sit in her favourite place at the edge of the garden overlooking the adjacent field.

McTominay the old gardener had been yesterday and mowed the lawns, so they still held that freshly cut smell. Robins and wrens hopped about on the immaculate blades searching for worms or seeds. A tit piped loudly in the bushes as it was joined at the feeder by several others. Small fluffy heads became busy at the bird table on the edge of the lawn.

Jane took a brush from underneath the wooden chair and swept off the dry leaves that had accumulated on it. She relaxed into her favourite seat and closed her eyes to listen to the prolific sounds of nature. The rustle of the willow herb grown tall on the fallow field, the brush and sweep of the unfettered apple tree as it swayed against the wall, and of course the hue and cry of the many little birds that lived in the gloriously overgrown bushes that surrounded the garden. She tried to isolate the individual songs of the birds, but she just heard a high-pitched cacophony. She would have picked out each individual flute or viola if it were her own orchestra, so why could she not do the same with the birds? These were instruments with which she was less knowledgeable, but surely she should be able to rely on her innate ability?

Jane closed her eyes. She imagined her baton in hand before her. A high piping sound came to her in quick bursts. She pointed her mind's baton in its direction and opened her eyes. A small brown bird hopped on the ground, its little stubby tail held high. A wren then. Jane circled her baton around it and in her mind she removed it from the garden. She closed her eyes again. Next the liquid warble of the robin. That was easy to isolate and move on. A machine-gun assault on a piccolo. A high C. Jane's baton located the culprit up in the tree ahead. A chaffinch. This was easier than Jane thought, though it was second best to actually conducting a fully assembled orchestra, each musician hanging on every twitch of her baton. Then the twitching nervous call of a magpie silenced the other birds. They'd not want their nests robbed of precious eggs. And she had heard that magpies eat young chicks whole. Some believed the presence of a magpie was unlucky.

Jane's thoughts turned to her real orchestra. She missed the LSO during its summer recess and couldn't wait to get back to start the autumn season, even if it did start with the Proms. The audiences' flag-waving and tub-thumping enthusiasm for musical cliches left her bemused, but at least she would have her back to them. That was the one saving grace of conducting.

Only the instruments mattered to her. Only the call of the flute, the serenade of the viola and the thump of percussion. Nothing else mattered.

When she went back up to London for the new season, she'd have to turn her back on Haruki. She would leave him alone with his brushes and his growing strangeness. It wasn't that she didn't love him. She'd never countenance leaving him, or having an affair or anything like that. Theirs was just the kind of relationship that benefited from a few weeks apart once in a while. And that *while* was becoming overdue.

She would be thirty-six next month and although Haruki's junior, she often felt the older of the two. They had met on the south bank, at the Tate. A glittery celebration of London arts, populated by notable celebrities and illuminates of the scene. Haruki had been standing next to Lord Bragg and amongst other luminaries of the art world, but it was difficult to tell who was looking the most impressed. Haruki was doing most of the talking and the others were listening and nodding like Haruki was a great sage come down from heaven.

He was young and dashing then, Jane sighed. Oh well, she'd have her flutes and her violas to keep her occupied before too long. Then maybe she'd forget how much she missed the old Haruki.

He appeared in the garden. It looked like he had given up on his morning's work. She called out to him as he strolled past, ignoring her: 'Haruki?' He glanced in her direction, but she could tell that he didn't see her. His blind gaze fell on the chair next to her. She heard him sigh. She was losing him. He was worse than ever. She really must get him the help he so obviously needed.

She settled back into her seat, finding the piccolo again courtesy of the chaffinch. She noticed that it was being answered by another, a little way off, perhaps in another garden. She wondered what kind of conversation they were having. Was it cordial or an outright declaration of war? Birdsong always sounded so sweet to the human ear, but if she were tiny, like a bird, she might find it more intimidating.

Haruki came jogging back past her towards the house. Minutes later he bustled back the other way, back into the field carrying his brushes, his paint box, palette and easel. She was just glad that he'd found the urge to paint. There'd be no resolution of his current mental state until he'd finished a piece. That's how it was with him.

She went inside in search of food and by the time she came back outside into the garden it was the middle of the afternoon. Haruki hadn't yet returned and, growing worried, she set out to find him.

She found him in the middle of the field down in a large square pit. It was the most curious thing. Had Haruki himself dug this, or was it someone else's work? The farmer, perhaps, or detectorists? Nighthawks without permission, digging up treasures from the ancient earth?

Haruki's completed painting stood on its easel. *It's pretty good*, Jane thought. Perhaps even worth putting up with Haruki's strange behaviour for. He'd depicted the pit itself in his usual modern impressionist style, working new colours between the muddy browns, stabbing yellows and reds between the slabs of brown oil paint. And in the pit, at the bottom, Haruki had painted himself laying on his back staring up. And that's how Jane found him.

He saw her look down on him and he smiled. Jane's heart leapt at his return to relative normality. He said, 'Did you see what I did?'

'It's great, Haruki. Come up and explain it to me.' Jane reached her hand down and Haruki rose to take it. She helped him climb back out of the pit and she tucked her arm into the hollow between his ribs and his stomach. He was becoming emaciated. She should try to fatten him up before she went back up to London. She kissed him on the cheek and realised his face was wet with tears.

'Sorry, love. This one took it out of me, I think.'

The next morning, she awoke to flowers in the kitchen. He'd been out early and had placed them on the table together with some fresh bread and the goat's cheese she liked from the local delicatessen. And that was the moment that Jane Kensagi realised her relationship with Haruki was over.

She'd come to terms with the fact that sometimes his attention was not on her. That was all right, it meant she could concentrate on her music, but she had never considered before that Haruki would break her heart by bringing her flowers. It was an insult, really. Haruki was allergic to the pollen, yet he'd bought her flowers anyway. The first for many years.

She knew him, better than he knew himself. The flowers were an admission. It told her that he'd lost the ability to relate to her. You buy flowers when on a first date, or when courting, or when you need to say sorry or to express your condolences, or for birthdays, anniversaries. Any event or reason will do. But what you don't do is buy flowers for no reason. This is the action of a guilty man. One who has had an affair, or one who wants one.

To bring her flowers like this meant that he didn't know how else to communicate. They had lost whatever intimacy they once had. It meant they had come to the end of their relationship. Haruki had given up and the flowers were an apology. They were desperation. They were an end to things. And the worse thing was that she didn't disagree.

So, when Jane went up to London that week, she took most of her clothes and belongings. Haruki never questioned the extra bags. She left a note on the console table but felt he might not read it. Perhaps he wouldn't even notice she had left him.

STRINGS

They were not coming together as a section. Jane had been at this for months now and there were still timing issues with the strings. Granted, it was a tricky section of the piece that required the musicians to carefully feel their way through, but they needed to be better than this. This was the London Symphony Orchestra, for Christ's sake.

The orchestra was by far the largest that Jane had so far been entrusted with. It hadn't been easy working her way up, and proving she deserved the position through merit was becoming increasingly more difficult, especially in the current climate where positive discrimination was being openly discussed as a recruitment policy. Did they have any idea how hard she had worked to get here on her own accord? If these overprivileged liberal elites screwed it up for her, she'd never forgive them.

Eighty salaried musicians rehearsing solidly for five months. The salaries alone made her eyes water, and then there were the fees for the rehearsal facilities and much more. A seven-night performance run at the Royal Albert Hall beckoned and the expense of that was so sickeningly high that it turned her stomach to think that she wouldn't be ready on time.

The strings she had assembled should have been the perfect number for this symphony. Violas, cellos double bass and violins - on paper they should have achieved a perfect balance. Her musical director had originally specified more cellos than she currently had, but their power had the capacity to overload the bottom end of the music. Cellos carried a very big sound that stirred the air dramatically, and the instant Jane heard them in unison she knew that fewer would suffice.

There was nothing that stirred Jane more than standing in the midst of a full orchestral string section and feeling the air vibrate and crackle with their sonic energy. The layers of sound, the rich timbre, the power and the emotion. It was what she lived for. She had hired the best she could get at relatively short notice. Some of her first-choice musicians were seeing out their commitments in Stockholm or Vienna, but even her second choices were still very fine musicians.

The trouble was with the symphony itself. She had re-arranged part of a middle section to prolong the build-up and heighten the density of the string ensemble because she felt the piece deserved a more luxurious sound. But she had introduced a new twelve-bar instrumental section that looped back to join up with the original movement. The first part of the new section contained a high melody whilst the second part was based on a low-pitch, sustained A-minor chord. This shouldn't have been too taxing, but her cohort of string musicians just couldn't get it right. And what compounded the challenge was her own self-doubts. She'd spent weeks doubting herself - her rearrangement, her feel for the music and her ability to handle an orchestra of this size. It was only now that she was able to admit that there were still just too many strings.

'All right people. Let's try this one more time and this time, please watch out for the drop in melody. The chord change shouldn't be beyond musicians of your calibre. You've had enough time to figure it out.' *Last chance*, thought Jane, *before I pull in an extra double bass to keep time.* That would mean altering the balance of her strings. She would need to add more on the top end to compensate for the bass. More violas, fewer violins. Well, that would only serve them right. But then she'd have to start again. She'd have to undo months of hard work and cram for the next few weeks to get it right. That wouldn't go down well with her already over-worked team. She kicked herself for not being more decisive earlier, when she'd had more time to make changes.

'Hold it.' Jane held up her hand to stall the orchestra. They hung on the movement of her hands and her rosewood baton. She was the conductor, after all. Jane reached into her pocket, where her phone vibrated. She looked at the screen. 'Sorry, I have to take this.' Several of the violinists lowered their instruments in open frustration whilst most of the others used the pause to play silently through the tricky section. Jane took note of which violinists had the worst attitude. She would sack these first if it came down to that.

'Jane?' It was Thomas Peters, Haruki's agent. A thrill of concern moved through Jane. There were only a few reasons that he'd be moved to call her, and none of them were good.

'It's Haruki,' Peters said. 'Manchester have come in for one of his works. And I'm trying to get in touch. I need access to the house.'

'Why should that concern me, Thomas? You know that we're separated?'

'Yes, Haruki told me before he left. For what it's worth, I'm sorry.'

'Before he left?'

'He left London months ago. He's staying up in the Lakes. He went up there to recharge his batteries.'

'So, call him.'

'I can't get in touch with him,' Thomas said. 'I'd go up there myself, but I can't get away. I'm going through a few things with Lilly and the kids. You know how it is.'

Jane *did* know how it was, although she felt relief that there were no kids to complicate her own break-up with Haruki.

'Jane, he hasn't been heard from for three months. I was wondering if you could access the house – perhaps you could let me have a key?'

'I'm sorry, Thomas. But you'll have to take this up with Haruki. If you know where he is, you'll have to find a way to reach him.' She knew this was harsh, but if she allowed herself to get involved, Thomas would call her at every little eccentricity from her estranged husband.

'I'm worried about him,' Thomas said. 'He wasn't exactly in a healthy frame of mind when he left. I wondered if you'd care to—'

'No, Thomas, I wouldn't. I washed my hands of him months ago. I'm sorry, Thomas, goodbye.'

Jane snapped the telephone back onto her pocket and turned to her orchestra. 'Right. My apologies, everyone. Now, prepare yourselves. Let's try the section one more time. And this time let us all try to keep together; we need to make this one count.'

After the rehearsal, Jane sat in her office. She was pondering upon the changes she was forced to make when a knock at the door interrupted her train of thought. It was that time already. This was the least enjoyable aspect of her role. 'Enter,' she called.

'You wanted to see me?' Chiara White entered and Jane gestured for her to sit in the chair opposite. Chiara was a slim, demure woman in her mid-twenties. She wore a matching suit with a pencil-thin white skirt which she smoothed down before sitting primly in an exaggerated upright position. All musicians were like this; all held their superb posture like a badge of honour. As if it made their instruments sound more melodic. Chiara had repeatedly worn white to the auditions despite Jane trying to encourage a uniform assembly of darker colours. The idea was that the musicians were not distracted by their surroundings, but Jane couldn't help think that Chiara meant to undermine her, or at least draw attention to herself. She tucked her immaculately straightened blonde bob behind one ear and fixed Jane with a frosty stare that made her glad there was three feet of thick oak desk separating them.

'Chiara, this isn't easy, but I will do you the service of getting straight to the point. The string section is off-balance and we have timing issues.'

'And you think this has something to do with me?'

'No, but I need to make some changes. I need to thin out the violins. I'm afraid you are one of the changes I need to make. This is nothing personal, you understand.'

'I see.' Chiara slowly rose from her seat. Her face was a perfect mask of composure, but the cold sureness of her movements gave Jane cause for concern. She had plenty of experience with musicians. She reckoned Chiara wouldn't even make it half-way to the door before… 'You know, Jane, it's your bullshit arrangement that's to blame. A string quartet would have difficulty playing that in unison, never mind a whole section. You should look to yourself if you wish to make changes.'

'Chiara, I understand that you must be disappointed, but it is my role to—'

'I wonder who is it that you think you are, exactly.' Chiara's hair fell forward as she leaned menacingly over Jane's desk. The girl wasn't shouting yet, but her mask of composure had well and truly slipped. 'At Salzburg, I was the recipient of the Amadeus award – the youngest to ever receive it. And in New York I was chosen from a very strong field for the lead in Verdi's *Requiem*.'

'Chiara, what's your point?'

'My point is that you don't have the right to treat me like this. I'm the best violinist in this orchestra. Why sack me and not the others?'

'It's a fair question, Chiara.' Jane tried to keep her voice low and level. She tried not to flinch under Chiara's searching gaze. 'If anything, you're a little ahead of the others. You transition between the chords a little faster, but I need someone who will wait for the rest to catch up. I need more of a team player.' Chiara's face changed colour and Jane knew she'd said the wrong thing.

'Team player? You accuse me of not being a team player. That's rich from someone who deserted their mentally ill husband and packed him off to a nuthouse up north. Yes, that's right, I heard about that; we all did. Let's not forget that the art world is a close-knit community. Especially when you're well-connected. Though you wouldn't know what that's like, would you?'

Jane stood aghast and, for the time being, unable to defend herself.

'In fact, you are quite the talking point. Famous throughout London as the heartless bitch who put her career ahead of her sick husband. So, what right do you have to lecture me about being a team player? If it wasn't for your bullshit arrangement we'd be ready for Albert Hall by now. You've made this performance all about yourself. And what makes you think you're even qualified to re-arrange the strings? What makes you think you're qualified to lead an orchestra like this in the first place? You're a joke, Jane, a bloody joke. You people are all the same.'

'What did you say?'

'You heard very well, Jane. I told you that you weren't qualified to re-arrange the strings.'

'No, after that. You said, "You people are all the same." What did you mean by that? Who is *all the same*, Chiara? Do you have a problem with the colour of my skin? Do you think I achieved this position simply because I'm black? Is that it?'

'Well, you must admit that it can't hurt. You know as well as I do that there are quotas these days. But I don't care that you're black. You could be white, brown or yellow for all I care. But my point is that it is you *conductors* that are all the same. You think you're the stars, but it's the musicians that should get the plaudits. You know what they say: those that can play, play. Those that can't, conduct.'

'No, Chiara. The point is that you're nothing more than a jumped up, self-important little bitch with a sense of entitlement the size of the Albert Hall. You think I won't call you out on your casual racism? You're wrong. Now I suggest you get out of my office and out of my orchestra before I do something to you that I won't regret.' Jane stood up to her. She wasn't as tall as Chiara, but the musician shrank from Jane before turning and storming out.

'You'll regret this, I guarantee it. I'll talk to my father. You had better pray that you hang on to this position, because it will be the last one you will have for quite some time.' The door slammed on Chiara's way out.

Bloody musicians, Jane thought. *They pretend to be at the vanguard of culture and civilisation, but when things don't suit them their claws come out like the rest of us.* Chiara would not fail in making trouble for her; she just hoped that she was resilient enough to weather the storm.

But Chiara had made some of her words stick. They cloyed and clogged her mind to the extent that later that evening, she found herself driving down to Barnes, out to what several months ago she'd thought of as the family house. Haruki had always been eccentric, but just before she'd left him, his behaviour had left the realms of normality. She had known he was suffering some kind of breakdown and so if he was now in trouble, she surely had some responsibility towards him? Thirteen years of marriage couldn't be expunged so easily.

Jane liked to think that she went there for Haruki's sake, but she feared that the real reason had nothing to do with him and everything to do with her own career. If news of Haruki's behaviour had already bled into the arts scene, then if anything further happened to him, her own career might suffer. With her atypical background, the LSO were already taking a chance on her, and they had a reputation of their own to protect.

The last thing Jane wanted was to be known as the wife of the crazy painter. And looking at it the other way, if Haruki had a major exhibit in a national gallery, then that would reflect very well on her. It could tip the balance for her career. God knows, she needed all of the help she could get right now.

She went there to get a spare set of keys for Peters and to stop the man from bothering her once and for all, but she was beginning to have second thoughts.

Jane lifted the catch on the bottom gate and walked up the path bisecting the front garden. The hedges were still neat and the grass recently mowed, so at least old McTominay was still around and keeping the garden tamed. Inside the house it was a much different story. The place was in disarray. Her first thought was to call the police to report a burglary, but then she realised that it was Haruki's painting things that were strewn all over the house. Nothing else was touched; the antique furniture was all in position and the valuable pieces on the mantel were all still there, including the gold carriage clock and the ancient twin vases.

She wondered how she'd feel coming back to the house for the first time in months, but she hadn't reckoned on the place being such a glaring distress signal for her husband's mental state. Each room was strewn with the cast-aside accoutrements of Haruki's paintings. Snapped brushes littered the carpet. So too were tubes of paint, their contents were squeezed out and smeared over the floor and walls. Each room was like this, but their bedroom was worse. The sheets were cast aside, the mattress upended and slashed open in deep gouges. Stuffing and springs spilled out like guts. Their marriage bed sacrificed to Haruki's obviously deteriorating mental state.

But the worst thing was the paintings on the walls. The house had been filled with Haruki's most notable works of art. Those that he deemed worthy of display and which were not currently on display in a collection somewhere. But now the walls were empty. Someone had taken down every picture. And when Jane reached the conservatory, she could see why.

They were piled up as if composing a bonfire. The heap reached half-way to the ceiling of the conservatory's high glass roof and on the very top, above all of the others, was a painting that seemed fresh. She recognised the sheen and smell of a freshly painted canvas. Haruki always used a lot of paint and this one was no exception. It reeked of thick oils that slid down the canvas to form a rich but twisted landscape. The picture was of twin hills, one grey-green and the other golden-yellow, and what looked like black boxes littered the landscape. It amazed her why Haruki would spoil a perfectly good landscape by painting coffins all over the place. Coffins, or graves.

She picked up the telephone and dialled Haruki's agent to tell him that she'd be dropping off a spare set of keys. Then he could come here and sort out this mess. Haruki would then be *his* problem, not hers. But when Lilly Peters answered, Jane found it difficult to hang on to that frame of mind. Peters had said that his own marriage was struggling, but this was proof that the couple were working things out. And Lilly sounded so nice, and she was so sympathetic when Jane told her about the scenes of distress at the house.

'Tell me where he is,' Jane found herself saying, despite her better judgement. 'I'll go and find him myself.'

JIGSAW

Jane had a warm feeling about this place. It looked like an idyllic cottage and the best possible place for Haruki to recuperate from whatever he was going through.

She'd stopped for directions down in the village; the people she'd met there seemed friendly and they were keen to stop and talk to her. It was a good sign that there were people on the streets who were willing to take the time to wander around talking to each other. In London, no one had the time for that. Everyone had somewhere to go in a hurry. You were surrounded by folk but lonely all the same. Here it seemed different and she had the sense that everyone knew each other. If Haruki had the good sense to bring himself here to have his mid-life crisis, then perhaps he wasn't so ill after all.

She might even be able to have a sensible conversation with him about their future. During the long drive up she'd been giving that a lot of thought.

She opened the little gate at the top of the path and wandered into the little cottage garden that was fringed by a knee-high slate wall. An apple tree stood in the centre of a small lawn; a blackbird chirruped happily in its bare branches. It nibbled at the fruit that hadn't yet dropped.

As Jane approached the front door and held her hand over

the lacquered iron knocker, she heard laughter from inside which gave her pause for thought. What she had just heard didn't fit with the notion that Haruki was struggling and on the fringes of despair, but that's why she'd travelled all the way up here.

Instead of knocking, Jane crept away from the front door and looked in at one of the windows. She couldn't resist the urge to know what she was walking into, so Jane put her hand to the pane and peered in.

Haruki was stretched across a sheepskin rug; the dying embers of a fire glowed at his side. At his other side lay a slim girl, pretty and white. Both she and Haruki were naked.

Jane felt a wave of revulsion as she watched the girl's hand play casually across his stomach. She couldn't help feeling that this was a deliberate act of ownership. The girl was marking him as her property. Jane felt vulnerable outside. Did this woman know she was being watched?

The bile rose in Jane's stomach. She bolted down up the little path that led out of the garden, not bothering to shut the gate again after her. She almost took a tumble down the trail that led back down to the village, but she managed to stay on her feet and only stopped running when she reached the bottom.

Breathing heavily and slick with sweat, she rested her hand on the stile that led onto the road and reflected on what she had seen. It frightened her that her first instinct was to run away instead of confronting them. And she was more afraid because she hadn't thought that he still had the capacity to hurt her like this.

Haruki wasn't having a breakdown; he was just hiding up here, having absconded with a girl half his age. Damn him, for dragging her all the way out here. She'd been worried about him, and she didn't deserve for him to make a fool out of her like this.

She had made a terrible mistake coming all the way up here and now she just wanted to get away from the place, but as she approached where she had parked her Tesla in a lay-by at the bottom of the hill, she felt more frustration. Both her front tyres were flat.

She had no choice but to trudge back into the village and try to find a mechanic. Her phone hadn't been able to obtain any reception since she'd arrived here, but she'd seen a telephone box in the village next to the post office. It was one of the red old-fashioned types, but it looked to be stocked with a modern telephone instead of useless books or God-knows-what that most seem to have been re-purposed to contain these days.

The village was still littered with people, perhaps a dozen in total. They were stood around mostly in pairs, chatting, and when she walked past, they stopped their conversations and greeted her with a friendly wave or nod of the head. All wore wide, friendly smiles on their faces. An elderly couple dressed in matching light tan raincoats turned to watch her disappear into the phone box by the post office. She could feel their eyes on her even as she picked up the receiver.

She was out of luck. Try as she might, she couldn't get a dialling tone, so she decided to enquire within the post office.

'I have flat tyres.' Jane got straight to the point. 'Could I use your telephone?'

The old man sat back in his chair at the other side of the counter. He regarded his chocolates like a curator might a prized museum collection. He reverently adjusted the position of a Cadbury's caramel, perfectly aligning it with the others before saying, 'Frank doesn't own a telephone. They are bad for Frank's health.' He made a circling motion with his forefinger around the side of his head. 'Makes Frank crazy. That's why Frank likes living here. No interference. Does it want a chocolate?'

'No, I don't want a chocolate, I want a mechanic. I need to leave and I can't because my car needs new tyres.'

'Frank does not want it to worry. He knows of a garage, just a little way out of the village. If Frank wanted to go there, Frank would keep on down this road.' He gestured in a direction over Jane's shoulder before quickly jerking his hand back to hover over his chocolates. 'It should tell them Frank sent it. It would not be lying because I'm Frank.'

Jane sighed with relief. 'Yes, I realise that. But thank you, Frank. Just down this road, you say? I didn't notice a garage coming in here.'

'It wouldn't, but Frank knows, and it now knows Frank, so that is good.' He swept a fat hand over the chocolates. 'Frank would offer to take it himself, but he has to guard these treasures.'

'Really? Who from?' Jane glanced around the empty shop. Bare dusty shelves stared back at her.

'From those who like treasure. There are those who would seek to take advantage of Frank. But Frank is vigilant. They will not succeed.'

Jane left the post office, quite glad to leave him to his chocolates. The garage was apparently just down the road and she wanted to leave the village before suffering the embarrassment of Haruki realising she'd come here. She managed to get a hundred metres down the road before it started to rain heavily. The downpour turned the sky a dirty shade of grey.

The rain was so heavy at this point that Jane started to run. She was close to the position of the garage that the old man had described to her, but really hated to get wet.

She couldn't remember when she'd last moved her body at more than a sedate pace. Her arms and torso got enough exercise with her conducting and they were in perfect coordination, but the same could not be said of her legs. She knew she must have made an ungainly sight, her legs thrown out sideways too much as they kicked off from the ground. But it wasn't as if there was anyone around to see her.

Before long she saw a bright light appear and felt this to be the place. Then she saw another light further ahead, two in fact; they were car headlights. She slowed to a walk and watched the car come onwards, smooth and fast, a big black Mercedes with yellow writing on its side. A taxi.

A head turned in the side window. A man stared at Jane, meeting her eyes for a moment with a flash of recognition. Then the moment was over and the car slid past. It parted the surface water, leaving momentary impressions of tyre tracks in its wake. Jane stepped out into the road and stared at the back of the car. The man had turned in his seat to look at her through the back window. An Asian man, lean-featured, with a good head of hair and sad eyes. It was Haruki.

Jane stepped out into the road and stared in the wake of the car. The rain bounced off the tarmac and splashed above her boots and onto her trousers. She had found Haruki in the arms of another woman only minutes ago and now here he was, fully dressed, in the back of a taxi streaking towards the village as if he was only just arriving. The only explanation for this was that he had somehow noticed Jane up at the cottage and had come down to look for her. In which case, why didn't he stop for her? Didn't he recognise his own wife running along the side of the road?

A flash of anger invigorated her. She forgot all about her flat tyres and instead set off after Haruki's taxi. She no longer ran, even though it was still raining hard, but she walked with a cold determination. Why was she avoiding Haruki anyway? Why should she be embarrassed to have come to find her own husband? It should be Haruki who was the one who felt uncomfortable at her presence. It should be *he* who was embarrassed.

Jane stopped at the post office and ducked her head in. She didn't exactly relish talking to the strange old man again; he gave her the creeps. He triggered some deep-seated instinct from her childhood and was exactly the kind of stranger that she had been taught to stay far away from.

Frank was still hunched over his chocolate bars; he looked up at her, but his eyes could not seem to rest on her. They roamed around the room as if searching for her. She realised with a stab of guilt that the old man was blind.

'Frank? This is Jane Kensagi. I was just in here a second ago. Listen, I didn't make it to the garage because something came up. But if you see the mechanic, could you perhaps mention to him that my Model S needs two front tyres? I've parked by the path up to Hilltops.' Jane regretted her use of the word 'see'. She blushed at her own insensitivity.

'Jane, it says? Sorry, I don't know it, is it sure it knows Frank? He'd be glad to know it, if it wants to come in and spend time with old Frank. He has chocolates – does it want one?' Frank held up a Turkish Delight.

'I was in here just moments ago. You must remember speaking to me? You gave me directions to the mechanic, but I've just seen my husband and I need to go back up to Hilltops.'

'Hilltops, it says? It'll be needing a good pair of boots…'

Jane considered it useless to dally further with the man. She rushed out of the post office and up the road that wound up the hill towards where she had parked. She traversed the stile and scurried up the path towards Hilltops, thankful that the rain had abated.

For the second time in an hour, Jane stood at the threshold of where Haruki had been staying for the past three months. Her hand held the iron knocker. She paused, shook the feeling of doubt away, drew in a breath and let the knocker fall.

Voices from inside, a man and a woman. Her husband, Haruki.

The door opened; Haruki appeared. He was fully dressed in a blue shirt and trousers. He had lost nothing of his slim, athletic frame. He blinked in the doorway, as if he were trying to process too much information. 'Jane? What are you doing here?'

'Hello, Haruki.' Jane stepped past him and into the house. Inside, the open fire smouldered, filling the air with a smoky smell. It filled her nose and pricked at her eyes. 'Jesus, you should open a window.'

'This is Maggie.' Haruki used his palm to indicate towards a slim, pretty woman sat at the table drinking tea in front of a huge jigsaw puzzle. It had only just been tipped out and all of the pieces hadn't been turned over yet. She was shuffling the pieces around but looked up at her with a smile that seemed genuine enough.

'I'm Haruki's wife,' Jane said, and regretted the insistency with which it came out. She didn't offer her hand in greeting but walked a wide circle to take in Haruki's front room. She went to the fireplace and examined the old-style hearth made of Lakeland grey slate. The mantel was a large piece of darkened oak. Both were soot-stained, as was the papered ceiling directly above the fireplace. She came full circle. 'So, this is where you've been holed up. It's charming enough, I suppose.'

Haruki started to say something, but whatever it was, he couldn't finish the thought. 'Jane, I…'

Jane opened her mouth to let her husband have a piece of her mind, but nothing came out. Now that he was in front of her, she didn't have the right words. Was she so shocked at seeing her husband naked with another woman, or was it that he now looked so innocent?

'Jane, you're all wet. Sit down and I'll get you a towel. I'll make some tea too. We can talk when you're more comfortable.'

Maggie left quickly, excusing herself to go and 'check on

her sister'. Jane noted the way she shared a glance with Haruki as she left.

Jane took Maggie's seat and by the time Haruki came out of the kitchen with a mug of tea, she had already completed a small section of the jigsaw puzzle at the upper right-hand corner. She found these things easy; it was just a matter of focus and application. The trick was to separate in your own mind the colours and shapes you wanted. You couldn't let the other pieces distract you.

'Your agent has been bothering me,' Jane said. 'He's not heard from you. He's worried. Oh, and Manchester Gallery wants you. They want your work at the centre of a new collection.'

Jane watched Haruki blink away any excitement at that prospect. She realised with some surprise that he was focusing only on her. It was quite unlike him.

'Jane, why are you here? I thought we were done this time. I thought that was it. You stayed away for so long. No contact from you, none at all. I waited for so long, but you never came back.'

'I know. To tell you the truth, I thought we were finished too.'

'And now? Why are you here?'

'I don't know, I really don't. I wish I did.' Jane blew on her tea. She used the time to arrange her next words. 'I saw you, Haruki. I saw you and that girl, Maggie.'

Haruki looked confused. 'What, here? With the jigsaw puzzle?'

'No, not with the puzzle, with your naked body, and hers. Down there by the rug. I saw you both, so please don't try to deny it.'

'I don't know what you're talking about, Jane. Maggie's just helping me get settled. She's like the caretaker; she looks after the property.'

'I'm not a fool, Haruki. I can see the way she looks at you. How long have you been sleeping with her? The least you could have done was drop me a line and let me know you're okay and that you'd found someone else. It's really okay. You have that right at least, after the way I treated you. But you should have let me know.'

'I'm not sleeping with Maggie. I only just met her. She lives with her sister down the hill. If you don't believe me, that's your choice, I suppose. It's always your choice, Jane, isn't it? It was you who walked out on me. It's you who chooses whether or not to come back, while I just mope around trying to paint and wondering if I'll ever see you again. It's always you, Jane.'

Jane pointed her finger at her estranged husband. 'But this time, you've made it about you, haven't you? You disappear for three months, leaving everyone wondering if you're in the midst of a mental health trauma. I was worried about you, but here I find that you're shacked up with a girl half your age.'

'I told you, Maggie and me, we're not... but what do you mean, three months?'

'Three months. That's how long you've been gone, in case you've forgotten. In case Maggie has fucked you out of all your senses. I walked out on you in February. Peters says you moved up here in May. It's now the middle of August.'

'What are you talking about? I've only just arrived here. I left London this morning.'

'Either you genuinely think that I'll believe what you're saying or you're playing stupid games with me. Either way, I'm not going to play along. I came to see if you needed help. You don't. Goodbye, Haruki.'

'Wait, don't leave. I don't know what's going on, you're confusing me, but it's really good to see you, Jane.'

'I saw you, Haruki. Just now. I saw you with that girl. On the rug.' Jane pointed but was shocked to see that there was no sheepskin rug in front of the fire, just a threadbare old Persian.

'I don't know what you saw, Jane, but it didn't happen. Really, I promise you.' Haruki was so insistent, but Jane knew what she had seen through the window. But then, the rug.

'Haruki. How did you get here?'

'By taxi – I took a train to Oxenholme and pre-booked a cab from there.'

'I saw you down in the village. Black Mercedes, yellow writing. You looked back at me. You saw me but went past anyway.'

'I remember. I saw someone that reminded me of you, but I couldn't see clearly through the rain.'

Jane threw her hands up in frustration. Haruki was as intractable as ever. 'You don't need to spare my feelings by concocting this pack of lies. You made me angry, and I wanted to give you a piece of my mind, but now I just want to leave. It was a mistake for me to come here. I had to ask our musical director to cover for me - Sir John no less. Jesus, Haruki, the LSO doesn't mess about with unreliable conductors. I could already be in serious trouble. I need to get to a phone. I should let Sir John know that I'm coming back immediately. Before he starts to change things.'

'The only person I know with a telephone is the Captain. If it means that much to you, I'll take you there.' Haruki peered out of the cottage window at the sky that was brightening by the second. 'But please stay here tonight. Whatever is going on, we need to talk it through.'

'Haruki, I'm not spending a second more in this sordid place than I need to. I'll get my car fixed and get back to London tonight. Then I'll leave you to romance as many younger women as you want. No, don't say anything, really, I don't care.'

TELEPHONE

The silence down to the Captain's house was as stony as the path on which they walked. They came to a large white house nestled at the bottom of the hill. Haruki yanked on a bell-pull and Jane heard a tinkle from inside. A soft concussion of footsteps told her someone was coming downstairs and towards the door. It opened to reveal a man in his forties, boyishly handsome with gun-metal eyes, but with a dress sense that came straight out of the nineteen-eighties. He wore tight jeans and a denim shirt that was unbuttoned almost at the navel. Nevertheless, he had a pleasantly tight body under the shirt and the snugness of his jeans left nothing to the imagination. Bleached blond hair completed the look, although Jane didn't have a clue what look he was hoping to achieve.

The man ushered them inside, through a low-ceilinged porch littered with nautical-themed decor and into a grander reception room with dark wood wainscoting and a wonderful old Chesterfield sofa and chair arranged around a large fireplace. Above which a grand sweeping staircase wound upwards. 'Could we use your telephone, perhaps?' Haruki asked.

'Sorry, my friend. I don't have one.'

'But I heard one when I was here last.' Haruki was polite but insistent.

'Ah, that telephone.' Although the Captain spoke to Haruki, his eyes were firmly on Jane. She was keenly aware that they travelled slowly up and down her body. 'You are mixed race?' he asked Jane, abruptly.

She screwed her face up at the question. 'My mother was Welsh, and my father was from London.'

'Well, you're a beautiful concoction, don't you think, Haruki?'

'I'm not a "concoction",' Jane said. She hadn't quite allowed the Captain's engaging smile to disarm her just yet.

'I'm a mixed bag myself,' the Captain said. 'I'll tell you about it sometime. Please come this way, the telephone is through here.'

Jane noticed Haruki flinch when the Captain put his hand on the door handle, and she wondered why he might be afraid of entering. But when he threw the door wide open, Jane saw a perfectly ordinary kitchen. A large Belfast sink was the centrepiece of the kitchen with an island unit fixed to the floor behind. A Welsh dresser held all kinds of mis-matched china plates, and bunches of dried herbs and spices festooned the ceiling, dancing at head height over the island unit. It smelled of food. Rich and fragrant and with a hint of vanilla. Haruki paused at the threshold of the room.

The telephone stood on the central shelf of the dresser. It was a baker-lite antique with a dial instead of digital numbers. 'Sometimes the old ways are the best,' the Captain said.

She took out her mobile phone to access the number of her musical director. 'Excuse me,' she said, and began the slow process of dialling. It took her several tries as she kept snagging and scuffing her attempts at dialling.

'London Symphony.' It was Julien who answered, Sir John's assistant.

'Julien. Can you put me through to Sir John?'

There was a pause at the other end of the line. 'Ms Kensagi, is that you?'

'Yes, it's me, Julien. I want a word with Sir John – is he around? Hello. Hello, Julien?'

There was silence at the other end, then Sir John's voice, 'Jane, where are you? Are you all right?'

'Yes, of course I am. I'm up in the Lakes.'

'Are you with your husband?'

'As a matter of fact, yes. Why.'

'You should have sent word, Jane. It is most remiss of you, I have to say. We hadn't heard from you, Jane. You vanished off the face of the Earth. You should have called us. We've given away your position, you know. Had to. We couldn't wait.'

'You've what? Why?'

'Do I really need to say? You ran off mid-rehearsal. You asked me to mind your shop for a day or two at the most. Then we didn't hear from you for months. You can't be surprised that we took that as your resignation. I know you felt that you bit off more than you could chew, but really, Jane, I expected more from you.'

'Months, did you say? What are you talking about?'

'Look. I think you should speak with Constance. This is really a matter for human resources. It's not a musical thing. I'll ask Julien to patch you through to her.'

'Sir John, wait, please. I really haven't been gone long. I left to see my husband; I thought he needed me. But I just got here. I've only been gone a day.'

'I'm sorry, Jane, this is really not a matter for me. Let me transfer you to—'

'Just tell me one thing then: who did you get to replace me?'

'As it happened, we had a hell of a job replacing you. Most of the first-class conductors were spoken for. We tried to pull in Caspar from Munich, but he was already committed to the Berlin Phil. In the end we had to promote from within. You should have called us. You should have let us know what was happening. We could never have kept the position open, but at least you might have had some kind of opportunity to come back to.'

'Tell me you didn't give it to Chiara.'

'She was the most accomplished with the strings. And she proved most capable of simplifying the tricky new arrangement. So, yes, and she's working out fine, if you want to know. We'll be ready for the Royal Albert.'

Jane had no response to this. It was exactly as she feared. Her mind raced with possibilities. Could it be a joke? A carefully executed revenge manoeuvre of Chiara's?

'Jane, I'm putting you through to HR. For what it's worth—'

'Don't bother,' Jane said, 'I'll come back to see them in person. Thank you, Sir John.' Jane hung up. She turned to her husband. 'How much do you know about this?' But Haruki looked as confused as she was. 'Forget it, I'll find out when I get back to London. Someone is playing silly buggers with me.'

'I'm sorry, Jane, really I am.'

The Captain approached her; she was surprised that she allowed him to place his hand on her shoulder. He looked her straight in the eyes. 'Jane. I think I know what your problem is. It's very common around here. You see, we're in a bit of a bubble. It's easy for people to lose time around here.'

'What? Are you suggesting I somehow didn't notice that several months have just slipped by?'

'No, I didn't mean that you may have lost *track* of time. I said that you have lost time. There's a difference. But wait around for a while, you'll find it again. In time, you can make another telephone call. When you do, things will be different then. You'll see.'

CAPTAIN

She couldn't believe that she was foolish enough to have been concerned about Haruki. And because she'd allowed herself to become distracted with him, her career was in jeopardy. She suspected Chiara, of course. Perhaps she'd falsified attendance records or found some other way to raise a false complaint against her. Whatever it was, she'd get back and sort it all out. She'd sort her out.

A younger woman had stolen her husband, it seemed, but she could just about accept that. They were all adults, after all, and it was about time that Haruki was someone else's liability. But what she couldn't accept was that Chiara disrespected her enough to interfere in her life. How dare she try to play practical jokes with her private life? She thought of her father, and of her early years growing up in London Fields. What would her father have done to those who disrespected him? She shuddered at the thought.

But she had little choice but to spend the night at the Captain's house. She couldn't face spending it at Haruki's place after witnessing him cheat on her with such indiscretion. And the Captain had insisted, whilst also promising to arrange her car to be fixed. It wouldn't be ready until tomorrow because the tyres had to be ordered from Carlisle. They were to be driven down first thing in the morning. There were no hotels or guest houses in the area. If she was really honest with herself, she didn't mind too much. She found the Captain interesting. And if she wanted to get back at Haruki, there were worse ways to do that.

But for now she was on her own. The Captain had gone out on an errand and he wouldn't be back until after dark, he'd said. But she was comfortable curled up on the sofa. The fire was warm and comforting and she had found an old, dog-eared copy of Bulgakov's *Master and Margherita*.

An hour or so into the novel she began to feel hungry. The sensation was mirrored by what she had just read, or possibly it was the other way around.

'His wife brought pickled herring from the kitchen, neatly sliced and thickly sprinkled with green onion. Nikanor Ivanovich poured himself a dram of vodka, drank it, poured another, drank it, picked up three pieces of herring on his fork... and at that moment the doorbell rang. Pelageya Antonovna was just bringing in a steaming pot which, one could tell at once from a single glance, contained amidst a fiery borscht...'

Pickled herring sounded great, and if she could find something hot in the kitchen, like leftover stew, then even better. And she could use a drink. Some vodka might be just the thing to take her mind off Haruki, Chiara and Sir John. Though she still doubted it was even him on the telephone and not some stooge of Chiara's. Jane set down her book and plodded towards the kitchen. But when she pushed open the kitchen door, her mind reeled with confusion. It was not a kitchen but a white room, almost entirely plain and featureless. She had to focus hard to see that there was a white metal drain in the centre and a chair stuck upside down to the ceiling.

Stepping forward to inspect both, the sprung door closed behind her with a soft click. She'd obviously stumbled into the wrong room, a wet shower room, although it was too large a room for a single shower. Her instinct was to leave the room quickly, but when she tried the handle, the door was locked. Her neck prickled with rising panic. She was trapped in here.

And something else was in here with her. She was sure of that. Something was hiding in the brightness. Something she thought didn't want to be seen but was creeping closer. A thrill of fear fixed her to the spot as she stared into the room. She became hyper-vigilant to movement or to any anomaly in the smooth white walls.

Then she saw it. A translucent thing about a foot in diameter.

It made its way furtively down one wall. It looked like water, except it was moving far too slowly. It didn't look like it was under the direct influence of gravity either because the moment after Jane noticed it, it stopped moving.

As if it had seen her notice it.

Jane awoke in a bed. It wasn't hers, but she was thankful that it wasn't the Captain's either. She was wearing a man's set of blue and white cotton striped pyjamas that she certainly didn't recognise. Blinking around the room, she saw nothing of her own clothes or effects. But hung on the wardrobe opposite was a gorgeous green dress. Even from her bed, she could see that it was cut on the bias and would flow beautifully over her. She had reservations about wearing someone else's dress. And if it had been specially selected for her by the Captain then she didn't want to give him the victory he might claim if she wore it. But she also didn't relish traipsing downstairs in another man's pyjamas. That seemed far too intimate.

She must have fallen asleep downstairs last night. That wasn't unusual. She often fell asleep in her big chair downstairs, exhausted after a day with the LSO. Especially when she read.

She found the act of reading very relaxing. The words came one after another in a simple, one-dimensional way. She liked that simplicity, especially after trying to manage the multi-layered complexity of a full-sized orchestra.

But she was sure that she would have remembered waking and coming upstairs to bed. If she hadn't put herself to bed, then it must have been the Captain. She didn't know how she felt to think that the man had undressed her and put her into pyjamas while she was unconscious.

Jane had a nagging feeling that something might have happened last night. Something of which she had only a nascent, slow-dawning awareness. She hadn't been drinking, she never did find any vodka, but it felt this morning as if she had. It also felt as it her body had been through some physical challenge or ordeal. Had she been attacked or taken advantage of? She didn't think so, but she certainly felt a little different in some way. She examined herself. There were no bruises, and to her immense relief, there was no soreness to suggest that she'd been assaulted. But she still felt very uneasy about the missing timeline of last night.

Jane found the bathroom and showered. She brushed her teeth with a plastic-wrapped hotel toothbrush that was placed by the sink, and she fixed her hair. She didn't have any make-up, but she often went without, even at work. She was lucky to have good skin, and so why should she mess with what nature had given her?

She found the Captain downstairs in the kitchen. At the sight of him, her hackles rose, but she stepped forwards into the room. The Captain was wearing his dressing gown. He had omitted to tie it tightly and it was gaping open at the naval. He looked like he had just come from the shower and his tight stomach muscles glistened.

'How old are you?' Jane asked. She was sitting at the kitchen table whilst he dried his golden blond hair.

'Now that's a question you shouldn't ask a gentleman,' the Captain said. He put the towel around his shoulders and poured himself a whiskey.

'And are you? Are you a gentleman?'

For a reply, the Captain waggled his glass at her. 'Want one?'

Jane ignored his offer. 'Where were you last night?'

'Up on the hill. I'll have to take you there one day.'

'I'm leaving this morning. Were you with Haruki?'

'Haruki was there, yes. He's an important part of the community. He and I had some business to attend to.'

'But you're not telling me what.'

'Your car is ready to collect. It's where you parked it. I'll walk you to it after breakfast, if that's what you want?'

'Of course it's what I want. Why wouldn't it be?'

The Captain moved closer to her. She could smell him. A fresh, slightly sweet scent. She found herself breathing in heavily. Her senses filled with the aroma of vanilla and the sight of his smooth pectorals peeking out of the gaping dressing gown. 'I thought you might want to stay for a while,' he said, leaning close to her. Jane froze; she allowed the Captain to come very close. His face was an inch away from hers and his eyes burrowed into hers. They were steel grey, the colour of the moon. She could feel his breath on her lips when he said, 'I want you to stay. And I think you want that too.'

Jane's heart raced. Though she kept herself perfectly still, her mind reached out just a little way and imagined kissing him. Her tongue explored his mouth, tasting its electric, metallic tang. In her mind, she touched his chest. She ran her fingers down his body, inside his dressing gown. She imagined him sat on the edge of her bed, tenderly easing her naked body into his own pyjamas. She fumbled at his belt and it fell away easily, revealing his muscular body in all its glory. She lowered herself to her knees, reaching out for him.

The doorbell brought her out of her daydream. She was sitting at the breakfast table, blinking and breathing heavily. The Captain's face was close, but his dressing gown was fully closed and belted. 'We can continue this later,' he said.

When Jane was alone in the kitchen, the feeling of unease returned to her. And now when she blinked, instead of darkness she saw light. A bright white room. A chair stuck to the ceiling. Something translucent inched its way towards her. She felt as though the blood was draining from her face; the feeling of panic intensified. She didn't dare to make any sudden movements, but she desperately wanted to get out of the room. Slowly and carefully, Jane rose, then the panic got the better of her and she bolted, slamming the door behind her and taking a breath again only when she reached the safety of the hallway.

PART THREE

HARUKI AND JANE

RECURSION

Haruki woke on the sheepskin rug by the fire in the little Hilltops cottage. He hadn't been aware of himself dropping off and was a little disoriented when he came to. It took him a few moments to remember where he was and what he was doing there. Maggie stirred bedside him. She was naked, as was Haruki. The fire had subsided and was little more than a warm glow, just enough to dispel the growing chill of the night. Maggie walked her fingers down to Haruki's stomach. Her breasts draped across his chest. They were warm and tantalisingly close to his face.

'How did you get this scar?' Maggie asked, fingering a two-inch long smooth line that was darker that the rest of Haruki's olive skin.

Haruki looked down at his own stomach. 'I don't know. I don't remember.'

'Which is it,' Maggie said, 'you don't know, or you don't remember? There's a big difference.'

'Is there?'

'Who doesn't notice when they get a two-inch scar in their middle?'

Haruki twisted his fingers through Maggie's hair, eventually releasing it to fall across his chest. 'To tell you the truth,' he said, 'there's a lot I don't remember. Is that bad, do you think? I'm beginning to worry.'

'Not at all.' Maggie laughed. 'It's sometimes hard to remember things in this place. But let me show you something.' Maggie rolled a little backwards to reveal the same size scar and in the same position, though it was on her opposite side.

It occurred to him that their scars had touched together when she laid on top of him. They had probably lined up perfectly against each other. That thought gave him a new urge, and Maggie must have had the same idea because she walked her fingers slowly down Haruki's body.

'How did you get yours, then?'

Maggie's fingers paused, they stopped walking. Then she lifted them off his stomach and put one to his lips. 'Hush, that's a story for later.' She lifted herself on top and kissed him.

'Wait, Maggie. Slow down a moment.'

'What's up?'

'I don't know exactly. I just get the feeling that this is all happening too fast.'

Maggie put a hand on his chest and with the other she reached back and raked the inside of his thigh with her nails. It almost hurt, but she didn't stop when she ran out of thigh. The thrill of that raced right into his brain. 'Ow! Maggie, I'm serious.'

She stopped what she was doing with her fingernails and put both hands on his chest. 'Haruki, you are one of us. It's not just the ritual. You've always been one of us. You just don't know it. Or you've forgotten.'

'How can that possibly be true? I hadn't met any of you until yesterday.'

'This place is different. It's easy to forget things here. I told you that. Time is not so ordered here as everywhere else.

It doesn't exactly mean the same thing here. It's distorted, because of the entity.'

'The entity?'

'Yes, the thing we've been keeping away. Look, the Captain will explain everything to you, when you're ready. I'll take you to him if you like.' Maggie smiled, and brushed his cheek with her hand. Then she reached it back again. 'But not yet; there's plenty of time for that later.'

Sometime later, Haruki pushed back a lock of Maggie's hair and looked into her eyes. They were lying together on a threadbare Persian rug in front of a long-dead fire and the chill of the day was winning through. In truth, Haruki had lost track of whether it was day or night. The weak light at the undrawn windows suggested to him it was either evening or morning, but he couldn't say which. To him it could have been an hour, a week or even a month since they last spoke. He watched her wake. Her eyes fluttered slowly open and her pupils contracted as they focused on him. 'Maggie, when we visit the Captain, I want you to know that I'm going to keep my promise.'

'What promise?'

'You asked me to warn him off. You asked me to keep Judy safe from him.'

'Did I? When was that?'

'Yesterday. Don't you remember? I came in from a walk around the village and you were here. You were doing a jigsaw puzzle and you were quite upset.'

Maggie laughed. 'That was ages ago, when you first arrived, and it's long since sorted. Forget about it.'

'It was yesterday, just after I arrived. And what happened to the sheepskin rug?'

'You spilled wine on it, remember?' Maggie laughed again. She touched his face tenderly. 'Oh, Haruki. You really are confused, aren't you? We've been together for three months already, silly. Come on, let's go and see the Captain. He'll straighten you out.'

The Captain was wearing a dressing gown that was open at the naval. His smooth stomach glistened, leaving Haruki wondering whether he was wet from the shower or from perspiring. He held a tumbler of what looked like whisky, though it was almost full to the brim. 'Come in, children. I thought you'd pay me a visit soon. How long has it been?' He smiled and was rewarded by Maggie's laughter. If this was a joke, Haruki wasn't in on it. 'I know why you've come.' He spread his arms out wide to take Maggie in his embrace. He hugged her tightly, whispering something in her ear. Then, when he had finished, he took Haruki's face in both his hands and kissed him full on the lips.

Haruki came away feeling dizzy. He hadn't expected that and he certainly didn't expect to like it so much. His nostrils filled with the Captain's scent and his face flushed, full of blood. His heart pumped away madly. The Captain gestured for them to take a seat and they fell back into the soft folds of the antique Chesterfield. 'You know, Haruki, I always knew you had it in you.' He winked and touched Haruki's knee. Haruki inwardly recoiled at his touch, but when it was withdrawn, he felt disappointed. He watched the Captain's smooth throat open and close as the man gulped down a large swig of whiskey.

A noise came from the kitchen. The door slammed abruptly and a woman appeared, breathing heavily. She was tall and slim with glistening ebony skin and dark braids that dangled over her face and stuck up every which way. She wore a dark green, flowing dress that hung loosely about her shapely body and sat especially low at her front, revealing smooth, dark curves. It was his wife, Jane. And as she came closer and Haruki saw her at an angle, he realised that something had changed. His wife's body had changed. Her breasts were fuller, her face rounder. And perhaps it was his imagination, but her stomach might have had a slight swell to it that it didn't have before.

Slack-jawed, Haruki watched as his wife took the chair opposite him. Her movements were slow and precise, and she didn't look in his direction until she had taken her seat. Then she turned to him and said, 'Hello, Haruki.' Her voice was flat and her eyes listless. She seemed like she'd been using drugs.

The Captain beamed and opened his hands wide. 'We are all here together. We have answered the call.' The knot in Haruki's stomach hardened; it had emerged upon seeing his wife and even the Captain's easy tone could not dispel it. He sat back and waited for some explanation as to why Jane was still here, and why she was dressed like this.

Jane was looking around the room and blinking as if she was trying to see through fog. The Captain stood up; he opened his mouth to say something but was interrupted by a knock at the door. For the fleetest of moments, Haruki thought he saw the Captain's face show concern. If it did, the man recovered quickly to resume his casual smile.

Maggie pressed his hand and kissed him on the cheek. 'Back in a moment,' she said. Both she and the Captain answered the door and stepped out into the porch, shutting the door behind them. Jane stared at him blankly. She blinked slowly, then rose and went over to the window. He followed and from their angle, they could just about see the man at the door. A fat old black man wearing a maroon velvet jacket and matching slippers. It was the man from the post office that Haruki had met on his first day.

'How long have we been here?' Jane asked. 'I think I've lost track.' It seemed to him that she had changed completely from one moment to the next. Before it was as if she were encased in ice, staring out but trapped within. Now the ice had melted and she was newly animated. 'Haruki, we're in big trouble. We have to get away from here.'

Haruki opened his mouth but closed it again. He didn't know what to say to her.

'We shouldn't be here,' Jane said. 'We shouldn't have come. They're using us for something that we don't understand. Nothing makes sense and I can't think straight, especially when the Captain is around, but I know that if we don't leave soon, we may never be able to.' Her eyes widened, reacting to something she'd seen in his facial expression. 'You understand, don't you? You've seen it too, in the white room. You have.' Jane had raised her voice and now looked fearfully towards the front porch in case the others had heard. They were still talking to old Frank from the post office. Their voices were low and Haruki couldn't hear what they were saying, but he heard Frank's laughter, until the outer porch door closed shut.

'One way or another, I have to be free of him,' she said.

The door opened again and the others came back inside. The conversation at the door had come to an end, and quite crossly, it seemed. The Captain looked angry and Maggie's face was like thunder. 'What's wrong?' Haruki asked, and that seemed to break the ice. A new smile came quickly onto the Captain's face and made Haruki feel again like nothing was wrong in the whole world.

'Just a neighbour,' the Captain said. 'Just old Frank. I don't know what he's doing up here and I think he doesn't either. So tell me,' he collected his empty whisky tumbler and waggled it, 'who wants a drink?'

It was then that a new shadow passed over Haruki. It was a shadow of clarity, and of certainty. He had *not* missed any time; he did *not* have a faulty memory and he certainly had *not* spent the last three months in a relationship with Maggie. He was certain that he had only just arrived in Barrowthwaite and that Jane had arrived almost at the same time. These things he now knew, but he also remembered one other, very disturbing detail.

'No whisky for me, but I would like to know what you keep in the kitchen.' He found himself on his feet. 'And not the normal kitchen you show us when you want to. I mean the white room. The room with the chair, and the grating, and the thing crawling about.'

The Captain maintained a straight face; he shrugged and smiled sweetly. 'Come and see for yourself, Haruki.'

Jane stayed seated as Haruki followed the Captain to the kitchen. Maggie followed, her hand on Haruki's shoulder as the Captain threw open the door. 'See? It's just a kitchen. You're welcome to look around, but don't open the refrigerator. My casserole really is a frightening affair.' The Captain strutted around the kitchen pointing out mundane items with his hands. He used over-the-top gestures, like he was a game show host's assistant demonstrating the prizes to a hopeful contestant. 'So, are you satisfied, Haruki? Or do you need more proof that what you thought you saw doesn't exist? There's another ritual this afternoon and I was going to ask both of you to assist in it, but perhaps you've had a tiring day. Maybe it's best if Maggie takes you home and settles you in front of the fire?'

Haruki nodded. He suddenly wanted nothing more than that. To be in front of his fire in Hilltops curled up with Maggie by his side. He closed his eyes and sighed with relief. Jane had got him all spooked about the Captain and this room, and he was very glad to avoid any confrontation. It was just a normal, rather pleasant old kitchen.

But when he closed his eyes. The image of the white room came screaming back to him. He opened them again quickly.

'Is everything all right, Haruki?' the Captain said.

He felt Maggie's touch at his shoulder. 'Let's go home, Haruki.'

Haruki closed his eyes again and there it was still. He was standing in the white room. Suspended above him was the white plastic chair and below his feet a translucent slime inched its way towards him. It stopped moving when he looked directly at it. It knew it had been noticed. Then the slime continued towards him regardless. If anything it made faster progress. It was aware that Haruki could see it, and it no longer cared.

'Your eyes are closed,' Maggie whispered in his ear. 'What can you see?' Haruki kept his eyes shut, trying to step away from the thing crawling on the floor. 'What is it, Haruki? What's there?'

'Haruki?' the Captain said, much louder. 'Open your eyes.' He responded to the Captain's voice. It was almost involuntary as his eyes snapped open. A flood of relief washed over him as the white room disappeared and left him standing again in the cottage kitchen with Maggie draped over his shoulder, holding on tightly to his arm. That made him feel secure at first, until he realised that she wasn't holding him to support him; she was restraining him. His feeling of security melted away quickly when the Captain came closer and he saw what was in the man's hands.

He saw the syringe only a split second before he felt its needle prick his neck. The smell of vanilla filled his head and he had the sensation that he was falling backwards into a turquoise sea. He floated on his back, enjoying the warm water wash over him, and for some reason he was counting backwards. But he wasn't counting numbers; even through his drug-induced confusion he realised that these were dates. 'August twelfth, August eleventh, August tenth...'

Very soon after that he felt nothing at all as the world around him melted away into darkness.

TIME

'A king is nothing until anointed, but when he touches Him, who was once king, is now god.'

Haruki heard the Captain speaking as he found himself coming around. As he returned to consciousness his vision returned. The Captain's face loomed over him, the bright white smile captivating him once more, going some way to settle the nausea and dislocation he felt at having been unconscious.

'This substance transforms you,' the Captain said. 'When you touch Him, He touches you. You are more than you once were. As close to Him as it is possible for a man to get. It makes you more than a man. More than human. This is my gift to you, Haruki. This is Judy's gift to you.'

Maggie was in the room too. She stood by the Captain with her hand on his shoulder, smiling. 'How do you feel, Haruki? Isn't it great?' He keenly felt Maggie's gaze on him as he struggled to wake fully. It was as if she were attempting to read every twitch and expression he made. Her own face went through somersaults of expression in sympathy. Haruki was slumped in a plastic chair that stood in the centre of the white room. Directly above his head in the middle of the high ceiling was a white metal grating and all of the walls were converted in featureless white plastic. He suddenly felt dizzy. He felt as if he were suspended upside down and unsecured; he might slip out of his chair at any time and fall down to the ground or up to the ceiling. Whichever was which.

'It is too early for him; let us give him some space,' the Captain said. 'He'll feel the full benefits in time.'

Haruki could see that the Captain was carrying something. It rattled in his hands with the soft cadence of a morning alarm. It was quiet and almost politely insistent. Haruki wanted to turn his head and go back to sleep, but the tinkling gnawed away at him, refusing to let him slip away.

Haruki roused and felt he was capable of trying speech. 'What was that thing? What did you let it do to me?'

'Very soon, you'll understand everything. Trust me.'

'Trust *yourself*,' the Captain said.

Haruki felt very far from trusting anything right then, but he sat up and, having located the source of the insistent rattling that had tethered him to consciousness, he accepted the teacup and saucer from the Captain's outstretched hands. The tea was hot and strong, and Haruki felt life returning to his body.

In fact it was more than life. It was an improvement on the state of foggy confusion that he'd been in since he'd arrived. He felt clarity.

He felt certainty. And it was exhilarating for him to piece together the events of the past few months. He had felt like time had been his enemy. It had eluded him. It obscured the reality that he was trying desperately to connect with. He could never be sure whether the moment he was living in was the real moment or one that had occurred in the past, or indeed had yet to happen in the future. But this state of mind wasn't something that he was previously capable of recognising about himself.

It must have been the substance, Haruki thought. Whatever they had done to him in this room, it had woken him up. When he looked back, he found he was able to recall everything that had happened over the past few days. And it was only days, not months as he had previously thought. When he looked back, he could see time stretch away from him into the past. It was still jumbled up in places, but he felt he was able to unravel it, if he tried.

'Time isn't linear,' the Captain said, as if he had read Haruki's thoughts. 'It is not supposed to be. That's just how we come to understand it. The only way we know how to understand it. Time comes to us in waves, back and forth; it washes over us like the tide. It slips through our fingers. But we can observe. We can determine each particle of time. We can connect each to each. We can control it. It becomes our tool.'

The Captain put his hands on either side of Haruki's cheeks. Then he leant forward and pushed his lips against Haruki's. Haruki's cup rattled in its saucer. 'I'll leave you both to get re-acquainted. You can tell him everything. It's about time.' Maggie nodded, and when he had gone, she turned back to Haruki.

'What do you see? Do you remember anything about us? Everything you thought you saw may have happened. There are many different possibilities right now. If you wanted that to happen, then it did happen. You and I will fall in love, Haruki. At some point it will happen. It already has happened. Isn't that great? It's simple physics, once you know the truth. Once you are anointed.'

Haruki felt like he had indeed woken, but not from a dream. His mind was clearer than it had been, but that wasn't much comfort for him. As Maggie clung to him, the tighter she pressed against him, the more he realised that he'd left his wife at the mercy of these people. Jane had come here for him. She had come back to him. And he had messed it up. He had thrown away his last chance with her.

'Maggie, I just don't get it. Look, I'm sorry. I need to work out how I feel about, well, everything. I need to leave, and I need to take Jane with me. I hope you'll understand.'

Haruki left the kitchen and went to fetch Jane from the lounge. Whatever was going on, he understood that he needed to face it with her. He need time with her, away from the others. But when he walked out of the kitchen, he went cold. Over by the fireplace, the Captain lay face down on the deep pile sheepskin rug. A pool of thick black blood spread out from under him. A fire poker lay on the rug beside the Captain's body. It was sticky with blood and on the brass handle Haruki saw the brown smear of fingerprints.

'Maggie, call the police,' Haruki said, his voice almost breaking with the shock. 'And an ambulance.' His mind raced with possibilities, but as Maggie fled back into the kitchen to use the telephone, he realised what had happened.

His imagination searched for alternatives, but it circled back on only one thought. That Jane had killed the Captain. Jane's coat and boots were gone. She had fled the scene. He was certain that if the police examined the fingerprints on the poker, they would be hers.

Haruki took a handful of tissues from the side table and spat on them, using the saliva to clean the handle of the murder weapon. When the fire poker was devoid of prints, he tossed the tissues in the fireplace. It had long since died down to embers, but a few still glowed red and Haruki was rewarded with a sizzle as the tissues caught and flared yellow with flame.

He rolled the Captain over, intending to immerse his own hands in the man's blood, but then he saw something glinting at the side of the body. It was a knife. The same one, perhaps, that the Captain had used during the ritual on Noonday Sun. He could clearly remember that ritual now.

In his other hand the Captain clutched something else. It was a scrap of dark green fabric. Unmistakably part of Jane's dress; most probably it was torn off in the struggle. This theory seemed supported by the fact that the hearth rug was rucked up and a side table had been knocked over. The Captain had attacked Jane with the knife. He must have wanted to do the same thing to Jane as he had done to Judy during the ritual on the hill. Jane fought back and had killed him in the process. She had used the poker to bash his brains out.

But how was that even possible? The Jane that Haruki knew wasn't capable of such violence. But perhaps there was a side to her that was? The Jane that existed before Haruki knew her. Hadn't her father been some kind of violent criminal? A notorious figure in South London, killed by rivals in a drug war? Did the apple really fall so far from the tree? In defence of her own life, Haruki realised that Jane was probably most capable of taking matters into her own hands. And another thought troubled him. Hadn't she said earlier that she wanted the Captain gone? *One way or another*, she had said.

He could hear murmur of Maggie in the kitchen talking to the authorities on the telephone. He knew he didn't have long. He knelt down and picked up the knife. He hesitated. The knife hovered close to his own stomach. He closed his eyes and felt the knife in his grip. He suddenly wasn't at all sure about this. He didn't even know if it would work. What did he know about modern detection methods or crime scene analysis? But he held the knife and allowed it to feel its own way through the confusion. He gave it the power to make its own decision. Whether, and where, to cut. Would it stab or slice? Deeply or superficially? Haruki cared not: he let his mind go blank; he allowed the knife to feel him. He trusted it with his life, and with Jane's. If this didn't look good, then it would condemn Jane as the murderer. His decision was simple, selfless. He would take the blame for the killing. He would ensure Jane's safety.

Haruki held the Captain's blade in front of him.

The sharp blade hovered,
Decision yet to be made,
To cut, or sever.

Haruki was only dimly aware of the nascent haiku before he felt the blade come to a decision. An incision. It pulled his hands down with it as it plunged into Haruki's side. A centimetre or two in depth, below his navel and to the left of his stomach. It stabbed him exactly where his scar was. The one he hadn't noticed until Maggie had pointed it out. The pain should have overwhelmed him, but he reacted with cold indifference.

To cut, or sever.

The knife had decided to cut Haruki rather than allow him to sever his ties with Jane. It had decided he would give his life for hers. She would be free. Of him and of this place. She would get away, back to London, to her orchestra and her life. He would take the blame. He would cut himself rather than risk losing her to a murder conviction. And perhaps ultimately, he would strengthen his ties with her, not sever them.

He felt his wound as a cold thing. Like an ice cube had touched him. He looked down and saw the blood flow out of it. His shirt blossoming with red, the stain creeping quickly south, droplets falling to the rug beneath him, mingling with the Captain's own.

He became faint and he put one hand down on the floor to steady himself. The rug was wet with the Captain's still-warm blood and Haruki stared down as he upturned his palm. The thick black blood stank of iron. A butchers' shop smell that rooted into his brain through his nostrils. It suddenly became all he could think about. He had to force himself into action as he felt the last of his life flowing out of him. He was very tired, and he wanted to lie down on the warm rug next to the Captain. He wanted to close his eyes.

Haruki grabbed the poker. He had wiped it clean of his wife's fingerprints, but now he added his own. He daubed the handle of the poker with the Captain's blood, impressing his own fingerprints into the smooth surface. It was quite a work of art. Perhaps one of his finest. With it he had created something, but unlike his other works, this one was of real substance. This one meant something. It meant Jane's freedom. He had given his wife her life back.

Haruki closed his eyes, but before he succumbed to total darkness, he imagined something leaving his body. It was an inch-long translucent pebble birthed from the small hole in his side.

Through tunnel vision he watched it flop onto the carpet and inch away from him like a caterpillar. Then darkness folded around him and his mind leaped to embrace it.

ESCAPE

When Haruki had mentioned the white room, the Captain's face hadn't changed one bit. He maintained the cheerful demeanour that he always wore. And that's how Jane knew he was lying.

She had been around duplicitous people her entire life. People like Chiara, who thought she was so far above everyone else that she'd lie to your face without any sense of embarrassment. The Captain was one of those people, she realised.

She was going to follow the others into the kitchen, but a tap at the window kept her seated. At an angle only she could see, the fat old man. He was trying to make his way down the garden path using a white stick to guide his way. But when Jane noticed him, he turned and winked at her. He looked her directly in the eye.

Jane waited for her chance and then bolted for the door. But when she got out of her seat, her dress was caught on one of the brass upholstery tacks that lined the armchair. Her dress ripped and almost sent her tumbling across the room. She recovered and threw open the outside door. She was not surprised at that moment to see the fat old man directly outside. He wore a red velvet jacket and matching slippers.

'Hello, Jane, it remembers old Frank, doesn't it?' His eyes once again roamed around the space behind Jane's head. Everywhere except at Jane herself.

The funny thing was that Jane *did* remember him, from her deep past. There was something about his jacket, his slippers, his broad grin and his weird way of talking. The name still meant nothing to her, but the image came to her of some time in her early childhood. In her father's flat near the river. He was always in and out of prison, but each time he was released, he'd bring a man with him. A strange man. A man like this.

'Did you know my father? Are you from the Fields?'

'Frank is from everywhere. And also, from nowhere. He had a passing acquaintance with its father, but it could say that he had more of an interest in the daughter. Frank takes it that the... went well?' Here he threw his hands about himself in a haphazard way, but Jane knew he was miming the actions of a conductor.

The vivid memory came to her of standing in the doorway, watching her father with his guest. She often did this when she was little. She was always afraid of her father and of his guests. But this one in particular had seemed kindly and had given her a present. More than that, he had taken an interest in her. He'd even inspired her. It was this man who had given her the conductors' baton. It was he who had given her the tools that she needed to get away from her father at the earliest opportunity and move away from the Fields.

As if understanding what she was thinking, the old man said, 'Nonsense. It did all of that on its own. Frank may have given it a nudge, but its achievements are all its own.'

'What's going on here?' Her question was almost a plea. 'I don't understand anything about this place or these people.'

'Ah, but it doesn't need to understand, does it? It just needs to separate what it knows from what it doesn't. For this one, it should be as easy as discerning the French horn from the oboe. Concentrate on one and ignore the other. Use the baton in its mind to sever one from another.'

Jane hesitated, then closed her eyes. 'I followed Haruki here. He'd been missing for three months, but when I arrived yesterday it was only a day after Haruki himself arrived.'

'Good,' Frank said. 'It's made a good start. Now it will continue.'

'I saw Haruki and Maggie on the rug. I ran but came back. When I did, it was as if nothing had happened between them.'

'It must go on,' Frank urged.

'Haruki is acting confused, like he's in a daze. I think it is the Captain who had that effect on people. I can't think straight when I'm around the man.'

'Yes, he's a recursion.'

Jane stared at him. She eyed the path running up to the track that would take her back to the road. She considered immediately running away, but there was something about the man that compelled her to stay and understand more.

'It is sceptical, but it has felt the force that gathers here,' Frank continued. 'It folds back on itself. It occurs, and it re-occurs. It has happened, but it hasn't happened. It is happening, all the time. So, do tell, what else does it know?'

'I know that this is the first time I've been able to think straight in the whole time I've been here.' Jane paused. 'And I think that might have something to do with you.'

'Indeed, very good. Frank is the antithesis of the Captain. What it gathers, Frank casts asunder. What it calls, Frank dismisses. It has grown powerful. It has called many.' The fat man in the red velvet jacket and slippers winked at her. 'But some of those it has called have been called already. Not by it, but by old Frank.'

'You mean me? And Haruki?'

'Indeed, and there are others.' Frank stepped sideways. Jane hadn't noticed someone standing behind him. It was a young girl, in her late teens perhaps. She looked a little like Maggie but with lighter hair. She wore a scowl on her face, but Jane didn't think she meant any hostility to her but rather to those inside the house. 'Think of it like an orchestra with Frank as the conductor.' With a flourish Frank swept his arms in the direction of inside the house. The girl took this as her cue and went inside. 'That is my little harp. A subtle instrument to pluck the strings that need plucking.' He then used his hands to gesture that they should leave, flapping his hands and trying to sweep her up the path.

'We can't leave,' Jane said. 'What about Haruki? And you can't leave that girl at the mercy of the Captain. I think he abuses people. He has a hold over them. He's part of a cult or something. We need to stop him.'

'It has already happened; there is not much that has not. If it wants to, it can see through the window.'

Jane peered through and saw the Captain come out of the kitchen and into the lounge. He frowned and looked out of the window, but despite looking directly at her, she knew he looked *through* her. His eyes did the same random flickering from side to side that Frank's did. As if he were looking for something in the air around or behind her. Then he bent down to the floor and when he came back up again, he held a piece of green fabric in his hands.

He looked at the green fabric with a confused expression, then, shockingly, Jane saw a flash of dark metal behind him just before his head shattered. A splatter of blood splashed against the windowpane directly right in front of her.

'Jesus Christ!' Jane shouted.

Another flash of dark metal, another spray of blood reached the window. Jane's mind screamed at her to run, but her legs wouldn't move. She watched through the blood-spotted window as the Captain sank to his knees. Behind him stood the small figure of a girl. She raised the poker above her head and Jane saw lumps of beige fall from it. A clump of long blond hair dangled from its point.

The girl brought the poker down onto the Captain's head one final time. He slumped to the carpet. Blood and brain oozed out of his head. He stared at Jane, unseeing. His wide moon-grey eyes now fixed upon her in the moment of his death.

'You did this!' Jane screamed at Frank. She watched in horror as the girl calmly picked up the white blobs that she had bashed out of the Captain's head. She placed each carefully on her outstretched palm and when she was sure she had them all, she came back outside. Frank was dancing on the spot with glee, his almost too-small slippers a blur of frantic motion. His hands flapped with excitement. 'Excellent. It's done very well. It's done very well indeed. Let Frank have it, give it to Frank.'

The girl offered her palm to Frank, but instead of him reaching out and taking what it contained, he took hold of her wrist. He brought his wide face up to her palm and opened his mouth. A huge tongue lapped out greedily at her palm as Frank slurped up what it contained. 'Yes. Very nice. It does not know how long Frank has waited for this. How long he has planned. How much time and effort he has put into this. Mostly time.'

'You murdered a man.' Jane was breathless, but this time her legs did work. They exploded into action. The fear compelled her to move, to get away from there. She bolted up the cottage path towards the stony path that would lead her to the road. She didn't care where she ran. She didn't care for how long she ran. She ran to get help.

PART FOUR

FRANK

BIRMINGHAM, 1985

Frank pounded the pavement as he hurried to his next rendezvous. Although he was running late, he found the time to mutter to himself. It wasn't a meeting, no. Frank wouldn't do anything as mundane as attend a meeting. It was a *rendezvous*. Definitely a rendezvous, complete with all of the mystery and intrigue that the word conjured.

A car backfired. An old Austen A40. Though it was well over twenty years ago since he'd worked at the factory, Frank remembered the familiar sound of spark plugs igniting unspent fuel. Nowadays, the cars were all soullessly engineered. Robotically assembled 600 series have nothing of the flair and artistry, no character. He closed his eyes and imagined the explosion inside the chamber escaping through the exhaust valve, pushing out all that air and a little flame. And people criticised Frank for his timing issues. If only they knew what it had taken to birth the A40 through fire and molten steel. The intellect it had subsumed to graft the engine to the body. The elbow grease to polish and raise up the gorgeous creation and roll it onto the streets in all its glamour and beauty. That was decades ago. And it was today. It was tomorrow too. Frank didn't care about which order things happened in. For him, it was all happening at once. All in the same moment.

Frank crossed a street and hurried in front of a taxi that was preparing to push off. He caused it to brake abruptly, and to stutter and stymie instead of rolling out of its space gracefully. He heard shouting in his wake and turned on his heel to address the driver. 'Frank apologises,' he said, 'for the intrusion onto its rightful thoroughfare. Please accept this humble man's contrition but know that it was all in good faith. For Frank has a destination, a mission. His carriage is of so great an import that he thought nothing of waylaying you. But though the delay is small, imposition is imposition and never let anyone say that Frank is impolite. Forgive him, my fellow traveller, but now he must leave it to go its noble and erudite way. For isn't it true that he and it are both students and masters of the road, eh?'

Frank spun on his heels; behind him in the cockpit of the taxi, a mushroom cloud of expletives blossomed out into the rusty sky. For a big man, his feet were dainty, and like a dexterous hammer thrower, he launched himself back into his direction of travel. His burgundy slippers slapped the concrete. His wide-cut trousers flapped around his ankles and the buckle of his tan mac swung uselessly behind him as it dangled idly from its belt loops. It had been half a century since Frank had been able to close it around his widening stomach.

'Should have been briefer,' Frank muttered. 'But Frank was never such a sole born into brevity, was he? No, not brevity, but the ability to at once pose himself a question and at the same time answer it? Definitely.'

He stopped, looked up and into the past. The Bullring. Corn Cheaping. A hoop of iron dedicated to bovine torture, but in this moment now a most edifying structure of concrete and steel. No cows here to torment today, but many ruminant humans shuffling from side to side as they entered the giant slaughterhouse of the shopping centre.

He tipped a nod to the Rotunda towering over his head and slipped inside, taking a series of switchback escalators until he reached the fourth floor. There he found whom he was looking for. A man in a shabby brown suit and crumpled hat pulled himself off the wall where he was leaning. Though he now stood upright, he still looked like he was lounging, so laconic was his attitude and demeanour. His upper lip bore a scratchy moustache, mousey brown with white flecks, though there was not the hint of crows' feet at his temples.

'So, you're the one,' the man said.

'The brown man addresses old Frank, but does it really know what it is that it's dealing with?' Frank said. 'Does it know what Frank is?'

'We know enough to know that you are not welcome. You can't come here.'

'Some of Frank is already here. More than you know.'

'We've gathered the pieces,' the brown man said, 'but we have put them where you cannot find them. Or if you do, you cannot reach.'

'Is it sure about that? Frank has ways. And means.'

'You are not the only one who has means.'

'So true,' Frank said. 'But Frank will be. His day will come. And Frank will come too. All of him. Everything is in motion; he is already happening. He cannot be stopped.'

'We will stop you.'

'You cannot. He has already happened. What it experiences now is just an echo of a time before. Frank knows this because he is there, right now. And he is here. So he knows, he has known and he will know. But it is stuck on its tightrope of time and can only move forward. And slowly at that.'

'If you say you can see into the future, you should know what will happen next,' the brown man said.

'For Frank there is no future and no past. Everything for him happens in the present. There is only now. Was it not listening?'

A movement at the side of Frank's vision spun him around. A woman was cutting through the traffic of people, scything her way between shoppers and heading directly towards him. Frank looked again and saw not one but two. Then three and four, all coming at him from different directions.

'Ha! If you are as you say, you should have seen this coming,' the brown man said with a cruel smirk. 'You have a few seconds left, I would say. Not one of my disciples will hesitate to cut you down.'

'Frank wouldn't do that if he were it, or if it were he. Frank would be more respectful.'

The brown man laughed scornfully. 'Ha! What is there to be respectful of? A fat old clown in absurd slippers? Against a dozen of us. There are many of us and we are all around. Many have answered my call. This is over for you. Goodbye.'

'It should not be so sure of itself. It has not yet seen the full conflagration of all Frank's hidden powers. Frank is constructed of cosmic forces that the likes of it can never hope to understand. Its mind is simply not flexible enough for the concepts involved.' And with that, Frank suddenly threw his arms up into the air and disappeared. Where Frank was a moment ago, only an oversized tan raincoat floated to the floor like a giant autumn leaf.

Frank giggled as he sped across the floor. He heard the brown man let out a cry of outrage and knew that his minions would be hard on his heels. His short, fat legs pumped away and his body jiggled. He knew he had all the grace of a waterlogged canoe, but that didn't stop him trying. His velvet slippers made short work of the polished shiny floor of the precinct as he steered upstream against the flow of the crowd of shoppers.

Frank rounded the corner, taking shelter against the wall of a tiny cobbler's booth. He'd lost them, for the time being. He willed his little fat legs to carry him off on a flying carpet of blurred motion. Outside, along the concourse, past the

Midland bank. He stopped alongside Woolworths. From waist height down, the long plate glass window was opaque from the crud and splatter of dirty rainwater, but he saw a hundred shoppers milling and spinning in the pre-Christmas rush. A huge queue for the tills left the red-jacketed staff frantic with despair. With their backs to him, Frank recognised the round slump of shoulder, the hang of the head that went with total misery. But Frank's eyes lit up. There was one place where he could lose himself.

Along the aisle, Frank jammed an armful of wrapping paper into the crook of his elbow. Three, four, five rolls now stuck out at odd angles. They obscured his face. Disguised his form. Frank joined the back of a very long queue. He watched.

A dart of movement along the shop front outside told him that his pursuers were abroad. Two men and a woman paused outside the window and peered in. Frank stood still, confident in his plain sight hiding place. His enemy hung around for a while, evidently confused as to what their next move should be. They had lost him.

The queue shuffled forward and as Frank glided forward he saw a head turn. It was the woman. Her dark hair fell forward about her young face and as she brushed it back behind her ears, her bright blue eyes looked inside through the window. Frank stood stock still and watched her gaze sweep around the shop like a search light. It passed over him and he held his breath. He tried not to meet her eyes, but to look away now would be a flinch of movement too far. He maintained a bored aspect and met her stare. He saw no hint of recognition in her face before she looked away. Frank let out a breath of relief.

He was too far from them and behind a half inch of plate glass, so he could not hear what they were saying. But he was not so far that he couldn't see clearly the lips of the two men. When the woman turned around, she stood with her back to him. For her, Frank could only use body language to guess at her meaning, but for the men, he could lip read everything they said.

'How could you lose him?' the man with a moustache said to the woman opposite him. She shrugged, and Frank did not see her reply.

The other, an Asian boy in a white shirt, had short, spiky black hair. He nodded crossly. 'I don't know how. He was here a moment ago.'

The woman shook with animated conversation. Then Moustache said, 'We've done enough here already. There's no way it's coming through tonight and we still have all the pieces.' Frank saw the man glance down at his own stomach and had an idea.

'It will try to come again,' the Asian said. 'Do we know where?'

'The Captain does. We should go back to him,' Moustache said.

'You two go back, I'm hungry. I'm going for a Wimpy,' the Asian boy said, and when the group disbanded he left their company and went into the fast-food outlet next door.

Frank maintained the wrapping paper pattern disrupter as he pretended to browse. His hand flashed out and articles flew from the shelves to meet him before being enveloped in the voluminous folds of his purple velvet jacket. His toes twitched in excitement at his newly hatched plan.

He waited for the Asian boy to get settled at a booth, then he walked out of the shop and into the food outlet next door. It adjoined Woolworths and Frank dropped his wrapping paper just in time to avoid any suggestion he was attempting to carry it illegally out of the shop.

The Wimpy burger bar was a miasma of aerosolised fat and grease. It coated the red plastic seating and the white square tables. There was a sheen covering the insipid mauve floor tiles that made them slippery to walk on. Frank's slippers could not achieve a decent purchase on the floor.

Unburdened with the rolls of paper obscuring Frank's face, the Asian boy recognised him immediately. He moved to stand, his mouth opening in outrage, but Frank quickly inserted himself into the booth alongside him, pressing him in. The boy's arms were trapped at his sides. The place was so jammed with bodies and the high chatter of families, that no one noticed the little flurry of activity.

'Frank smells hot dogs.'

The boy looked confused, especially when Frank extended his hand. 'Frank is pleased to meet you.' The boy could not get his hand out from his sides, he was so squashed in by Frank's corpulence. 'Never mind,' said Frank, 'but Frank would at least like to know to whom he addresses.'

'You'll get nothing from me, fat man.'

'Ah, it speaks at least. Well, that's a start. A very palpable start. But will it answer a question? Will it tell Frank why it follows the brown man?'

'Let me out,' the Asian boy said through gritted teeth, though his tone was set as one who was trying to avoid the attentions of the other restaurant-goers.

'It won't cause a scene, will it?' Frank said. 'Because then the game will be well and truly up. For both, he thinks. So, it keeps its voice down and it tells Frank why it wants to kill him, when a perfectly amiable bargain has been struck?'

'You're trying to bring that thing into our world and we won't let it. You can go to hell if you think we won't fight you. We'll never let it in, never.'

'It speaks as one who fears. Perhaps it doesn't know the whole story? Shall it listen whilst Frank tells it the truth?'

'No,' the boy hissed. The family in the booth opposite was alerted to his sibilant tone and spared glances in his direction, but Frank surmised that they had not yet realised that something was up. Frank smiled pleasantly at the family and rubbed his tummy whilst pointing to the children's food. He made a little boy laugh before his parents scolded him for bothering the man. 'You had better kill me here, fat man. Because as soon as I am free, I'm coming for you. We all are. And there's nowhere you can go that we won't find you.'

'A pleasant thought for old Frank indeed. It may wish to consider that Frank does not wish to hide but wants to be found.' Frank produced something out of one of his voluminous sleeves and held it out in front of him. It was the thing that he'd stolen from the aisle in Woolworths next door. A twelve-inch plastic ruler. At the same time a number of chocolate bars fell out of his sleeves. 'Whoops, those are for later,' Frank said as he quickly scooped up the illicit confectionary and put them back into his sleeves. 'It won't tell on old Frank, will it?'

Frank's attention returned to his ruler. 'You know, in a few years' time, Frank wouldn't be able to do this,' he said as he snapped the plastic ruler in two. It left a triangular point and a sharp serrated edge. 'Soon he will be blind. And besides, they will be shatterproof.' Frank palmed the two ends of the ruler and dropped his hands below the white Formica table.

The boy looked puzzled. 'Why are you…' But then his face widened in shock as Frank pushed three inches of the sharp plastic shard into his side.

Frank felt it stab through the Asian boy's skin just at the right place and he stopped pushing. It was a close thing. Too far and the boy was in danger of losing his life, such that it was. Too little and the thing would not be drawn out of him. The boy started and jumped backwards. He kicked and bucked, trying to get away. The boy shouted out.

Frank had to act quickly. He pressed his fingers a little way into the boy's side and muttered something under his breath. He then rose out of his seat, releasing the pressure, which gave the boy room to leap up and shout. Frank leapt out of the booth and grabbed both a fistful of paper napkins and a plastic bottle of ketchup that was fashioned in the shape of an oversized red tomato. It oozed congealed ketchup from its green top. As Frank allowed the boy out of the booth, he squeezed the bottle hard, so that it spurted everywhere, all over the table and all over the boy.

'Clumsy Frank,' Frank shouted. 'He did it again.' Frank thrusted the paper napkins into the Asian boy's midriff. 'It needs to clean itself up, it does.' Frank turned to the other diner and shrugged. 'Apologies, my friends, Frank is a clumsy oaf.'

A member of staff, a young lad of twenty with a spotty face, came running over and saw the scene. Ketchup spilled everywhere and Frank standing in the middle of the scene with crimson hands and a red face. 'The top just exploded,' Frank said.

By now the Asian boy was nowhere to be seen. Frank last saw him fleeing the restaurant clutching the paper towels to his side.

Time for Frank to make himself scarce, he thought. *Only a matter of time before its friends descend on Frank's location.* 'Something for your trouble, a thousand apologies for the mess.' Frank conjured a twenty-pound note and placed it on the table. It was folded in two and stood upright where Frank had laid it on a blob of ketchup. Or it could have been blood.

Frank walked out of the restaurant, his hands enclosed around what he had taken out of the Asian boy's stomach. It was a blob of a sticky translucent substance that writhed in his closed fist but remained perfectly still when he opened his hand to look at it. It was half covered in red sauce, but he saw it perfectly for what it was. Frank paused momentarily, shrugged, then popped the thing in his mouth. His tongue wrestled with it for quite a while and though he did so with some difficulty, he managed to swallow it down.

He burped, then, putting his hands to his mouth, he giggled.

He looked back, through the fog and distance of time. Although to him, it was all the same. Just another task to be completed. Or one that was already done.

LONDON FIELDS, 2000

Frank whistled a jaunty tune. He felt quite at home. But he also knew that these people would sniff out anyone who doesn't belong to the Fields. *There is a sense of community here, a very strong sense. But it is jealously guarded.*

He strolled through the market north of the river. Blue plastic sheeting billowed from one stall. A gust had got up and the owner struggled to tie it down in the wind. Frank gestured and an apple flew into his hand. Or his hand flew to the apple. Either way, the seller didn't see as he was preoccupied with the blue sheeting. Across from him, a trailer dispensed goat curry into yellow polystyrene trays for a small queue of hungry stall holders. 'A breakfast of champions,' Frank said to himself.

'What did you say?' A boy stepped forward. He was fourteen, perhaps. Young for sure, but old enough for Frank to take seriously. Not all soldiers wore their blades at their belts. He wore a grey hoodie and black puffy jacket. His jeans were old, worn and dirty, but his trainers looked brand new.

A girl next to him said, 'Be cool, probably five-o.' Frank looked down and tried to walk past. The last thing he needed was a confrontation here.

'Are you five-o, mister? Hey, you – yes, I'm talking to you. I said, you five-o, innit?'

'I smell bacon for sure,' the girl said.

A couple of older youths rounded the corner stall and came into view. Perhaps this caused the boy to become more emboldened. He stepped forward to block Frank's path. 'I said, I'm talking to you. Why do you blank me, fat man?'

Frank had no choice but to engage the boy. 'Good morning.'

'Good morning? It ain't no good morning. I don't see what's good about it, do I? And what are those things you're wearing on your feet? They ain't trainers, they ain't even shoes.'

'Slippers, Frank likes to wear slippers. He finds them both comfortable and practical. But Frank likes its shoes too. "Trainers", it says. Yes. Very nice. Comfortable too, Frank thinks. But we can't stand here chatting about footwear all morning, pleasant though the prospect might be. It should return to its normal activities, whatever they might be. Good day.'

'You disrespecting me?' the youth said. 'You'd better watch it, Grandpa, or you'll get some blade.'

The girl started tugging at the boy's sleeve. 'He's just a mad old man. Leave him.'

'Right,' said the boy, 'but he's just standing there. He's looking me in the eye, like he don't respect me.'

Frank knew enough to respect anyone occupying a street corner in London Fields. It really didn't matter how young they were; all it took to end a life was a jab with their mother's potato parer.

'Frank respects. He does, honestly. He knows what it takes to stand here. But does it know what it takes Frank to stand here too? Perhaps not, but here comes some who do. Let's see what it has to say on the subject of respect, shall we?'

Two men sauntered up to Frank. They were no taller than the boy but broader, and mean-looking. Frank knew that anyone of their age needed to be respected, even by him. With age brought authority. They had earned it just by staying alive that long.

Of the two, Frank knew one personally. He was the one with the swagger. He was the one in charge. The boy and girl shrank back nervously as he approached. And when he addressed Frank directly they looked incredulous.

'Got your message, fam. What's the deal?' The man offered a fist bump to Frank, who took it awkwardly in both his palms and pumped it up and down whilst muttering a greeting.

'You know this clown?' the boy said, and that earned him a clip on the back of the head from the man's companion. 'Ow! What was that for?'

'Disrespecting. This is Nikki's lawyer – he got him out of school early. Now shut up and cover your corner.' The man nodded towards a dirty couple winding their way towards them. The men shrank back to observe the boy's interaction with them.

'Got any food?' the woman said. She had scabs around her mouth and chin that she kept scratching at.

'Not for you,' said the boy. 'Move on.'

'Come on,' said the man. He held up an orange plastic bag. 'We got some p's.'

'That ain't p's,' the boy said. He snatched the bag from the man and took out a knackered old car stereo. 'What's this? It's useless. No one has these anymore. What is it, a CD player? They's all done. Now it's all iPods and that. Piss off unless you've got the p's.'

'P's?' Frank turned his question towards the man known as Nikki. 'What's it talking about?'

Nikki whispered, 'P's. Pounds. Money.'

'Ah, Frank sees that now. And "food" is drugs.'

Frank's attention reverted to the scene being played out in from of him. The boy was insistent. 'If you ain't got the p's, then fuck off.'

'Don't be like that,' the woman said. 'It's good. It works and everything.'

'Come on,' said the man, 'it must be worth something. Just a little hit. You've got to give us something.'

'I ain't giving you nothin'. I mean it, fuck off and take your scabby whore with you.'

'Allow Frank this indulgence,' Frank said, stepping forward. 'He wants to see how this works. How much does it need? Fifty, a hundred?'

'It's ten. Ten for a bag.' Nikki said.

'Right then,' said Frank. 'Ten it is.' He plucked a note out of his voluminous jacket sleeve and waved it in the direction of the underage drug seller.

'Don't give it to me,' said the boy. 'On the floor, innit.'

Frank stooped and placed the note carefully on the ground; as soon as he had straightened up, another child swooped in from an unseen location and gathered the note. It was a swift action and it looked well-practised. The boy then coughed up something in his hand and gave it to the woman. He made the exchange look almost like a handshake.

Frank turned to Nikki. 'Very nice. Frank sees that what it lacks in manners it more than makes up for in practised efficiency. Frank's compliments to the teacher who produces such adeptness in ones so young. How many does it have? One on each street corner, he supposes?'

'To tell you the truth, it's a constant struggle to keep up; we're having to recruit in schools, football teams, everywhere. What you see here is only a fraction of the operation. Most of the youngsters are out west. Reading, Slough, wherever. Too much competition in London keeps prices down. It's getting hard to make a living.'

'Indeed. It is most enterprising. But what do the parents say? Each of its workers must have a set of said guardians. And then there are schools and teachers. Surely someone notices if its little Johnnys are not in school.'

Nikki laughed. He shared the joke with his sidekick and

they exchanged fist bumps. Shaking his head, still laughing, he said, 'You crack me up. Come on, let's go to my place. I have a flat near here where we can talk.'

Inside, the colourful modern furniture was a great contrast to the stark white of the walls. In clear contrast to the outside, everything in Nikki's tower block flat looked very expensive. 'Cash. Got nothing else. No bank account, no savings, just cash. Brings in a few luxuries, though.'

'And cars,' Frank said. 'He sees from what it has parked outside that it likes its cars too.'

'Yeah, well, that's my business fleet. Company cars and that. I have a growing operation that needs to be mobile. You get me?'

'Frank gets it, for sure. He fully understands its side of the business and whilst he doesn't particularly have a good opinion of the object of its endeavours, he won't judge. It has to do what it has to do. Frank knows something about that, for sure.'

'Right. Then let's talk business. What do I owe you for getting me out?'

'Owe me?' Frank said. 'It doesn't owe me anything. Frank didn't bring it home because he needs money. Nor does he want any favours. Our relationship is pure, unsullied by the prospect of commercial exchange.'

'What do you want then? Why get me out of prison if you don't want anything?'

Frank didn't acknowledge that he'd heard Nikki's last question because he was distracted by someone who'd appeared in a doorway just off from the main living room. 'What's this vision of loveliness that Frank sees in front of him?' A little girl peeped out of a bedroom. She could have been eight years old, or she could have been fifteen. But the truth was somewhere in between. She had wide, birdlike eyes, thick dark ringlets and in contrast to her pallid father, she had beautiful dark skin.

'This must be Jane. Because no other girl is as lovely as Jane. It's true, I heard that from a man in the market. All over the Fields and beyond people are talking about the beautiful girl locked up in the white tower by the river. Some say it's a princess, others say it's—'

'Yeah, well, Jane's not one for talking much. And she never comes out of her room. I doubt you'll get anything out of her. Sometimes I think I should take her to see someone.'

'Nonsense,' Frank said, 'it's destined for great things. I know.'

'Come here, Jane, come and meet Frank,' Nikki said. 'He's the reason I'm sitting here with you today instead of having to go away for a long time. Come and sit with us.' Jane shook her head. The motion was just visible from behind the doorway where she was hiding. 'I said, come and sit.' Nikki raised his voice and the girl shrank further behind the doorway, but Frank could just about see that she hadn't retreated completely.

'Jane. It's okay. Frank understands if it does not wish to talk. Frank can be more than a little overwhelming at times. Even Frank finds it hard to put up with Frank. But if it does find within itself the curiosity to meet him, just know that Frank has a special present for it.'

'She don't need a present. It's enough that you got me out. She didn't expect to have her dad back for Christmas, did you, Jane?' Jane had edged back to her peeping position, where Frank could see all of one eye and most of the other. They were dark and wide, full of curiosity, Frank thought.

'If it doesn't want the present, that's fine. Frank will leave it here in case it changes its mind. But it needs to know first that this is a magic wand. The finest magic wand in the world. Frank looked high and low for this item of powerful sorcery.'

Jane shuffled a little out of her doorway and when Frank retrieved a long wooden box out from inside his sleeve, she came further out, eyes wide and full of intrigue. She wore a little blue dress and had her hair in bunches. A picture of innocence in a cruel, rough place. Frank waggled the long, thin box and offered it to Jane, who walked slowly up to him to take it. She didn't look him in the eye, but her smile told him that he was winning her over.

'Before it opens its present, it needs to know something about magic.' Jane looked at Frank, just for a second, and at that flash of attention, he saw the girl's intelligence. 'Not many this young are wont to listen to old Frank,' he said to Jane, 'but I think this one is special. Yes, it's very special.'

'Why do you talk funny?' Jane said. Her voice was small, and both Frank and her father were straining to listen.

'Jane. That's not the way to—' Nikki was silenced by Frank's hand.

'It's okay, Jane. It can ask me anything it wants to. Frank will answer its question before he leaves, but not yet. Come on, it should take its present.'

Jane reached out and took the box in both hands. Frank didn't release it yet but held on to it firmly. Jane too didn't relax her own grip on the box.

'Ah, it meets Frank's grip with iron resolution of its own. Fantastic. But before it opens this, it needs to know what kind of magic it can perform. It is not the immediate kind where it can turn its father into a frog.'

Jane giggled.

'Or create gold coins from thin air.'

Jane smiled broadly at that.

'But whilst the magic takes longer and requires more from its user, it is much more powerful that the immediate kind. With this kind of magic it can change its life. It can turn itself into anything it wants to. It can give it everything it desires. It will allow it the freedom to make its own choices. It can leave this place and go wherever it wants, do whatever it wishes and with whomever it chooses. It just needs a little patience. And hard work. Yes, hard work and intelligence is a pre-requisite, but something tells me that this is not going to be a problem for Jane. Is it?'

Jane shook her head and Frank let go of the box. With wide eyes and quick fingers, she opened the box. Inside was a wand. A twelve-inch length of thin wood, painted white, with a polished rosewood handle.

It was a baton. A conductors' baton.

Frank watched Jane as she regarded the wand with awe. She came over and sat with him, and although she hardly said a word, she listened as he told her what it was and how it could create sounds and music from thin air. How it could control an army of musicians just with the smallest flick of the wrist. Frank was impressed that she didn't even flinch when he told her of the years of patient study she'd need before she was able to even learn how to use it. 'That's where the magic is,' Frank said to her. 'The source of the magic is in the effort it puts into it. More effort means stronger magic.' Jane nodded and it seemed to Frank that the gesture was to herself more than to anyone else.

When he was finished talking with Jane, Frank rose from the sofa and addressed Nikki, who had been chopping onions in the kitchen. 'A scene of domestic bliss. A far cry from the street corners.'

'Yeah, well, I've got a crew to do all of that for me.'

'Indeed.' Frank nodded and grinned. 'Now, far be it for Frank to tarnish our friendship with transactional matters. But he does have one or two requests.'

'Sure, anything. You're family now. Whatever you need.'

'Frank was hoping it would say that.' He produced from his sleeve a round, translucent pebble about an inch in diameter. He held it on his palm and showed it to Nikki.

'What's that?'

'This is Jane's present. Her birthright, you might say. It's for luck. Keep it in the house. Under her pillow, perhaps. Yes, that will do nicely. But don't let her see it.'

'Worth much, is it?'

'Not at all, not to anyone but Jane, but worth is relative, of course.' As Frank handed him the stone, he was pleased to see it behave itself and maintain its placid, neutral state. 'Well, Frank must be going. He suddenly finds that he has no more time.'

On his way out, Jane tugged at his oversized velvet jacket. 'You never said why you talk funny.'

Frank bent down and whispered very quietly into her ear. 'Don't tell, but it is because Frank is not from around here.'

'Where are you from?' Jane asked.

Frank pointed a finger upwards.

'From the high-rises?'

'A little bit further up than that,' Frank said, and winked.

BIRMINGHAM, 1985

Frank looked back at the scene of confusion he'd left in his wake. He had a sense that the diners and staff still thought of the disturbance as an exploding ketchup incident. So, the police would not be interfering anytime soon, if at all. But he had to find the Asian boy again. There was something important that he hadn't done the first time around.

Contrary to appearances, Frank wasn't making everything up as he went along. He knew the outcome already, so he already knew what to do. Yet what kind of a life was that? Frank was a colourful character. He needed some colour in his life, same as anyone. He always knew how to manipulate events in his favour. A nudge here, a wink there. But sometimes he let things play out, just for the hell of it. Sometimes he even allowed the universe to intervene, at which times he'd revel in the beautiful chaos that was created. Otherwise it was too easy. Colour was what Frank was all about. He liked things colourful. Colourful made him cheerful.

Frank whistled a jolly tune when he next came upon the boy. Wounded, though not badly, there was a lot of blood. So, the boy had run to the nearest washroom to clean and patch himself up. He wouldn't risk going to the authorities, and he wouldn't go immediately back to his superiors. What Frank had taken from him had been entrusted to him. He wouldn't readily admit that he'd lost it to an old man. Even now he'd be plotting to get it back.

'Look no further,' he loudly announced, walking into the washroom and seeing the boy desperately holding paper towels to the wound and trying to wrap a whole toilet roll around his middle to keep the makeshift dressing in place. 'Frank is here.' Frank coughed up the translucent blob and held it out to the Asian boy. It squirmed slightly under his touch. 'It wants this back? Be his guest. But be warned, Frank has a prior claim on it. It is a piece of him now, and he is a greater part of it. Here, take it. It won't get a better offer from Frank or anyone else today.'

The Asian boy reached out tentatively, but Frank giggled and popped it back in his mouth. 'Frank expects the brown man will want it to apprehend him.' The boy's eyes narrowed. 'Kill him, perhaps?' The boy's fingers twitched towards his back pocket. Frank made a gesture and then relaxed. 'So, go ahead. What are you waiting for? It should take the knife out of its pocket and try.'

The boy didn't move. He eyed Frank suspiciously.

'Reluctant, is it? Good, it should be. It is wrong to try and keep us out. It is fighting a losing battle. It is pitting itself against a law of nature.' The boy's eyes fell on the distance between himself and the exit. Frank had positioned himself to block the boy's escape.

'It is preparing to attack Frank, is it? Or maybe it wants to get back to its master? It doesn't know that Frank is its master now. Frank has almost all the pieces he needs. More than enough to make it forget about the brown man. And if it is ever drawn to him again, Frank will be waiting. And when the time's right...' Frank licked his lips. He was suddenly famished and his thoughts turned to the chocolate bars he'd purloined from the shelves of Woolworths.

The boy edged nervously around the side of him, towards the exit, but then he decided upon action. He put his hand behind his back and produced a butterfly knife. With a flourish he opened out the blade and fell into a low knife-fighter's crouch. 'Aha! An artist! But is it good enough to paint with Frank's blood?'

The boy lunged, closing the distance with deft footwork. Almost before he had started his attack, Frank began to narrate the boy's movements. 'It lunges, but Frank dodges aside. The blade cuts the air harmlessly where he has been. It swivels neatly on its two feet and slashes out. Frank uses his meaty forearm to block its attack. He grapples its wrist and twists painfully. It backs away, but it still has its knife.'

The boy now stood two paces away, panting. Frank eyed him impassively. 'It wants to make another attempt, but it is confused.'

The boy shifted his footwork and prepared for another attack. 'It prepares. It strikes. Its knife goes one way, but it is a trick and its fist comes thick and fast. Frank is equal to it; he catches its fist and once more, its attack is repelled.' Frank smiled. 'But it will try one last time.'

The boy shouted with rage and rushed at him. This time he did not attack with the knife but clearly intended to push past Frank and get out of the toilet, to freedom. 'Frank allows it to come forward, then he spins on his feet and pushes it off course. It careers out of control, and slips. It falls to the ground. But then it comes forward once more, low and hard, with its knife out again. Only this time it is not a knife.'

Frank stood still, grinning as the boy stabbed him in his fat stomach. True to Frank's words, it wasn't a knife point that pushed into his flesh; it was an inch of soft horsehair bristles. In the boy's hands was a delicate paintbrush.

Frank grabbed the boy's wrist and twisted it so that the boy half turned and fell, grimacing, to his knees. Frank maintained his grip, leaning heavily on the outside of the boy's elbow joint. The boy dropped the brush. 'Oh no it doesn't,' Frank said. 'It will be needing that. It has nice hands, very dextrous. But it will use this tool in future. That's how it will serve. That's how it will survive. It will learn to paint, yes. Frank knows. Frank sees it already, although it will have to wait. It will answer the call, not Frank's, but another.' Like lightning, Frank pushed out his fat hand and, with a podgy finger, he prodded the boy on the forehead. 'When it awakes,' Frank said, 'it won't remember. But it will answer the call. And Frank will be ready.'

The boy fell immediately into a deep sleep as he collapsed onto the floor.

'Good night, Haruki,' Frank whispered. 'See you in the north.'

PART FIVE

LAW AND ORDER

JANE

Jane ran from the Captain's house at breakneck speed, skidding and sliding down the long, winding path. She almost lost her footing several times and once nearly brained herself on a low-hanging branch that the recent rain had lowered to head height. She had no further plan other than to get away as far as possible and raise the alarm, and when she reached the road, she gambled and turned right. After forty-five minutes of running, a triumph of stamina over her ungainly technique, she concluded that it was the right decision when she reached the outskirts of the neighbouring village and soon after that she came to the police station. Throughout her flight, there was no sign of Frank, Judy or anyone else, though she kept looking over her shoulder.

Cragside police station was set back from the street and raised up on the hill. She counted thirteen steps to the front door. The walls were constructed of the local blue-green Lakeland slate and a blue glass lantern looked down on her as she breathed heavily, trying to compose herself. She approached with trepidation because she didn't know exactly what to say. She had never reported a murder before.

As soon as she stepped within the vicinity of the building, her telephone chirruped. *Thank God*, she thought, *a signal at last.* She approached the large arched doorway and pushed open one side of the black double doors, passing into the premises of Cumbria Constabulary.

The desk sergeant sat on a raised stood and looked down on her from behind a toughened plastic screen. When he spoke, the sound carried through tiny speakers set into the outside of the desk. 'Hello, madam, how can I help you?'

She took two deep breaths. 'I want to report a murder and an attempted abduction.' She tried to look the sergeant in the eye, but the sheen of the Plexiglas-glass distorted the light and she couldn't see his face clearly enough.

'Those are serious crimes, madam.'

'I know they are serious. That's why I want to report them.'

'But they are very rare. Nothing like that happens around here.'

'You sound as if you doubt me?'

He shrugged. 'Just stating a fact, madam.'

The man took her details, punching them slowly into a keyboard using only one finger at a time, then he said, 'Please take a seat. One of our officers will be with you shortly.'

Despite the characterful exterior, the station was like every other institutional building she had ever been in. It looked like a bank but much dirtier and ill-kept. The linoleum floor was besmirched with black scuffs and pock-marked with used chewing gum. In places it was even burned, the floor blackened and distorted where it had melted.

'It's a bit shabby,' said the sergeant, 'but you wouldn't believe how many visitors we get through these doors in the summer.'

Jane looked at the row of dirty plastic seats that lined the far wall facing the desk. On one, it looked as if someone had thrown up all over it; yellowed stains spotted the back rest. And someone had obviously tried to set alight to another of the chairs – the seat was buckled and melted. 'What kind of person tries to set fire to a police station?' Jane said.

'You'd be surprised. But we're not responsible for the upkeep of the place. That's hired out to a private company. We get on at them all the time, but nothing ever seems to get done.' Jane nodded but didn't really accept that as a viable excuse. She was about to make further comment when an almighty clanking and slamming of doors emanated from around the corner.

'Spillage in interview room six,' a woman officer announced. She was short and had a thick utility belt around her large waist. She wore black trousers, a white short sleeved shirt and an armoured waistcoat with 'police' written in clear letters in several places.

The desk sergeant didn't look up but scribbled something down with a cheap plastic pen. 'Okay, Charlie, thanks. I'll get on to the cleaning company. Might be an idea to shut the room up until the morning. You know what response times are like.'

The woman officer frowned and ran her hair through her straight chestnut bob, scratching her head at the side. 'Okay, I'll switch him to the other. Give me a sec, will you?' Jane didn't know whether she was talking to her or to the desk sergeant, but she was left hanging around the entrance for another ten or fifteen minutes before she approached the desk again. It seemed to Jane that there was an overt lack of care on display, and she wondered if it was motivated by the colour of her skin. Apart from Frank, she hadn't seen another person of colour.

'Do you keep everyone waiting like this?'

'Sorry, madam?'

'I mean, I've just come here to report a series of serious crimes. Nothing important or anything.'

'Madam, I can assure you we value your custom, and just as soon as the next officer becomes available your statement will be taken. Please be patient.' Either the sergeant didn't recognise her sarcasm or he'd been trained to ignore it. He sounded like he'd once worked in a telephone call centre.

Down the corridor, Jane heard further sounds of doors slamming and keys turning, then laughter. She peered around the corner and through the thin vertical window set into the reinforced door. In the corridor beyond, a man and a woman were talking in low voices. They were both police officers. The man noticed Jane and nodded in her direction. His colleague turned around and Jane saw from her nametag that this was DC Matthews. Matthews noticed Jane looking, but then she set her back towards her and continued the chat.

'Please take a seat, an officer will be with you just as soon as one is available,' the sergeant reiterated, this time without the rehearsed neutrality but with an open and growing hostility. Jane thought he didn't take kindly to people showing their faces at the inner sanctum. Especially if the face was a black one.

'What about those two?' she said. 'They look like they're available.'

'Madam, please take a seat.' His tone was becoming harsh. He put down his pen and took off his glasses. He looked like he was preparing to come out from behind the armoured plastic of the desk. She knocked on the door to get the attention of the police officers on the other side. Matthews looked at her and when Jane locked eyes with her, there was a short battle of wills. Matthews sighed, said something to her colleague and came to the door.

'Name?' Matthews said.

'Jane Kensagi. Yours?'

The officer raised her eyebrows and almost rolled her eyes. With a sigh, she said, 'I'm DC Matthews.'

'Is there somewhere else we can talk?' Jane asked. 'I'd feel more comfortable if we did this in private.'

'All of our interview rooms are occupied. And I'm not at liberty to interview at my desk. Address?'

'Flat four, Bryer Court, Barbican.'

'Birmingham, did you say?'

'No, Barbican. You know, in London.'

DC Matthews wrote that down, saying, 'Sorry if we're not that familiar with the nation's capital as you people.'

You people? 'What do you mean by that?' Jane said.

Matthews shrugged. 'Southerners, Londoners. Off-comers. Take your pick. Age?'

'Thirty-five.'

'Sex?'

'Look, I really must insist that we speak in private. I'm not comfortable with doing this in a public area.'

Matthews put down her pen and folded the paper form that she had been writing on. 'Have it your way, madam. Please take a seat.'

It must have been at least half an hour before anything else happened. She'd sat on the scruffy, ripped and burned seats, trying not to think about what was spilled down the back of the one next to her. Jane perused her emails and checked her social media profile.

It was her biggest fear that she had indeed lost three months of time, but she was relieved when she saw the date as August twelfth, only a day after she'd set off from London. Her posts, emails and everything else looked in line with her expectations and there was nothing from the LSO. She wanted to call them and make sure but was afraid of looking stupid if she were to check in so soon after taking leave. She'd give herself time to think of an excuse to call in, maybe tomorrow.

A cleaning woman came in and was buzzed by the desk sergeant into the back office. She heard some conversation, then a melodious whistling. Jane thought about engaging the desk sergeant in conversation, but something about the man's body language made it quite plain that he'd had enough of her and wasn't going to allow her to interrupt his sitting back and staring into space. He made it impossible for her to meet his eye.

After another ten minutes, she considered that inviting his wrath was the lesser evil to waiting around for an indeterminate amount of time. 'Will this take much longer?'

'All in good time, madam. You requested a private interview room and we have to wait for one to become vacant before we deal with your enquiry.'

'Enquiry? This is more than an enquiry. I've been attacked and abducted. I'm in fear for my life. Someone has been murdered.'

'So you say, madam. But we won't know that until we take your official statement, will we?'

'But I know!'

'Please calm down, madam. I would ask you not to raise your voice.'

'Why not? What will you do? Arrest me? You don't have the room, evidently. But if it will help me to get seen earlier, that's fine by me.'

'I don't care for your tone, madam.'

'And I don't care for your attitude. I come here to report a string of serious crimes and you keep me waiting like this. Then you give me this attitude. It is completely unacceptable.'

'Please, madam, don't get so angry.'

'Why not? I've been taken advantage of far too much already.'

'Madam, may I just check something? Amongst these crimes you want to report, you wouldn't have been attacked in any way that is *more* than physical, would you?'

Jane knew what he was getting at and thought about this. Could she be really sure that she hadn't been violated in some way at the Captain's house? She blinked and saw the sudden image of the white room and the insidious crawling thing. 'Yes, I think that I have definitely been violated in some way.'

'You mean to say that you are the victim of sexual abuse?'

'Can you define sexual abuse?'

The man pecked with one finger at his keyboard and waited a few long seconds. He read from the screen, 'Any sexual contact without your consent is sexual assault and is a crime. Would you like to report such a crime at this time?'

'I don't know, I'm not sure.'

'You don't know if you want to report it, or you're not sure you've been a victim?' The sergeant squinted at his screen. 'I should advise you that contacting the police will start the process of investigating your attacker, but our priority is safeguarding you. If you choose to support a police investigation, you will be supported every step of the way. If you are reporting domestic violence or abuse then getting help is perhaps the most important thing you can do.'

'Are you reading all this off your screen?'

The desk sergeant pressed a buzzer and spoke into a microphone. 'DC Matthews, please come to the front desk. We have a possible section forty-nine offence.'

Jane heard the response through the thin speaker, though the sergeant took pains to shield the sound by cupping his hands around it. 'That's a priority code, I'll be right there.'

'What's a priority code?' Jane asked.

'Each month we've been asked to put a priority on certain types of offence. This month it's sexual abuse. You're in luck.'

Matthews came bustling in. 'You should have said something,' she said to Jane. 'You poor dear, please come through. Can I get you a tea? Coffee? Have you eaten? Do you like Chinese food?'

Half an hour later, Jane was cradling her hands around her third hot steaming mug of tea and DC Matthews was leaning backwards, pushing a foil takeaway carton away from her. Jane hadn't touched hers. 'So what happens next?' Jane asked.

'Well, the crime number has come through, so it's now just a matter of assigning you an SIO, a senior investigating officer, to your case. I should imagine they would want to interview you first thing in the morning. Is there anywhere safe for you to go?'

Jane shook her head. 'Not unless you can get me back to London?'

'Whilst you are not under any obligations whatsoever, I would strongly advise that you stay in the area. I can notify social services and they can find you room at a well-women's centre. They'll know how to give you the support you need.'

'Support I need?'

'Yes, you've been the victim of a serious sexual assault. You'll need all the support you can get.'

'But I just reported a murder.'

'You told the desk sergeant you were sexually assaulted, and your welfare has to be our priority.'

'I said I wasn't sure. I feel like something happened, but I don't have any physical signs.'

'So, all of this paperwork is for nothing?'

'Didn't you record what I told you about the murder?'

'Yes, of course I did, but that's a matter for the serious crimes department in Carlisle. They've got their hands full at the moment and it could be days before they are in touch. The most important thing now is for you to get help for the section 49 offence. Victims always need far more support than they realise.'

'I told you that I wasn't sure whether anything happened.'

'So, you wish to retract these allegations? Is that what you are telling me?'

'Yes, if it helps you to investigate the murder. That should be the priority.'

DC Matthews stormed out of the interview room and came back a few minutes later with another officer. It was the man with whom she'd seen Matthews sharing a joke when she'd first arrived. Both sat down opposite her. Matthews had a black look about her, but her colleague seemed more friendly. To Jane, it seemed as if he were almost embarrassed to be there. Matthews leaned forward and pushed a cassette into a large, heavy tape deck and pressed a grey button that was worn with use. A long note sounded from the machine and when it subsided, Matthews said, 'Interview of suspect Jane Kensagi, conducted by DC Matthews and DS Booth. Since the suspect has admitted to an offence, this interview is now being conducted under caution.' She looked at Jane the whole time but only now addressed her directly. 'You don't have to say anything, but it may harm your defence if you fail to mention something under questioning that you later rely on in court and, of course, anything you do say may be used as evidence. Do you understand?'

Jane frowned in disbelief.

'For the benefit of the tape, the suspect nods her assent.'

'What are you doing?' Jane said. 'I come here to report a crime and I find that I'm the suspect. What are you accusing me of, exactly?'

'You have not been accused or charged with any offences at this time. This is an interview under caution as there is suspicion of offences under section forty-nine of the police and criminal evidence act of 1984, namely making false accusations of sexual assault. Would you like your solicitor to be present at this time?'

'But I didn't—'

'Ms Kensagi, for the record, did you or did you not inform the desk sergeant that…' Matthews flicked open her pocketbook with a flourish, 'and I quote, "I think I have definitely been violated in some way."'

'Yes, I did say that. But that was an hour after I tried to report a murder and attempted abduction. What have you done about those? Nothing, absolutely nothing. I want to make a complaint; this just isn't acceptable.'

'Madam, you have every right to make a complaint, of course. But let's establish the facts of this other matter first.

I am concerned over your lack of remorse. Making false allegations is a serious offence and in some cases can lead to a greater charge of perverting the course of justice. It will help your defence if you give us your full cooperation.'

'If you want facts, why don't you mention that you also asked me if I thought I had been sexually abused. I said that I couldn't be sure. That's a fact. It's also a fact that you only became interested in me when you realised that you had a priority code. That's what you said. I suspect that you are only interested in targets and performance indicators. I'm willing to bet that making false allegations about sexual assault is also a section forty-nine offence. Am I right? You don't care about the murder, do you?'

The growing tension was interrupted by a knock at the door as the desk sergeant tried to get the attention of his colleagues. He beckoned them outside. DS Booth reached across his colleague towards the tape machine. 'Interview terminated,' he said, hitting the big grey button, then the two officers left Jane on her own for a few minutes. She used the time to process what was happening. In many ways, she felt more in control in Barrowthwaite. That place was a waking nightmare, but this was also unbearable.

Matthews and Booth came back into the room. 'Ms Kensagi, I am recommending to the CPS that there is no case to answer. You are free to go. Please accept our apologies for keeping you and you have our thanks for assisting in our enquiries.' It all sounded like Matthews was well practised at this little speech.

'What about the murder I reported? Don't you people even care about that?'

It was DS Booth who spoke next. 'Madam, I have authorised DC Matthews to accompany you to the scene of the alleged crime, but you should know that there is a complication. The crime you have reported happened three months ago. A man from London has already been charged and has been remanded in custody awaiting trial.'

Jane went cold. Her mind reeled with this new revelation. 'My husband, Haruki?'

Booth did not deny this. 'And you, Ms Kensagi. It seems that you have shown up on our missing persons database. In fact, one of the charges that have been brought in this case relates to your own disappearance. You have been missing since the incident.'

'Oh shit,' Jane said. 'Not again.'

'I'm sorry, Ms Kensagi, is there an additional statement you would like to make? Perhaps something that can help us clear up the matter of where you have been since August thirteenth?'

'Am I a suspect?'

'Why would you imagine you would be a suspect?'

'Am I a suspect?'

'Not at this time, and you are no longer under caution, but we would ask that as a person of interest you remain close by. We will almost certainly arrange for you to come in for questioning at date of our choosing. May I ask you where you will go? Where will we be able to contact you?'

'I'm going to visit my husband,' Jane said, 'but after that, I *do* want one of you to accompany me to Barrowthwaite.'

HARUKI

Haruki was woken by an elbow in the face. It wasn't one levelled at him in anger, he would surely know about that if it were, but in many ways he would have preferred that.

As his eyes flickered open, he realised he was sleeping on his side and facing the man squatting on the toilet. 'Better turn your head,' the man said. 'There's trouble brewing.'

It was like this each morning; Redrum was regular. But if regularity was a virtue, stinking out the tiny prison cell for most of the morning wasn't. Haruki had stolen a couple of lemons from the kitchen last week and he still had one dried husk hidden under his pillow. He turned to face the wall, rubbed the lemon on his pillow and daubed a little juice under his nose.

It didn't really work. It didn't change the smell of faeces that rushed into his nostrils. Now it just smelled of excrement and lemons. He doubted he would ever be able to eat lemon again when he got out of here. If he ever did get out of here. His trial was closing fast and his legal representation wasn't hopeful. That was fine; he was resigned to that outcome because if he were acquitted, then it would be Jane that they would most likely go after next. The investigation would continue and they might look again, or more deeply, at the evidence.

Redrum farted and followed through with a tumble of liquid into the stainless-steel toilet basin. 'Oh my God, what did I eat?'

'You ate Skinny Jesus's dinner. You threatened to eat *him* if he didn't hand it over,' Haruki said. He considered moving his head up the other end of the bed, but then he'd only have to look at the man, and Redrum didn't like eye contact, especially when he was on the toilet. He could be very touchy about things like that and Haruki knew that his survival was contingent on learning very quickly what all of those things were.

Redrum wasn't his real name, of course. Behind bars, no one went by their real names. He claimed the name came from being hung like a horse, but others had said it referred to his conviction. Redrum was murder backwards and the victims of his murder habit were often left in extravagant circumstances that resembled scenes from Stephen King novels. Prison names here were very apt and Haruki supposed that came from the inmates having a lot of time to sit around thinking them up.

In between the offensive bowel movements, Redrum said, 'Aha! You're right. Thanks for… ah… reminding me. The little bastard must have known I'd take it from him. He put shit in his food, didn't he? And it was meant for me.'

'You don't know that for sure,' Haruki murmured, trying to open his mouth as little as possible. 'And you shouldn't jump to conclusions.'

'You know, Picasso, you're the only one who gets to speak to me like that. But it's fine. I like you. You tell me how it is.' Haruki's prison name was disappointingly obvious, but he didn't have any choice over it.

'If you say so.' Haruki plugged his fingers into his ears so that he didn't have to hear. He didn't really care what happened to him in here. From first arrival he'd been put in with Redrum, Hawkmoor's most notorious inmate. A serial murderer and man-rapist. The staff must have seen that as some kind of joke. The cultured artist with the famous musician for a wife, slim and ageing, bunking down with twenty-five stone of murderous sexual aggression.

Except that the pair had got on much better than anyone would have imagined. Redrum enjoyed his company and they often talked well into the night when the lights were turned off.

It turned out that Redrum himself had an aptitude for painting and that had been one of the reasons that N4S, Hawkmoor's operating company, had introduced art therapy classes twice a week. They must have seen an interesting reverse correlation between the regularity of art classes and the propensity of Redrum to beat both inmates and wardens within an inch of their lives.

Having a dangerous cellmate brought Haruki certain advantages that on balance outweighed the morning toilet ritual. The other prisoners saw him as either on friendly terms with the notorious rapist, or on terms that equated to a little more that friendship. Either way they left him alone. They even afforded him some respect. And that was something that Haruki was keen to trade on. He'd taken over teaching the art therapy class in an attempt to inculcate friendly relations with some of the other prisoners. If anything should happen to his protector he needed to be sure there were others that would sponsor him. At the very least he considered it important that the other prisoners saw him as a person in his own right rather than simply Redrum's plaything.

More straining and watery sounds pouring into the toilet basin. 'Fuck. I hope that's the last of it. I'm going to kill Skinny Jesus. I'm going to strip his corpse naked and then I'm going to… Hey, I've just had an idea. What if I save some of this shit and use it in art class tonight? I bet no one's done that before, eh? It'd be a first. I'll probably get a Turner prize for that, right?'

'Actually, Chris Ofili won in 1998 for painting with elephant dung.'

'So, not human shit? Good. And not his own. And if I mix it up with some of Skinny Jesus's blood, then there's more meaning in that, isn't there? I'll call it *The Produce of Violence and Retribution*. That's good, isn't it? Now you just need to coach me on what to paint and how to paint it.'

The thought of standing over a bucket of blood and excrement and advising his cellmate how to smear it over a canvas turned his stomach. He thought he might be needing the basin himself before too long, but then a buzzing at the door distracted him. It indicated that one of the guards was entering.

'Stand away from the door.' All the guards were employed by N4S, the private company that operated Hawkmoor under licence. All the officers read exclusively from a script that they carried with them at all times in the form of a handheld tablet. Ask them any question and they would scroll down to the appropriate response. If there was none, they would ignore the question.

'Haruki Kensagi, answering yes or no only, do you accept to see your solicitor at this time?'

'It is about the trial?' Kensagi asked.

'Answering yes or no only, do you—'

'Yes, of course.'

The two officers watched as Haruki dressed. They accompanied him to the washrooms and stood inside the door as he cleaned his teeth and brushed his hair. It was a pity he didn't have time for a shower. It was still out of hours and the cubicles were free. Normally there was a long queue. A long and dangerous queue if you happened to join it at the wrong time. The presence of Redrum mitigated the danger, but only slightly. He was more likely to cause the danger himself than to prevent it from happening.

'Answering yes or no only, are you now ready to see your visitor?'

'Yes,' Haruki said, 'lead on.'

The interview room was down a corridor, through five sets of gates, each with an entry and exit procedure that required following to the letter. Barcodes were scanned, times noted and keys cross-checked before opening or closing anything. The whole rigmarole took around fifteen minutes to travel fifty metres. When Haruki eventually reached the interview room he was asked to 'answer yes or no only' to a serious of banal and useless questions. Like, 'Do you understand that the prison health and safety policy applies to interview settings?' and, 'Are you fully aware of the inmate code of conduct, especially with regard to sexual harassment, including inappropriate eye contact and abuse of power in a relationship?'

Haruki assented to each. He imagined a small transaction occurring after each yes or no answer. It wouldn't have surprised him if he learned that N4S were paid per question, or per gate. He also knew that to answer in anything other than the affirmative would result in an aborted visit. That had happened more than enough times to Redrum, causing no end of difficulties for all concerned.

When Haruki was finally admitted to the interview room, he nodded a greeting to Fargher, his lawyer. Fargher was a small man in his fifties, who always wore a wide herringbone tweed jacket with a turquoise pocket handkerchief. Alongside this, he wore either matching trousers or mustard-coloured ones. He put his eccentricity of dress down to his Australian nationality, but Haruki suspected that the man was colour-blind. Today he sported the mustard trousers, but that was only a passing observation as Haruki had just seen whom Fargher had brought with him. It was Jane.

She looked exactly as he had seen her last. She wore walking boots and a waterproof overcoat, and underneath that he saw the flash of a green dress. Jane looked up at him with wide, dark eyes. 'Hello, Haruki.' She reached out tentatively across the dividing table, glancing at Fargher to question whether it was okay to touch. Fargher nodded and they held hands. Haruki didn't know what to say. He just stared open-mouthed at his wife.

Fargher took control of the situation. 'Haruki, we sought an immediate interview with you because of new evidence that has come to light about your case. Now, as a member of the public, normally Ms Kensagi wouldn't be allowed to see you outside of visiting hours, but today she is here in an official capacity as a witness. Jane is the new evidence that has come to light. Now, as you know, Ms Kensagi has been missing since the incident you are charged with and one of the charges against you relates to her disappearance. Because that has now been called into question, we have reasonable grounds to request an extension whilst we process the new evidence.'

'I thought you'd get away,' Haruki said. 'I'd hoped you'd go back to London and pick up your life where you left it.'

Fargher was quick to get the interview moving. 'Now, let us deal with the facts of the case in a more private setting, shall we? What is said here is under legal privilege between myself and my client, Mr Kensagi. But your own status needs to be worked out, Ms Kensagi.'

'No, it's okay,' Jane said. 'I already told the police what happened. I've nothing to hide. They'll surely investigate again and come to the right conclusion.'

'Which is?' Kensagi asked.

'Which is that Judy killed the Captain. She was working for Frank.'

'The strange blind man from the post office? Why would she do that?'

'Does it matter? Now that we know the truth, we need to get you out of here and back home. We'll go far away from here, leave the country if we need to. Anything to put Barrowthwaite behind us.'

'I am afraid it is not as simple as that,' Fargher interjected, talking to Jane. 'Your eyewitness testimony could be called into doubt. If so, it's inadmissible. If allowed, it would be just one piece of evidence amongst many. The forensics are against my client, as is the testimony of the other witnesses. And Haruki could still be seen to have had the means, the motive and the opportunity. And of course there is the matter of his confession. That can't be so easily overlooked.'

'You did that, Haruki? You pleaded guilty?'

'He's admitted killing the victim but not to murdering him. We are claiming self-defence.'

Jane's voice was thick. 'I get it. You did this for me. I don't know what to say.' Haruki was thrilled when Jane squeezed his hand and continued to rub her thumb alone the back of it. It was the most intimate gesture he'd shared with his wife since he didn't know when. 'Just tell them you made a mistake, that you were not thinking straight. We can go back to Barrowthwaite and show them how strange it is there. We can show them the white room. That's all it will take, surely.'

'I doubt the police will want to re-investigate. They have long since released the scene of the crime back to normal use, so that avenue of enquiry won't be available to us. We'll need to think about this,' Fargher said.

'No, it's already arranged. They'll take me up there to gather evidence. I'll not allow my husband to rot in this shitty prison. And afterwards, we'll sue their arses off. They should have known that Haruki wasn't in his right mind.'

Haruki noted the fierce determination in his wife's eyes. He hadn't seen her this animated for years. In fact he couldn't remember when they last had such a strong connection with each other. He nodded to Fargher. 'Yes, do as she says, please.'

'Okay,' Fargher said, 'but one thing at a time. I suggest we go over the main evidence against Haruki. Then we can discuss our next steps.' Both Haruki and Jane nodded their assent.

'Good. Firstly there's the forensics. DNA and fingerprints on the handle of the poker. Prints all over the house. Small drops of blood in the kitchen. All match the control prints and DNA that they took from Haruki, with a probability match of ninety-nine point nine. That's as close a match as they can get.'

'An open and shut case,' Haruki said.

'Except we have to consider what they don't have.'

'What they don't have?' Jane asked.

'They don't have any of Haruki's DNA on the victim. The existing evidence support the scenario that there was a struggle, through which Haruki was stabbed but after which he killed Mr Brown.'

'Mr Brown?' Jane asked.

'John Brown.'

'That's the Captain, right? That's his name?'

Fargher nodded. 'But as I was saying, although there was evidently a struggle, there was none of Haruki's tissue under his nails, none of his clothing fibre on his clothes and, most importantly of all, none of Haruki's blood on his hands.'

'So, that's that then. Haruki couldn't have done it.'

'Not quite. An absence of evidence is not evidence to the contrary. We'll need something stronger than that. The police allege that Haruki arranged the scene of the crime to make it look like there was a struggle.'

'Are they saying that Haruki stabbed himself. That's ridiculous.'

'I *did* stab myself,' Haruki said. 'I wanted to take the blame because I thought *you* had killed him.'

'Stupid man – after all these years, you really don't know me at all. I'm not my father.' Although Jane's words stung him, her tone was not unkind and she squeezed his hands as she spoke.

'There's another spanner in the works,' Fargher said. 'They have an eyewitness too. An independent one.'

'That can only be Maggie, but how is *she* independent? She's working for the Captain and she's the sister of Judy, the real killer,' Jane said.

'Well, now that we know that, we can begin to construct a case. We don't have to prove that Haruki didn't do it. We just have to throw enough doubt onto their version of events.'

Haruki was comforted that Jane was with him and he was thrilled with their new intimacy, but the matter of Maggie still haunted him. He'd known her for only a day or so, but part of him felt that he'd been with her for much longer than that. When he thought of her being the main witness against him, he couldn't help but feel betrayed. He'd had to endure endless police interviews where they threw all kind of accusations at him. If the charges were not so serious, he would have found it laughable the extent to which they'd used their imaginations to drum up all kinds of false theories which they put to him in ways that became more and more aggressive.

And then they tried to ladder the evidence, so that they could add more charges to the list, probably to meet some target or other. *Perverting the course of justice*, was one, which was an absurd tautology. If he was convicted of murder, then of course that was a perversion its own right.

And when Haruki agreed to a guilty plea of manslaughter, the horse trading really began. 'Are there any other offences that you would like us to take into account at this time?' they asked. The offers came flying in thick and fast. Plead guilty to this and that, have these sins absolved, no extra penance. Theft, assault, coercion and, of course, perverting the course of justice all carried no additional penalty, according to the senior investigating officer. Haruki doubted that, but in any case, just the one killing was more than enough for him to martyr himself for at this time.

'So currently they have a strong case. They have passed the evidence threshold test with flying colours. They can establish the opportunity, the means and the motive,' Fargher said.

'What motive?' Jane snapped. 'Other than to protect me? And we've talked about that.'

Fargher glanced at him seeking permission to disclose something. Haruki gave it with a nod. 'It was Maggie who gave them the motive,' Fargher said. 'She claims Haruki was jealous of the Captain, who was Maggie's ex-lover.'

'My husband had only just met the woman,' Jane said.

'Maggie claims that she and your husband were cohabiting,' Fargher said.

'None of that happened,' Haruki said. 'But apparently it's going to. Jane, none of this makes any sense. And ordinarily, I'd expect anyone that listened to me to think I was insane. But you've been to Barrowthwaite; you know what it's like there. Time is all wrong, and so are the people. There's nothing right about the place. You yourself claim to have seen me with Maggie. But I never was, or at least I don't remember. She told me that it was going to happen in the future, but that's all.'

Jane withdrew her hands from Haruki's and spoke to Fargher. 'Do they have any evidence of a sexual relationship between Haruki and Maggie?'

'Not beyond her statement. They would have to disclose it if they did.'

'She's protecting Judy,' Haruki said. 'That much is obvious. But they would say the same about you, that you are protecting me. So it's a case of your word against hers, but that's only as far as the motive goes. The evidence against me is far stronger than that, even if I did falsify it myself.'

'I wish you hadn't,' Jane said. 'There was no need.'

'I thought you had killed him and I couldn't have your life ruined. Not when it was all my fault that you were there in the first place.'

'But there's something more, isn't there? Something you're not telling me.'

'Or, something I hardly know myself.' Haruki felt a tear escape and run down his cheek. It had appeared so suddenly. 'I don't know. I got so confused whilst I was there, but I have this nagging feeling that I did something I should feel guilty about. That feeling has grown whilst I've been in here. But it's more than that. I like it in here, Jane, can you understand that? I think that somehow I'm supposed to be here. I think that I deserve to be here.'

Jane's anger was swift to appear. 'No, you don't. Don't you dare.' Her fist came down on the table. A startled Fargher jumped in his seat. 'You didn't do it. You didn't kill the Captain, and you didn't do anything else. You've nothing to feel guilty about and I'm going to get you out of here.'

'Jane, listen—'

'No, you listen to me. I'm going to make you a promise. I'm going to get you out. I'm going to figure out what happened. I'm going back to Barrowthwaite.'

JANE

On the way into Barrowthwaite it started to snow. At first it was only a smatter, tiny spots of wet sludge lingering on the windscreen of DC Matthews' service vehicle, but then the flutter turned into something more serious. Before long the wipers had to work overtime to keep the Volvo's windscreen clear. Outside, the flakes floated down incessantly. They stuck to the ground, onto the drystone walls and onto the roofs of the little village houses, building a slow blanket of white wherever they touched down. In a few short minutes the whole village was covered. Jane had never seen such a whiteout.

The roads had started to become slippery and even with Matthews' advanced driving skill, she doubted they could go much further. 'It's early,' Matthews said. 'We don't usually get this until January.'

'It's unheard of,' Jane said, 'to have this much snow in mid-August. And you'd never see this much down south.'

She received a quizzical look from Matthews. 'It's mid-November, madam.'

'Call me Jane.' She tried to hide the stomach-churning thought that it was all going to happen to her again, that she'd get stuck in the village, ensnared by the Captain.

'I get it,' Matthews said. 'You've no recollection of the last few months. You've been missing all this time and you want to get some answers. Well, that's why we're here, isn't it?' Jane let the rhetorical question float around like a snowflake in the air. 'Don't worry, this happens sometimes,' DS Matthews said after a while.

'Does it?'

'It's consistent with being involved in trauma.'

Jane let the conversation fall there and Matthews drove on in silence. For Jane, the implication was clear. The police considered her involved. Not a witness but actually, physically involved. They must have dropped their notions of bumping up their section forty-nines in favour of a more serious charge. She was a murder suspect. That's why Matthews had been only too keen to drive her back out here. She wanted to be the one who implicated her in the murder. She wanted to be the arresting officer. Jane had more to worry about than losing track of time; if she wasn't careful, she'd be arrested and thrown in jail. Then she'd be of no use to Haruki or anyone.

As they passed into the heart of the village Jane began to see the warm lights shining out from inside the villagers' homes. She envied them their cosy warmth and security, tucked up in their homes whilst she was outside in the cold feeling scared and uncertain. With no answers as to what had happened to her and Haruki in Barrowthwaite, she couldn't go back to London. She had to resolve things up here first.

They passed the old post office and Matthews slowed to negotiate an icy sheet on the road. Jane first noticed the old red post box sat atop a drystone wall. It wore a thick crown of white that threatened to slip off. The old-style telephone box stood next to it. It had lost many of its windows. Blackened jagged shards of glass held on to the dull red frame, the paint split and peeling. The post office building itself was a similar model of disrepair. The windows were boarded up and it looked like someone had tried to start a fire in the recess that housed the front door. The Lakeland slate of the outside wall was chipped and scuffed, and moss grew between the cracks.

Matthews drove out of the village centre and climbed uphill. After a steep switchback, she pulled up the Volvo alongside what looked like a snowbank, but she soon recognised it as her own Model S. 'That yours?' she asked.

'He was going to fix it for me. I had a flat, two of them.'

'You mean John Brown, the one who was murdered?'

Jane nodded. 'They called him the Captain.'

'We cross-checked with both social security and the border force, and there is no mention of him, anywhere.'

'I didn't know him well.'

'Well enough for him to fix your car. Well enough for you to spend the night at his house.'

'I didn't have a choice.'

'If you say so, madam.'

Matthews parked the car next to the Tesla and fetched her coat out of the boot. Jane used the time to examine her wheels, brushing back the snow with her foot. The front two were brand new. Matthews handed her a spare coat and Jane shrugged it on. She followed the policewoman across the road, over the stile and down the path that led to the Captain's house. The snow under Jane's boots crunched and squeaked as it compressed, and she was glad of the warmth of the borrowed coat, and even for the fact that it was a gaudy high-vis jacket. She supposed her body would be found sooner if something happened to her here.

The Captain's house was exactly as she'd left it. Tentatively, she approached the window through which she'd witnessed his murder. She peered inside. A light shone from an adjoining room, and when Matthews strode right up to the front door and knocked the light changed as a shadow passed before it. 'Someone's in there,' Jane said.

'Probably the caretaker,' Matthews said, 'Margaret Robertson.'

'Maggie? But it was *her* sister who I saw kill the Captain. She bashed his head in with a poker.'

'The forensic report pointed quite clearly to your husband's involvement.'

'What about my witness statement? Does that mean nothing?'

'Let's see what Ms Robertson has to say about this, shall we?'

Jane heard some footfall and a door close from somewhere inside. Then a figure came into view, disturbing the light from inside. It reached the front door and unlocked first the inner, then the outer door. It creaked open. Jane expected to see Maggie and was preparing for what she would say to the girl. She had more than a sneaking suspicion that all of what was happening right now was Maggie's fault.

But it wasn't Maggie; it was a man. Tall, long blond hair, tied back into a bun. He wore nothing but a towel around his waist, and his smooth tanned torso glimmered with a slick sheen. He radiated health and fitness. He smiled as if he were genuinely pleased to see the police officer at his door. It was the Captain.

'I saw you murdered,' Jane said, those being the only words she could summon.

Matthews stepped in front of Jane to take control. 'Good evening, sir, please forgive the intrusion. I'm DC Matthews from Cragside station. I would like to speak with the caretaker, if you wouldn't mind.' Matthews was straining her neck to try and peer around the Captain and get a good luck at the inside of the house.

'It needs to come in,' the Captain smiled, 'and it should know that the Captain is the proud homeowner. He lives here; he *owns* it.' She watched Matthews screw her face up in confusion as she took out her pocketbook and flicked back through the pages. 'You are Mr Brown, John Brown?'

The Captain nodded. 'It takes out its notepad and it finds a name.'

Matthews snapped shut the pocketbook, giving Jane a withering look before saying, 'Mr Brown, there seems to be a few irregularities on your records – would you mind if I asked to a few questions to clear some of these up?'

'It comes in and it sits itself down.' The Captain gestured towards the sofa. He winked at Jane.

'You'd better explain,' Jane said. 'Haruki is in prison.'

'It knows why it came?' the Captain said to DC Matthews after he waited for her to take a seat on the sofa.

Matthews wriggled, looking increasingly uncomfortable. 'Go on.'

'It has come because it has been called.'

Matthews soldiered on. 'Sir, someone of your description was involved in an incident several months ago and I'm here to establish the identity of that person. May I see some form of identification, please?'

'It sits and waits, but first it tells what *incident* means.'

'A serious crime was committed. A man is in custody.'

'It means murder.'

'You are already familiar with the case?' Matthews' eyes narrowed. 'Can you tell me how you came to live in this house? Do you have any proof of ownership?'

'It wants to know about life and it wants to know about death?'

'Are you playing with me, sir? This is no laughing matter.'

'It doesn't want to laugh, but it hasn't considered the alternative. It thinks this matters, but there is no matter. Matter hasn't happened, and when it does, it does not matter as much as it thinks. It wants to know about crime, but there is no crime. Take it from someone who is murdered.'

At that, he jumped up and almost danced into the kitchen. 'But is it thirsty?' he called. 'Does it want tea? Coffee? Biscuits? Yes, it must want biscuits. It wants the nice chocolaty ones that are wrapped in foil. It stays sat whilst biscuits are fetched.'

The Captain had already disappeared into the kitchen before Matthews could remonstrate with him. She turned to Jane and whispered, 'This is the person you saw murdered?'

Jane nodded. 'He's acting strangely, but yes, this is him.'

'Then can I ask you what the hell is going on here? Your husband is being held for this man's murder. There are fingerprints, DNA analysis, forensics, a murder weapon. There was a body.'

'It thinks that, doesn't it?' he called from the kitchen. 'But it looks again and it finds differently.' He came back into the lounge with a plate of round biscuits. They were all neatly wrapped in foil. 'It takes gold if it likes milk and it takes silver if it wants dark. It takes the green. Ah yes, it takes green if it wants… mint!' He practically shouted that last word, causing Matthews to jump. Her hand shot down to her belt towards the bright yellow content of her holster.

'No chocolates, thank you, and no drinks. But I must insist on some form of identification and I have to advise you that if your proper identity cannot be ascertained at this time, then you may find yourself under arrest.'

'It is nervous. It follows the Police and Criminal Evidence Act, note 2D. It warns. It warns! Whoops…' The Captain's towel dropped from around his waist, but he caught it in the nick of time before he exposed himself. 'It wants to see more. It follows with its eyes.' The Captain danced away upstairs. Jane heard the footsteps on the floor above. It sounded as if the man was skipping.

She turned to DC Matthews. 'He wasn't like this before. He's changed.'

Matthews' voice was gravel. 'Whatever this is, you're on the hook for it as far as I'm concerned. If I don't get answers soon, I'm taking the both of you into custody.'

'On what grounds?'

'False accusation, perverting the course of justice, fraud. I'll find something if things don't start to make sense very quickly.'

Despite the frustration she felt, she had some sympathy for the woman; she knew exactly what Matthews was going through. Nothing here made sense. 'Look, I just want to clear the charges hanging over my husband's head. You've seen that the Captain wasn't murdered after all, so please don't lose sight of that. Haruki can't face charges for something that hasn't happened yet.'

'Yet? You said, "yet". What the hell do you mean by that?'

'Nothing, I must have misspoken.'

The Captain came floating back down the stairs. This time he was wearing a red velvet dressing gown and matching slippers. 'It wants biscuits, but it hasn't been able to eat because it's been talking.'

'Mr Brown, you have been reported as dead. Murdered, in fact. A man has been arrested and awaits trial. I require your identification immediately. And I must warn you that I may have reasonable grounds to suspect that you are involved in a hoax of some kind. Do you know what? Forget the identification. These are questions that are better asked back at the station.'

'It wants to make an arrest. It wants to go back, but it can never go back.'

'Was that a threat? Right, that's quite enough. John Brown, I am arresting you on suspicion of—'

The Captain grinned. 'It is reading his rights, but it must see something first. In here.' He indicated towards the kitchen.

'Don't,' Jane said. But Matthews was already up and heading in the direction that the Captain, smiling sweetly, was indicating for her to follow. Jane rose from her seat. The woman didn't know what she was heading into. It was a mistake to bring Matthews here. Haruki's freedom notwithstanding.

'Sit down,' Matthews barked at Jane. 'Stay here.'

Jane had little choice but to comply. Matthews had her hand on the hilt of her taser. A bright yellow and black presence at her side that she now looked just as likely to use on Jane as much as on the Captain.

When Matthews saw inside the kitchen, she did not hesitate but to pull the weapon from her holster. 'Don't move,' she shouted at the Captain. 'Down on your knees, now!' The Captain obliged, the smile never fading from his lips. She cuffed him and only when his hands were secure behind his back did she re-holster. Jane could not resist a look into the kitchen and, despite Matthews' insistence that she stay where she was, she got close enough to the kitchen door to see what was beyond.

It was Judy. And it wasn't the kitchen. It was the white room. She was suspended from the ceiling and her arms dangled down below her. She wasn't moving of her own volition, but she swung softly as she dangled. A thick white rope was tangled around her ankles. Her head lolled to the side, facing Jane. From her mouth and eyes jutted dirty white fur-like growths. There was no blood, but what looked like grey snowflakes rotated in lazy circles around her, defying gravity. A white viscous liquid dripped from the fur growing around her mouth. It dropped onto the floor and inched away down the drain. It looked as if the walls were dripping with liquid too.

The Captain was kneeling at Matthews' feet, but he turned his head towards Jane. 'It sees what happens when it is away. It takes to Judy. Judy takes to it.'

'Quiet, you sick fuck,' Matthews said, kicking him with her foot. 'And you, I don't know what your game was, luring me here, but you need to stay well back. Don't make me use this on you.' She tapped her taser and that was enough for Jane to back away. She inched backwards towards the front door as Matthews fiddled with the police radio on her shoulder.

'Despatch, this is DC Matthews. Be advised of a homicide. Request backup. Full forensics and everything you've got. I have apprehended two suspects.'

There was a silence on the other end of the line. 'Despatch, this is DC Matthews. Please respond.' There was no response.

'It talks into its little machine, but does anyone hear? Does it need a telephone? There is one in here.' The Captain nodded in the direction of the white room.

Matthews didn't take too kindly to that. She yanked on the handcuffs behind his back and brought him somewhat painfully to his feet. 'Mr Brown, or whoever you are, I am arresting you on suspicion of murder. You do not have to say anything at this time, but if you fail to mention something that you later rely on in court, it may harm your defence. Do you understand?' For his response, the Captain giggled. 'Right, well, anyway, you're coming with me.'

And to Jane, she said, 'You too. I'm not arresting you yet, but as far as I'm concerned you are on thin ice. In any case you'll need to accompany me and undergo a new interview under caution. Do you understand?'

Jane shrugged; she didn't care as long as they left this place quickly.

As Matthews wrestled the Captain to his feet, Jane closed the door to the white room, preserving the scene of the crime and shutting in Judy and whatever else was in there, but she couldn't shake the thought that by the time the police had sent evidence teams and scene of the crime first responders to the location, all they would find was a normal kitchen. Complete with island unit and Belfast sink. She wouldn't be surprised if when the police came Judy was sat sweetly up to the island unit drinking tea or eating cake. Probably Maggie would be there too. They were all in this together.

But before Jane could close the door fully, something white came licking out of the inch-wide crack. It flew past her face, right in front of her nose. She shouted in alarm and threw herself onto the floor. It was rope, or a tentacle or something. It retreated back into the white room as she scrambled to her feet. Then she watched in horror as it came back, snaking out from behind the door, but it didn't come for her.

As it snaked towards Matthews she went to step over it, but it moved with alarming speed and easily wrapped itself around her ankle. It drew tight around her foot. Jane rushed to help. She got a grip on the rope and pulled. The strange thing was that she couldn't feel it. She knew she was gripping the length of something smooth and white but only by the evidence of her own eyes. Nothing else about her hands or body told her she had hold of it. Nevertheless, there was no denying the obvious strength that came from it as it started to pull Matthews inch by inch towards the white room.

As she tried to help Matthews as much as she could, Jane had the strange insight that the pulling force came not from the rope thing, or even from conventional physics like matter and energy, but from something deeper, something more profound. Like gravity.

Shouting abuse at her, Matthews fell to the floor and kicked out at Jane. She was the only thing within Matthews' reach that could afford her some purchase, but once Jane had been knocked flying, Matthews had nothing to stop her from being pulled into the kitchen.

The door opened wider and Jane again saw the kitchen beyond. This time, Judy was upright but slumped backwards on a chair by the kitchen table; the awful fuzz of mould was still growing out of her open mouth and now it was around her eyes and ears. At her throat her skin was translucent. Through it she could see glowing and pulsating lights inside her. But the most awful thing was that the white rope that was attached to Matthews, emanated from Judy's own mouth.

Matthews was at the door now and braced herself with her arms on either side of the door frame. Two more white tendrils unfurled out of the fuzz around Judy's yawning mouth. Three or four of these tendrils rose high and waved around in the air like the tentacles of a kraken. Two of them snaked towards her. They were going to fasten themselves to her and, like the one that had already snared Matthews, they would draw her towards Judy's husk of a body. Towards that yawning mouth, towards the horrible fur, the pulsating lights. Jane screamed.

A flash of light and a loud clicking sound, like a thousand magpies laughing at her. Then the tendrils retracted. The kitchen door slammed shut. 'What the fuck was that?' DC Matthews said. She had regained her feet and stood over Jane, brandishing her taser; its own tendrils had reached deep into the kitchen beyond the closed door.

'You used it on those tentacle things?' Jane said.

'Not quite,' Matthews said, panting heavily, a look of wild recklessness about her.

Jane suspected that the woman had buried the tasers hooks into Judy's body.

'I don't know what the fuck is going on, but I do know that twenty thousand volts are enough to persuade anything to let go. Jane, you need to tell me right now what that thing was. Otherwise I might have to use the second charge on you.'

Jane looked at a heavily panting Matthews. She saw the wild frenzy of panic in her eyes, but she also saw the calmness and clarity of her police training taking over. Her face was a picture of both these things, competing for control. Like a strip light flickering on and off: one instant, panic, the other a calm determination. Matthews' face flickered like that for a few moments, then it seemed that the calm police officer had won through. She re-holstered her taser and tried her radio again.

Jane didn't hold out any hope of the radio working, no communication ever did in Barrowthwaite, but then she watched Matthews' face drop with relief as she received an answer. The line crackled with the hope of salvation. 'Despatch.'

'This is DC Matthews. I need urgent backup. My location is the old cottage up at Barrowthwaite, the one where the murder happened late summer. I have a homicide and one suspect under arrest. There are others, hostile and dangerous. I am currently under attack.'

'Received. Officers despatched to your location, stand by.' There was a pause, then, 'DC Matthews, is that really you?'

'Yes, of course it's me. Why do you ask?'

'Come on, Matthews, you have to ask? You've been missing for a month. Where the hell have you been? We have a nationwide search on our hands, for you.'

Jane saw the policewoman's mouth open wide with shock. Matthews' eyes roamed from side to side as if searching for some information that could make sense of this for her. Then her eyes fixed on Jane and widened. She looked like she was about to speak, but she held that position for a moment, without moving or without blinking. She looked like she'd been frozen in time.

Then she crashed to the floor, and behind where she had been standing, the Captain appeared. His handcuffs were gone and his dressing gown had fallen open, revealing his naked body underneath. He had lost nothing of the conditioning that Jane had noticed at their first meeting; his stomach was tight with flat muscle. Beneath his stomach dangled twelve inches of thick, flaccid penis. It swung like a pendulum back and forth. It reminded her of the ends of those ropes in the gym that she'd had to climb at school.

His penis jiggled. She was captivated by its awful size and watched it swing and dance. Then she realised that the Captain was laughing. And in his hands, he held a knife. Blood was on it. And all over his hands and wrists. It dripped onto the carpeted floor before her. It trickled down his arms to his elbows, disappearing into the folds of his dressing gown. The Captain grinned.

The radio crackled. 'DC Matthews, are you still there?'

The Captain laughed. His face was wider than she'd seen it before. His grin was huge. It went from ear to ear and looked far too big for his face. She saw too that he had too many teeth for his mouth. Perhaps twice as many as was normal.

'DC Matthews, please respond.'

The Captain dropped the knife. It fell onto the carpet with a weak thud. It was so small. Just a thin sliver of metal, really. Yet it had had such a devastating effect on Matthews.

She didn't want to take her eyes off the Captain but had to check on Matthews. She had fallen forwards, face into the carpet. Blood poured like water from a tap out of a hole in the back of her neck. Jane didn't think but just reacted. She took off her jacket and used it inside out to try and staunch the wound. She bundled it up in her fist and pressed down hard. She wasn't sure whether she'd damage Matthews in this position but considered it her first priority to try to stop the outpouring of blood. She was aware of the Captain grinning madly over her, his terrible nakedness at odds with the blood on his hands and the knife that he'd dropped.

But the Captain didn't need a knife to be a threat to Jane. She felt his hand around her neck. Her skin crawled at his touch and at the horrible realisation that she should not have tried to save Matthews. She should have run. She promised herself that in future she *would* run, if she ever got the chance again. She'd run far away and never come back. Not for Matthews, not for Haruki, not for anyone. His hands closed around the back of her neck and she felt herself being lifted off the floor. With a shake of his wrists, he flung her away from Matthews' still-warm, wet body and she landed crumpled like a discarded doll at the foot of the stairs.

HIDE AND SEEK

She must have hit her head, or passed out, and by the time she recovered herself, shaking the confusion from her slowly returning vision, the Captain was bent over DC Matthews. Jane heard what was happening before she saw it.

Wet sounds, like a dog thirstily lapping water from a bowl, came from the Captain's mouth that had closed over the back of Matthews' neck. He noticed Jane's return to consciousness and lifted his face. Blood covered the lower part of it, from his ears to his neck, Matthews' blood. He grinned and now she saw that his too-many teeth were smaller than usual, crowded in multiple rows in his mouth, and they were pointed, like the tips of a kitchen knife.

Matthews' wound was bleeding profusely as the Captain lowered his head to it once more. He flicked his tongue out and licked his lips and chin. His tongue distended future and further until it was a good twelve inches from his face. It searched for the hole in Matthews' neck and when it had found it, the tongue disappeared inside. For all Jane knew it was growing larger inside her. Perhaps it snaked down the entire length of her? The Captain's eyes budged horribly as he drank up her insides.

Jane recovered her feet. She hadn't forgotten the promise

she had made to herself. She had to save herself. She had to run.

She started to dash for the front door, hoping she could make it past the Captain whilst he was distracted with Matthews, but when she took a first step in that direction, he shook his head, the tongue still far inside Matthews' body. The warning was clear, so Jane ran the other way, back into the house, up the stairs towards the bedrooms.

She must have tried a dozen windows, frantically clawing at the sash mechanism and at the brass locks holding them in place. Short of breaking the glass, there was no way to open them. She considered doing just that, but then there would be razor shards around the frame and even if she could make it through without slicing an artery, she'd be on a steeply sloping roof and facing a cruel fall to the ground below. Running was one thing but crippling herself was quite another. She'd only be doing the Captain's work for him.

And Matthews had made the call on her radio. Help was on its way. So, instead of running, she tried hiding.

Visions from her childhood swept through her mind. The ghosts of childhood games of hide and seek. She'd never played it with other children, but it was a game she knew very well. When the police came to her home, she would hide her father. When the social services came for her, she'd make herself small and find somewhere ingenious to wait them out. Somewhere they would never imagine a child to be. Now was the time for that again.

But this house was unfamiliar. It wasn't her own, where she knew every nook and cranny. Yet, houses were houses. She'd make do somehow. She had to believe that she could hide. At least until the police arrived.

The bedroom where she'd stayed was one possibility, but an obvious one. It had a large wardrobe, a four-poster bed and vast chest of drawers. She was drawn to those possibilities but knew that the Captain would be too.

The first room she came to was the bathroom. An old iron roll-top bathtub might make her feel safer but would be no use at obscuring her. She could crawl underneath its feet, perhaps? That was a distant possibility.

'It tries to hide,' the Captain called from below, his voice thick and wet. 'What fun?' He giggled. 'He'll count to fifty?' He began his count.

Jane gave the bathroom a second glance. Her fear had made her overlook it. She'd discarded a perfectly good place to hide because her head wasn't thinking straight. The terror she felt was winning over. She tried to gather herself. She closed her eyes and tried to blot out the sound of the Captain's mad chant below as he counted down to the game of hide and murder. She imagined she was back in the LSO, conducting Mozart or another complex piece with a lot of instruments. She'd have to separate one sound from another in her mind; she'd have to isolate and compartmentalise each instrument. And she applied this technique now to her situation. Rooms, furniture, hiding places. Where would her body fit?

'Forty-six, forty-five…' The Captain giggled. 'Is it having fun? It likes its games, doesn't it?'

Then Jane knew what to do. To the Captain this was a game. And games had rules. One of the rules of hide and seek was to look away whilst counting.

She hastily took off her boots and socks and tossed them under the bathtub. She put the metal plug in the hole and turned on the taps. Soon the upstairs was filled with the sounds of the bath running. Then, with bare feet, she held her breath and crept back along the landing to the top of the stairs.

'Thirty-two, thirty-one… Ha ha! It is having a bath! Is it done? Is it hidden? Can he come? No, he mustn't. Rules are rules.' He almost had to shout over the sound of the running water. The sound resonating from the old metal bathtub carried impressively throughout the house.

She peeked at him from the top of the stairs and saw that he was indeed dutifully looking away with his hands over his eyes. She crept along the outside of the staircase rather than the middle, hoping that it wouldn't creak. The slight squeak and tread of her bare feet were obscured by the Captain's rambunctious counting and laughing. At the bottom of the stairs, she saw him at an angle. The dressing gown hung loosely on his square shoulders, blood clung to his shoulders and arms.

'Nineteen, eighteen…'

Jane put one foot on the ground floor and twisted her body. She felt a rise of panic as she put her back to him, but it was necessary. Once she was around the bottom finial of the thick oak balustrade, she would be out of sight.

'Fifteen, fourteen…'

She found a door to a cupboard under the stairs. It was made of the same oak wainscoting that clad the entire downstairs, but it opened easily at the slight pull on its small wooden handle. She opened it a fraction, and though to her the slight squeak of the hinges sounded like a trumpet blast, when she spared a last glance at the Captain, he didn't seem as if he had heard anything. He was shouting now, perhaps thinking that she'd made it into the furthest recesses of the house. She began to regret that she hadn't. The bathroom, the master bedroom, or even the attic, part of her wished that she had tried to put as much distance as possible between her and this monster. The space under the stairs seemed far too close.

'Nine, eight, seven…'

With seconds to spare she inserted herself into the space under the stairs and closed the door behind her as quietly as possible. Her fear raged against shutting herself up in a hole with no escape if she were to be found. But then her reasoning told her that it was the right thing to do. She had felt his awful power when he'd cast her aside like she'd weighed nothing.

There was surely little chance of fighting him off, even if she were out in the open. Her best chance lay in keeping still and keeping quiet.

'He is coming, ready or not.'

It was pitch black in the cupboard. It smelled like old coats and leather, damp soil and furniture polish. She didn't know what else was in here, so she dared not move a muscle. Even her breathing had to be shallow, lest she dislodge something and make a noise that would give her away. Her heart hammered inside her chest and the blood rang in her ears. Both of these sounded so loud to her that she had to tell herself over and over again that *he* could not hear it. She had to keep still. Hold her breath.

Above her, light streamed through from the cracks in the staircase. She tried to change her focus to see if she could see anything above her – the ceiling, perhaps. But a sliver of light was all that filtered down to her hiding place. The Captain was right outside her door now; she was sure of it. She though she heard him snuffling and scratching at it like a dog. But then his voice rang out from the other side of the staircase. 'It hides in the dark, somewhere. It is listening. It is waiting to be caught? It knows that it is already found, but it likes its games. Has it already seen the outcome? Is it cheating? It thinks about what will happen to it when it is caught. It knows it will get eaten, like its friend.' Jane's body shook at the thought, her breathing threatened to hyperventilate. 'It wants to be eaten. It wants to be drank. It wants to be drunk.'

One foot on the first step. Jane heard it creak under the Captain's weight.

'It wants to become like Judy. It will make a nice host. It is very welcoming.' The Captain's tone was light and his voice had a sing-song quality. As if he were in a playground or reciting a nursery rhyme to a child. 'It will come out to play sooner or later. It hides, but it wants to come out, doesn't it?'

A second creak, then a third as the Captain lightly treaded up the stairs. A shadow passed over the cracks in the stairs above her head. She had a sudden urge to leap out and run away, but she thought it through. Was he far enough up yet? Would she make the front door in time? Once outside, could she outrun him? Was the front door locked? Was there a back door?

She decided to risk waiting a little longer, so she would have a better chance when she made her move, although she dreaded making it. When she closed her eyes, when she blinked, all she could see was that toothy grin and the impossibly long tongue snaking down into the back of Matthews' neck. And his member had been exposed throughout. His foot-long genitalia had twitched and slapped against his inside thigh as he devoured the poor policewoman.

'It shouldn't worry. It has been chosen. It belongs here. It is anointed. It won't be eaten. Not today. It is just playing a game, not a matter of life and death.'

Jane steeled herself to move. The Captain had reached the top step. She was about to bolt out of her hiding place when something stopped her. It was something the Captain said. 'Anointed'? 'Safe'? What did all of that mean? That time in the white room where she was sure she had been attacked by something, perhaps even violated. Was that what he was referring to?

'It remembers. Long ago, when it was little, yesterday, when it was small. It received a visitor. It was set on a path. Does it remember what else it received? Does it still have it? Has it kept it safe?'

The Captain was now in the bathroom. He switched off the taps and the sudden loss of that sound was shocking. She could clearly hear him, even though he had lowered his voice almost to an intimate whisper. 'It was set on a path. And it was drawn to the other. The two of them together, they were both here and they will be again.'

Was he talking about her and Haruki? Did he know her as a child? Jane found it unsettling beyond words to think that it was more than an accident that had drawn both she and Haruki here, to Barrowthwaite. Had they both somehow been manipulated in ways they couldn't possibly understand?

Jane listened to the Captain's footsteps head further into the top of the house; she heard the squeak of complaint from the hinges on a far bedroom door. Now was definitely the time for her to make her move. It was now or never.

She drew a deep breath and put her hand on the cupboard door. Wincing as she pushed it open, dreading to come out, she also dreaded the click of the door as it opened. Any noise was anathema to her. Without the taps, everything was so quiet. She could hear the Captain muttering to herself from far upstairs and she decided that he hadn't heard. So she pushed the door open and stepped out of the cupboard under the stairs.

'There it is. Does it want to play?'

A flower of pain burst around her heart caused by the shock and the breath was knocked right out of her. The Captain had been right outside the cupboard door all the time. Through his bloody face a grin of mammoth proportions cut through the grime and gore. He licked his lips. She thought of where that tongue had been and screamed. In her panic, she lost her footing. That, or her legs simply gave way in fright.

From the floor, she saw the Captain's prodigious penis swinging in front of her face. It was flaccid, but as the Captain noticed her looking, it twitched and jerked as if it were coming alive. Far above that appendage his grin got even wider. Jane screamed again as he reached down for her.

He picked her up like a stuffed toy and held her in front of his face. He was about to say something, but his grin changed shape, taking on a different characteristic. It looked strained now, as if he was in pain. It was only then that she realised what was happening.

The Captain collapsed to the floor. He jerked and convulsed like a tap dancer. A woman stood over him. She wore a loose white cotton shirt and jeans. It was Maggie. And in her hands she held DC Matthews' taser. Its second payload of electrocuting hooks were attached to the monster on the floor and it was still dispensing as much shocking force as Maggie could get out of it.

MAGGIE

'I'm sorry. I should have been here sooner. Are you all right?' Maggie reached out a tentative hand of support but then thought better of it and retracted it.

'No, of course I'm not all right,' Jane said. She looked down at the Captain, who lay unconscious on the floor. 'What is that? It's not the Captain, is it?'

'It was once. But now I don't know what it is.'

'Is it dead?'

'Frank tried to kill him, but I think they just merged somehow.' Maggie prodded the body with her foot. 'I think they underestimated each other. They were both very potent. But this,' she prodded the body again, 'this is something different.'

'Is it an alien?'

'They were both people, once. I knew them both from before.'

'It killed Matthews and… oh shit, Judy. Maggie, I'm so sorry.' She remembered that Judy had died in the other room.

A shadow drifted over Maggie's expression. She went to the kitchen door and opened it. Jane knew she'd be haunted by what happened next. The look on Maggie's face, the shock of seeing her sister in that state, overcome by those alien spores, turning her dead body into something grotesque. If she were in Maggie's shoes, she would not go in. She would rather not see anyone she loved dead and rotting in a chair, brutalised with putrid decay.

Maggie caught one glimpse of her sister and was wracked with convulsions. She retched, sending the body-warm contents of her stomach splashing to the floor. But she stood stoically with her hands on her knees and never once took her eyes off her dead sister. When she had finished vomiting she emitted a strange, high-pitched keening noise that Jane hoped never to hear again as long as she lived.

'Oh God, what happened? What is that stuff?'

'I found her like this. I'm sorry, Maggie.'

Maggie pointed to the lights pulsating inside her through paper-thin skin. 'There's something inside Judy.'

'Whatever this is, it's not Judy. She's gone. All we can do now is to save ourselves. We have to get out of here. The Captain will wake soon and he'll kill us.'

Maggie wiped away the spittle that was hanging like a rope from her mouth. She was still unable to tear her gaze away from the gently glowing body of her dead sister. 'He wasn't keeping the entity away, was he? He was calling it here. We all were. He was using us. He brought it here and then he gave it Judy. That thing ate her, the Captain fed her to it. Oh God, what have we done?'

'Maggie, we have to get away.'

'He said we'd be safe. The anointment was supposed to keep it away from us.' Maggie looked at Jane in horror. 'Christ, the ritual, he took it from Judy. He cut *all* of it out of her and gave it to Haruki. She wasn't protected, because of Haruki.'

'Maggie, it was Judy who killed the Captain, not Haruki. Did you know?'

Maggie shook her head sadly. 'If she was no longer anointed, she would have been under Frank's influence.' Tears welled in her eyes and dripped down her face. 'I thought we were doing good. I thought we were keeping it out.'

Jane heard the Captain stir behind her. 'Hit him again,' Jane said.

'I can't,' said Maggie, impressively turning to practical matters of survival. 'I used the last charge.'

'Then let's go.'

'I can't leave Judy.'

Sirens ripped apart the air outside. The police were out at the top road. Car doors slammed; the bark of radios cut through the air. 'Maggie, listen, we can't trust the police.'

'What do you mean?'

'An officer has been killed. They'll see us as part of this; they'll see us as murderers. They'll think we're part of a cult, or label us terrorists. And we have no explanation that will set it right. By the time we see a solicitor it will be too late. We'll be powerless to resolve whatever is happening here. We've got to get away and buy ourselves time to think. Whatever happened to Judy is going to happen again, unless we find a way to stop it.'

'Where will we go?'

'London, I remember something from my past that I need to check on. We're going back to London.'

'Why there?'

'I'm not sure, but it's something the Captain said. I think I need to make a collection.'

HARUKI

Haruki considered it ironic that it was in prison that his mind enjoyed the most freedom. There was nothing to do here but paint. There was nothing to think about here but painting.

At home, he'd been unsettled. Jane had drifted in and out of his life over the last few months, coming and going, leaving and returning. He felt that her absence, or presence, was now beyond his control. And then there was the troubling events at Barrowthwaite. He was still confused about what had happened there, but after two months inside, he'd managed to find some peace in the stable routine of prison life. He would be here for a very long time, and he felt a perverse sort of comfort in that. Here, there was no block to his creativity and he had begun to produce art that began to approach his former standard.

Word of his creativity had quickly spread, and inmates flocked to the classes that he was trusted to run. The prison bosses soon realised the value of art and self-expression; they told him they welcomed it because it made for a more peaceful bunch of inmates. And so far he'd received all the materials and resources he needed. There was even talk that he'd be allowed to paint full-time as a kind of resident artist, and if there wasn't a Turner prize in that, he'd be sorely disappointed. So, in truth, he had all that he needed in life.

Here, he was able to express himself. Here, he could experiment with his art. He could try new things and he could push the limits of his creativity. After he'd discharged his expected duties towards his cellmate, Redrum, and his other students, Haruki's time was his own. There were no critics, no clients, no confusion.

But that was until Jane had stepped back into his life. She was an oscillating constant, a metronome. Each time she seemed lost for good, she found a way to come back to him.

He mulled over yesterday's visit. She seemed genuinely touched at his sacrifice. Though she must have thought him gallant and stupid in equal measure. He smiled at the thought that, despite everything, he'd proved his regard for her. Despite their recently rocky relationship, the long periods of separation, the depression and the indifference. Despite their separate lives. Despite all of that, he had shown her that she was still important to him. He had sacrificed his freedom for hers.

He dwelled on the last few years with her and it seemed to him that the two of them had either been living together *apart* or living apart *together*. The sad truth was that he felt closest to her when she was gone. It that sense his imprisonment was ideal: Jane needed her freedom and he needed a safe and secure routine. Except now that she had re-opened up his mind to the events of Barrowthwaite, he could not get a certain someone out of his head.

He was still attracted to Maggie. And he knew this feeling was mutual. Yesterday, like so many other things, he had put it behind him, but today he felt it as a physical force. It was a compulsion, an obsession. He longed to be close to her like an addict needed a hit. Despite all of the madness, and the betrayal, he wanted to see her. He loved Jane, but Maggie was an itch that he needed to scratch. The strong prison walls protected him from his feelings. There was energy within, enough to fuel his painting but not enough that he couldn't keep it under control. But if he got out, what then?

Haruki put down his brushes. He'd been thinking about all of this whilst painting. Or he'd been painting whilst thinking about all of this. He hadn't been truly aware of what he was painting, or how he was doing it. His art came to him these days like driving a car. He could do it autonomously. He simply channelled something through him and onto the canvas.

He stepped back and saw what he had created. The outline of a tree, daubed in black, the rough texture of the bark recreated in layers of thick paint. Branches reached out from the trunk like hands. Blackened fingers held a yellow ball of light. At its core a round mosaic pattern, white with red outline and delicate tracery. No pattern, just wild flicks and curls of the knife, applying red paint like an incision. It felt more symbolic than it did a mature and blended piece of art. It was a mandala of brutal representation and he knew that it was connected to the events at Barrowthwaite, as if the colours clearly represented something, or someone.

Redrum viewed it later when he came for the evening class. 'A painting of all colours,' he said. 'You know, it's Jungian.' To him, everything was Jungian because his was the latest therapy they had him on to curb his enthusiasm for sexually aggravated violence.

'I know what it means,' Redrum said with childish glee. 'You're Chinese, aren't you? So the yellow is *you*.' The casual racism washed over Haruki like water; all his life he'd had to suffer people making wrong assumptions. 'And your wife is black, so those tree-like hands belong to *her*.' Haruki looked again and saw that his cell-mate's naive interpretation was nevertheless interesting. 'She's holding *your* life in *her* hands.'

'And the other colours?' Haruki said.

'There's that white girl you talk about in your sleep,' Redrum offered. 'And as for the red.' He chewed his lip then closed his eyes and grunted. 'Nah, don't know what that means.'

'Are you sure?' Haruki said. 'You seem like you have an idea at least.'

'Okay, since you asked. The red clearly represents violence.'

'Violence?'

'Trust me. I'm an expert. Most likely this is about unfinished business. Is there someone you badly need to hurt?'

Haruki almost dropped his brush because he suddenly felt the true meaning of the painting.

His cellmate continued. 'The first time I picked up a brush, it was all about the red, which was good because it helped me to remember where the children's bodies were buried.' Redrum winked, but Haruki didn't know if he was entirely joking. 'But listen, I've had an idea for my own piece of work. If I combine all my bodily fluids into one…'

Redrum droned on, but Haruki had stopped listening. He watched a guard enter the corridor outside and stride with purpose towards the art room. Something was up.

'Kensagi, visitor.' The man stood square-shouldered in the doorway. He was new, but he was of the type that Haruki saw a lot of in here. The type that Redrum would enjoy tussling with. He was a big man, huge even, heavily muscled and gym-fit. He'd no doubt think himself more than a match for any prisoner, but if it came down to violence he'd soon find himself on the ground with Redrum sat on his back, sucking on his toes. He'd seen it happen, more times that he'd cared for.

'Now,' snapped the guard.

Redrum squared up to him. 'We've not finished our session yet,' he said menacingly. Haruki moved swiftly past the guard and out of the art room because he didn't want to get caught up in this. His cellmate had a Jekyll and Hyde quality. There was a second person within him always watching the first and waiting for an opportunity to break out at the slightest provocation.

'Not my problem – playtime's over, girls,' the guard said. A violent departure from the Hawkmoor script to which the others religiously stuck.

A brush snapped.

Haruki knew the way to the visitor's centre and took himself off there quickly, leaving in his wake whatever was going to unfold behind him.

He registered with the guard, who oddly didn't raise an objection to him arriving unescorted, and he was shown into the meeting area. He couldn't help thinking about the violent aspect that Redrum was so sure was behind the red part of his painting. What his cellmate had said seemed to trigger some latent memories for him. A tip-of-the-tongue feeling that there was another side to what occurred in Barrowthwaite. When he closed his eyes and tried to force the memory; the only faces that came to him were Maggie's and Judy's.

Fargher was waiting for him in the open meeting area. Jane wasn't with him. 'We don't need a closed room,' he said, rising to shake Haruki's hand. 'Great news, you're getting out.'

'Out?' Haruki wasn't prepared for the news. 'What about my painting?' he asked.

Fargher ignored that. 'There's no evidence, or not enough to go to trial. They've closed your file. Congratulations, you're a free man.'

'I don't understand,' Haruki said. 'What about the body? The poker, Maggie's statement?'

'My office sent a disclosure demand to the CPS in preparation for the forthcoming trial, but nothing came back and less than a day later they folded. I suspect that they don't have half the evidence they said they had, or it's contaminated, or lost. I'll be asking what evidence threshold they had thought they'd passed, and if I don't get the right answers, we should be looking to sue for wrongful imprisonment. We should be looking at compensation in the region of six figures – seven, perhaps, if we push for a loss of reputation. But the important thing is that you can come with me, right now.'

On the way out, Haruki looked back. He wondered what would become of his paintings and that thought tugged at him. This didn't seem like freedom to him, but like loss.

Jane's Model S crunched the loose stones littering the drive up to the prison gates. 'Well, goodbye, Haruki,' Fargher said. 'I'm glad this has all worked out for you.' They shook hands and Fargher turned away as the passenger door opened. Jane's face peering through the gap. He longed for the safety of his cell. For Redrum's snoring and farting. For the safe isolation of the night-time. He realised then that the outside held nothing for him but anxiety and consternation. He realised that he was afraid, very afraid.

'Haruki, get in.' Jane's face was far from the kind expression of concern she'd held for him when he saw her last. And there was something else. Someone else was sitting in the back seat.

As Haruki peered in, a slim white face peered out. She was very pretty with golden freckles and light brown hair falling around her head in a cascade of ringlets. It was Maggie.

Haruki had never experienced such a difficult atmosphere inside a car. He was in the front seat next to his wife, but Maggie, the girl that he'd become infatuated with was, directly behind him on the back seat. She was breathing down his neck. He felt guilty for the time he'd spend with her in the past, behind his wife's back. And he felt ashamed about wanting to spend much more time with her in the future. Maggie had once said that they *were* going to get together. She told him that either it had already happened, or it was going to happen. The Barrowthwaite time paradox left him unsure of what had actually happened, but he knew how he felt about her, and that was enough.

But during the long drive down to London, neither Maggie nor Jane hardly paid him any attention. They seemed to have more intimacy amongst themselves than with him. As if the two of them had more in common with each other than he had with either of them. That led him to wonder whether if it were *he* who was frozen out, would he be more jealous of Maggie or of Jane?

He listened to their account of the encounter with the Captain, and though it raised his hackles to think of the frightful incident, he tried to think it through. His first thought was that it at least explained why he was released. If there was no body, there was no murder.

'He wasn't himself,' Maggie said. 'He acted more like Frank.'

'The weird guy from the post office?' Haruki said.

Maggie nodded. 'Perhaps they've merged somehow?'

'How can two people just merge?' Haruki said.

'We don't think they're people, not any longer.'

Jane spoke calmly and precisely, as if she were giving notes to a section of her orchestra. 'We have to go back and kill it,' she said, her eyes still on the road. 'Whatever killed Judy will take more lives, and it will spread.'

'So, call the police,' Haruki said.

'It will just reset time, or whatever it does. They won't find anything. But we're all part of this – we can get close enough to stop it.'

Haruki found himself close to panic at the thought of going back and this was his chance to get through to the two women. 'But what good can we do? We were all in thrall to him and if we go back, he'll just wrap us around his little finger. I've no wish to become his puppet again.'

'We won't be,' Jane said. 'I wasn't. He attacked me and I nearly died, but I wasn't changed like before. I wasn't confused.'

Haruki stared at his wife; at that moment be both loved and feared her. She kept her eyes forward and her hands on the wheel, and from the whiteness of her knuckles, he knew how determined she was. 'What do you have that makes you think you can protect us from him?' he asked.

'I think the only thing that can protect us from him, is more of him,' Jane said. 'We've all seen them, haven't we? Those crawling, translucent things. I think that's what the Captain has put inside us. That's what he's anointed us with.'

'The ritual,' Maggie said. 'He uses it to harvest the thing in people. When they dig holes, they draw the stuff to them.'

Jane nodded. 'I think it's all connected. I think those things, the substance, the Captain, the entity he says he's trying to keep out. They're all the same. It's all the same. It's not a "them". It's just one big "it".'

'That's how Frank speaks. He says *it* when he should mean *you* or *they*,' Maggie said. 'As if he's never really understood the difference.'

'What if both Frank and the Captain were collecting the substance? And when there's enough of it in one location, it interfered with the physics of the place,' Jane said.

'It's alien,' Maggie said. 'Time and space can get messed up when it's around.'

'And whoever has enough of the substance has the power to influence others and can get them to do what they want. Like the way Frank used Judy,' Jane said. 'It's about time we got some power of our own.'

'And where are we going to get that?' Haruki asked, fearing the answer.

'I remember something from my past,' Jane said. 'I was only a little girl, but if I'm right it might still be there.'

PART SIX

RECURSION

THE HOMECOMING

'This is where you grew up? I had no idea it was like this.'

'That's because you never paid me much attention,' Jane said. She fixed Haruki with a scolding look but allowed a trace of a smile to break through. She was rewarded by seeing his face scroll through several emotions one after another. From shame to relief.

Jane realised that in truth, she'd been careful not to be totally honest with Haruki. From the outset of their relationship, she kept from him the details of her humble background. He was the established artist, the *enfant-terrible* of the art scene, and although she was never ashamed of where she grew up, neither did she wish to play on her working-class roots. Her career success would be entirely on merit. But there was working class, and then there was this. London Fields' inner-city gang culture. She saw the signs of it everywhere. The kids on the street corner. Dark hoodies, diligent hands in pockets poised over bright new trainers. The empty plastic wraps on the pavement. The hush descending over the few shoppers who trudged past trying to ignore the trade under their noses and outside their doors.

She hadn't been back here for years, but she was born to this as a lord to a manor. This was her home, her family, her blood.

'Is it safe?' Haruki asked, gripping her hand as they walked through the market. Billowing sheets rustled on the market stall selling used DVDs and Blu-Rays. A fast-food van steamed in the morning cool, the smells of curry and spice leaking out of a little plastic chimney set into the ceiling. Its conical top gently steaming.

'It is for me.' Jane grinned.

'We left Maggie in the Tesla.'

'They'll think she's police,' Jane said. 'She's good for about an hour, I'd say.'

A kid on a BMX whizzed past. He, or she, broke into a wheelie and revolved the handlebars through 360 degrees. Then he executed half a dozen bunny hops before landing on the front wheels and cycling away at some speed. 'We've been marked,' Jane said, squeezing Haruki's hand.

'You lost or summit?' A willowy young girl appeared from behind a corner and drifted up to them. She kept her hood up, but Jane could see that one half of her head was shaved and the other sported long dark ringlets that draped over her pale face. The girl chewed gum ostentatiously. 'You police or what?'

Jane had to laugh at that. She'd been so shy herself at this girl's age, but if she'd stayed here, she would have probably turned out just the same way eventually. 'What's your name?'

'Josie.'

'How old are you, Josie?'

'Fourteen. But what's that got to do with—'

'And where do you live?'

'Castle Black. But you ain't got the right to—'

'That's where we're going,' Jane said. 'Why don't you take us there and buzz us in? Who's running things here now?'

'Ghana Boys,' Josie said. 'And they don't like intruders. Know what I'm saying?'

'The Ghana Boys? Well, we're here now, so go and tell them, will you? Tell them that we're coming. I'm Jane, Nikki's daughter. They'll know who I am.' Josie raised her eyebrows at the mention of Jane's father.

'Nikki's not been seen for ten years, innit.'

'You think I don't know that?'

'Yeah, whatever.' Josie broke off and ran towards the towering block of flats that rose up over the market.

Jane felt Haruki at her back. His hand laid on her shoulder and he rubbed some warmth into her, though it was not a cold day. She shuddered. 'Difficult to be here?' Haruki asked.

'It hasn't changed. Not one bit. That's the hardest part. You'd think they would have done something about this by now. You'd think they'd clean it up somehow.'

Castle Black was what they locally called the large three-storey building south of the Fields that overlooked the river. It was where Jane had lived with her father. It was where he had run his drug-dealing empire, and it was where he had died.

Her father had met a violent death. That wasn't surprising. What was surprising was that he'd reached his mid-forties before meeting his end. By that time he'd run the drugs trade in South London for almost half his life. He was a legend in these parts. And regarded as such not in the least by the gang who'd gunned him down and taken his place. The Ghana Boys.

A boy slouching in the doorway straightened and approached. 'You got beef, or what?'

'No beef,' Jane said. 'I just need a favour, that's all. Then we'll be out of your hair.'

'We don't do favours.' The boy backed away but only to circle the newcomers. He looked them up and down ostentatiously, sizing up Haruki and feeling up Jane with his eyes. He clicked his teeth and whistled. 'Wow, girl. Nikki did something right.'

'I'm not a girl. I'm nearly twice your age, so show some respect. And this favour benefits both of us.'

'Go on.'

'I want to see my old flat. And I want to recover what's inside.'

'Ain't nothing inside. We cleaned it out long ago. And it hasn't been yours for years, so why would we let you in there?'

'Because I know where my father hid things. And he hid them in places you would never find. Let us in, and any money or drugs are yours. But we'll keep whatever else we find. Deal?'

'Dunno. I'd better take this to Sharky. He'd want to know why Nikki's daughter is hanging around.'

'Sharky?'

'Yeah. Sharky runs things now. He took over from T-Spoon last summer.'

'Right. And what would Sharky say if you went to him empty-handed rather than having taken the initiative to bring him money and drugs? Free money and drugs, no strings attached. That's if you *do* bring them to him. If we were to leave promptly, you might say it was as if we were never here.'

'Nah. Can't do that. Josie saw you.'

'But Josie won't see us collect my father's stash, will she? And Josie is also your insurance against our return.'

'How do you make that out?'

'Well, if you take the drugs for yourself, and you don't give Sharky his dues, he'll surely kill you if he finds out. So, if that's the route you choose, you'll have to kill to protect your secret. The only person who knows we were here is Josie. Josie won't know about the drugs, so she'll only be a thorn in your side if we were to return to rat you out to Sharky. She'll back up our story, if she remembers. If we return, you'll have to kill her, and that's enough to ensure we won't return. I won't be responsible for her death. But if anything happens to her, then we'll surely rat you out. Understand? You might say that she's a hostage. Keep her safe and she's your insurance policy. What's your name?'

'Clinton, but my friends call me Cardz.'

'Spelled with a "z", I suppose.'

'Yeah, that's it.'

'Well, Cardz, I've no doubt that you now see the wisdom of this deal and the opportunities for both of us. May I take it that we can proceed?'

Cardz clicked his teeth and nodded.

'Pretty nice logic,' Haruki said as they approached her old flat via the back stairs. 'I had trouble following it myself.'

'Yeah, well, I don't think Cardz did, but all you need sometimes is to give people a reason – if they want to believe something, they will.'

'I'm impressed you thought it through about Josie. You really know these people, don't you?'

The flat was not as she remembered. It was tiny, for a start. And it was dirty. Disgustingly dirty. The green bamboo pattern wallpaper was clad in an ombre of filth that started thick at the floor and thinned to a grey coating closer to the ceiling. The floor was covered in broken bottles, syringes and used condoms. Jane's heart froze in sadness as her hands shrank inside her coat sleeves. She didn't want to touch anything because surely an irreversible disease awaited anyone who did. 'I'm sorry,' Haruki said at her shoulder.

'Don't be. My father was a piece of filth, so it's only fitting. This place has caught up with him, that's all.'

'Still,' Haruki said, and Jane wondered what he meant by that. In truth, Jane wondered a lot about what Haruki said and thought. She wasn't used to having him around. Even when they were together, he used to be an empty presence. He was never all there. His body might have been close, but his head was always far away, lost in the detail of a landscape, or in the crease of a client's face. But she could feel that things had changed. Now she felt him right here, beside her. He really did understand her. So, how had that come about? And what had woken him up?

'Where do we look?' Haruki said. Cardz was waiting outside the drug den that was once her family home. He wouldn't be patient for long.

In a way, the putrid state of the flat made it easier to do what she needed to next. If it were more like the image in her head, she'd find this much harder. As it was, Jane suffered no regret as she took out a screwdriver from her pocket and dug the flat blade into the top flange of the holding pin that joined the two sides of the brass hinge of the kitchen door. The top pin came out easily enough, despite the encrusted dirt. The middle pin came out relatively easily too, but she needed Haruki's help with the last, bottom hinge. He held the door straight and steady, so that as little pressure as possible was applied to the hinge. When the door came away from its frame, Jane allowed it to drop heavily on the kitchen floor with a crash. It was like a loved tree being felled in the forest. But one that was rotten, so that in the end it was a kindness.

Jane's screwdriver worked the top of the door and prised out a foot-long sliver of wood that had been wedged into the top. It revealed a hollow inside the door itself and soon she had managed to worry out a plastic-wrapped A4 folder. Flopping it down on to a bare section of the breakfast bar, she unwrapped it. Inside was a pile of newspaper cuttings, certificates and the occasional rosette. Testaments to Jane's early career in music school. 'That's you!' Haruki exclaimed, snatching up a newspaper clipping showing a twelve-year-old Jane accepting a scholarship award to the Royal Academy of Music.

'My father has made quite a collection,' Jane said as she fingered through the collection of papers. She felt Haruki's hand on her shoulder and thought she knew what he was going to say. He would tell her that this was proof that her father loved her. The man might have found it difficult to show or tell her, but there was no doubt that he was proud of what she'd accomplished.

'Is that him, behind you?'

'Yes, he looks so young.'

She'd always thought of her father as an older man. Someone who'd stretched further into the future than the child Jane could have thought it was possible for someone to do. He was her father, her protector, her king. But looking at the newspaper photograph, she realised that he was not old. He was never old. And he was just as lost as any other young man trying to make his way on the streets of London. She realised that Haruki had taken his place in her life. He now provided for her what her father had. A male presence and whatever protection that provided her, but like her father, Haruki didn't pay her all that much attention. But what she lacked in stability, she gained in fluidity. She grew up having to tend to herself. Daily, in fact, as her father tended to his crime empire. And for longer stretches as he either had to go into hiding or was held by the police, or remanded in custody for a time. Then it was a game to dodge social security, who would have put her into care, itself a prison imposed on the innocent for the sins of their fathers. She always found one of her father's crew to pose as an uncle or aunt and falsify a few reports, so she could stay home alone.

But then one day it wasn't the police or social services at the door. It was the Ghana Boys. The rival crew from south of the river. And they had killed him. They gunned him down in his own home. In her home.

'And who the hell is that in the background?' Jane had been lost in her thoughts, but Haruki had been studiously examining the stack of newspaper clippings. 'Look here, and here.' He stepped the images on several pages that he'd laid out next to each other on the kitchen work surface. 'On all of these, look who it is.'

Jane picked up one of the clippings and held it to the light. It was a picture of her and the other students outside Albert

Hall. They were holding their instruments up to the camera and laughing. Jane herself flourished her conductors' baton as if it were a magic wand. Members of the general public were gathered around them, applauding. 'Students celebrate public performance', was the caption underneath the photograph, but Jane was staring at one of the members of public in particular. A small fat man, dressed flamboyantly. The newspaper was printed in black and white, and she couldn't discern the colour of his jacket, but there was no doubt that this was Frank, smiling and cheering the students on.

There he was again on another, and another. On each picture containing the general public, Frank was somewhere to be found amongst them. Jane shuddered. This meant that the creepy, murderous man had stalked her for almost her entire life. She was just like Judy, she realised, an intended future plaything for a malevolent man.

'There's something else in the door,' Haruki said. 'Give me a minute to prise it out.' With his slender fingers, he pinched and pulled, until a plastic-wrapped small box emerged from the top of the hollow door. He tossed it to her. 'What is it, a ring?'

It was a ring box. The type that engagement rings come in. Like the one that Haruki had offered her one day. He'd knelt in the boat off the Californian coast. They had been surrounded by humpbacks when he offered his outstretched hand in marriage. It still set her heart racing to think of that one act where her life had been joined to his. Where her story had been indelibly written alongside his.

A presence at the front door caused her to turn. 'You've had enough time. Now for the big dog to have a look, innit.' Cardz carried a big red fire axe. It looked like the one in the stairwell that was kept behind the emergency glass. It was designed for breaking down doors. 'Stand back.' Rather than swinging it long and high over his head like he would do if he were chopping logs, he held it high on the handle and attacked the door in short stabbing motions. It was effective enough and caused her to wonder how many doors he had broken through like this in his time. Or people. Before long there was a foot-long rift in the centre and Cardz pulled a series of white and brown plastic bags through it, one after another until a large pyramid of them piled up on the kitchen surface.

Cardz unfolded a knife and stabbed it into one of the white packages. He licked the flat of the blade, a broad grin appearing on his face. 'Candy.' He laughed. 'Three kilos. And I think there's more in there?'

'What's in the brown packages?' Haruki asked.

'Coffee,' Jane said. 'It disguises the smell from any police dogs.'

Cardz whooped with excitement as he took the axe to another part of the door. More bags appeared, but Jane and Haruki didn't hang around to see what was in these. Jane had got what she had come for. She signalled to Haruki and they left Cardz to his excited demolition job.

'What's in the box? Did you get it?' Maggie asked, when they had retreated to the relative safety of Jane's car. Although the gleaming white Tesla had attracted some attention from the local kids. They circled the car on their too-small bicycles, like sharks dogging a wounded whale.

Jane handed the small jewellery box to Maggie. 'See for yourself.'

Maggie lifted the lid. A bright white light shone out and filled the car interior. 'Jesus, where did you get this?'

'You said yourself that the Captain had called us all to him. That made me remember a visit I once had as a child. An old man, who dressed and talked funny. It was Frank. He gave me that and my dad hid it. He kept it safe all these years.'

'Why did Frank give you this?' Maggie asked.

'That's not the point right now,' Haruki said. 'The question is whether we should be taking it back to him?'

'We've all taken a bit of that thing inside us,' Maggie said. 'And Judy had the same thing inside her too until the Captain cut it out of her.'

'You think she died because she no longer had it inside her?' Haruki said.

'Maybe it no longer recognised her, so it killed her,' Maggie said.

'Killed her?' Haruki said with panic in his voice. 'From what Jane described, it *ate* her.'

'I don't have all the answers, Haruki, but we have to try, don't we?' Jane said. 'I think that as long as we have this inside us, then we won't be controlled by the Captain and we won't end up like poor Judy. I think it has the power to protect us. Who knows, perhaps the more of it we have inside us, the more power we might have.'

'We need to kill it,' Maggie said, delighting Jane with a resolve that matched her own. 'Whatever it is, we will kill it. But to kill it we need to get close to it, and I'm willing to do whatever it takes.'

THE MOULD

The flurry of snow that had appeared just south of Kendal dissipated as they approached Cragside. The sun burned its way through the steel clouds until it shone bright and warm through the windscreen. She slowed as the police station came into view, the car silent, running on its electric batteries. It was a risk to approach the police, but it would tell her much about what to expect on the return to Barrowthwaite.

Haruki hopped out and skipped up the steps leading to the large glass double doors. She saw him raise his hands to shield his eyes from the bright sunshine. He shrugged as if disbelieving the sudden change in weather, then he went in.

They sat in silence, waiting.

'You do that a lot, don't you?' Maggie eventually spoke. Jane was staring at herself in the vanity mirror behind the sun visor. She hadn't been aware she was doing it. 'What are you looking at?'

'Not *at*,' Jane said. '*For*.'

'I did the same when I was first anointed. You get used to it.'

Jane turned; she saw Haruki come flying out of the station and down the stairs. He ran the short distance across the road and jumped into the car, slamming the passenger door shut. They both stared at him. 'Please, just drive,' he said.

'Haruki?'

'Just give me a minute.' Haruki had his head in his hands. He was shaking. Jane pressed the pedal and the car drifted slowly and silently away. 'It's bad,' he said. 'Those white spores you described. They're everywhere. All over the police station, all over the police. They're dead, I think, covered with that stuff. We should never have come back.'

'Or, we shouldn't have taken so long to do it.' Maggie's words stabbed at Jane's conscience. She had torn Maggie away the last time they were here. It meant she could not retrieve her sister's body.

'So, what do we do?' Haruki asked. His face could not mask the terror he must have felt.

'Haruki, what exactly did you see in there?' Jane asked.

'I told you. Bodies, fur, mould. It was horrible. It was growing all over them, inside, outside and all over the station. Bits were floating in the air. I didn't go in; I couldn't. I'd be infected. We'll all be infected. We can't go back to the village. We have to leave.' It sounded like Haruki was panicking again.

'No,' Jane said, 'we have to be firm. We have to go back, and believe it or not, I think this is a good sign. It means that time is back on the right track. We are re-entering Barrowthwaite after we left, so it means that time is no longer disrupted.'

'It's calling us back,' Haruki said, the panic still prominent in his voice. 'It wants the stuff that's already inside us. We might be all that it needs to make it complete. Then they'll be nothing to stop it covering the whole country. It will be the end of everything.'

Jane couldn't say that he was wrong, but they had to try. Besides, they were already here. She slowed the car. The village was quiet. No one was on the streets and there was no sign anyone was in their houses. No smoke from chimneys, no lights in the windows. Only the birds flew overhead, free and uncaring. Finches darted from the bushes and rooks cawed their way across the sky, surrounded by family. Jane envied each and every one of them.

'I'll walk the rest of the way if I have to,' Maggie said. 'I need to know what happened to Judy. I should never have left. I should have stayed.'

'Stayed?' Haruki's eyes were red; his hands shook. 'You would all have been killed and eaten by that furry mould. You'd be nothing more that plant pots for that thing. It would be growing inside you, eating you. And if we go back, it will eat all of us.'

'Haruki, that's enough. We've come this far and we're going on.' Jane squeezed the pedal and the prodigious acceleration pushed then back into their seats. The tyres struggled for purchase on the ice and slush, but the car avoided fishtailing and soon it was heading quickly towards the centre of Barrowthwaite.

Further inside the village, the scale of the infestation was difficult to comprehend. Eruptions of furred mould was everywhere, but this time it didn't just grow on dead things; it grew independently. It pushed up the tarmac and jutted through the road. It encased trees and it grew around structures, houses and walls. There was very little in the village that wasn't plastered in dirty grey fur. 'Where are all of the people, all the villagers? I don't see anyone.' She didn't like to think about where they might be, or what might have happened to the police that had been despatched to DC Matthews' rescue. 'What had happened to everyone?'

'I'm not so interested in *what* as in *when*,' Haruki said. 'If this is happening now,' Haruki asked, 'whose *now* it is?'

Jane understood the question. Throughout her time in Barrowthwaite, she'd been the victim of time fluctuations. Haruki had slept with Maggie, then he hadn't. She'd spent an afternoon in the village only to find that she'd been gone for three months. Haruki himself had spent the last two months in prison, but to her it was only a couple of days at the most.

There was so much mould around that the village streets had become impassable. They would have to make their way on foot, which was fine because she didn't relish the idea of driving over or through the stuff. She tentatively opened the car door, holding her breath, fearing to breathe in the air in case it was polluted with flecks of floating mould. Slowly, she put one boot down on the road, then swung around in her seat to place the other outside the car. She stood and straightened. All the while she eyed the larger growths of mould around her. She didn't want to leave the safety of the car, but she forced herself to.

Contrary to her fears, nothing happened. The mould remained inert. She walked closer to one heap, past the point of return where she thought she might have a chance to retreat into the car. She went closer. She didn't dare touch it, but she was close enough to smell it. It had the odour of vanilla.

A sound at her back told her that Maggie had joined her; she came over and put a hand on her shoulder. 'Do you think it is the same thing that Judy...?' She wasn't surprised that Maggie didn't want to give utterance to what had happened to her sister. What could the girl say, anyway? *Is this the stuff that ate my sister? Is this what my sister is now, a heap of furry slime mould?*

The car door opened and thudded shut. Haruki's footsteps brought him close to her. She had her back to him, watching the mould carefully, studying it for any insight she could get. She felt his hand on her shoulder at the other side to Maggie's. They were connected now, all three of them. *Perhaps in some way we have always been connected*, she thought.

'Is it safe?' Haruki asked.

The moment his voice sounded, the mould began to react. At first it was just a slight quivering on the surface. The tiny cilia vibrating in unison.

'What's happening?' he asked.

'I don't know,' Jane said, but she realised that this was a lie. She knew that the thing had reacted to Haruki. It considered him an outsider.

'Shit, Haruki. You don't have any of the substance inside you, do you?'

'What do you mean?' Maggie said.

'The time distortion,' Jane said. 'In prison, Haruki has been on a different timeline. So, he mustn't have any of the thing inside him.'

Haruki shrugged. 'When I faked the Captain's murder, I cut myself. I think I saw some of it crawling out of me.'

'Haruki, why didn't you say something?'

'I didn't want that thing inside me again. I thought it would be enough to stick close to you.'

'Get back inside the car, quickly.'

Jane wheeled round. The mould began to emit a sound. It had the cadence of Haruki's voice but was distorted to the extent that she couldn't recognise it as such. It started softly, like a monk's plainsong chant, but then grew in intensity. It blurred. The cilia on the surface of the mould grew longer and rippled in unison. Then other voices joined it. All around them, the other growths were joining in. Adding the same dull modulation. She shivered at the eerie mix of alien voices.

Then the first tentacle shot out. It flicked by the side of her face like a tongue, but it didn't touch her. Then it flew over her shoulder to wrap around one of Haruki's feet. It started to pull him towards it, raising his foot in the air as he tried to resist, hopping on the ground and reaching out to her for support. She grabbed him, and Maggie did the same. Together they tried to put themselves between him and the mould, but it responded by sending out another ribbon of white to wrap around his standing leg. It pulled him off the ground.

They jumped on top of him, trying desperately to resist the pull of the tentacle. But she knew how strong it was; she had felt it before. 'Haruki, open your mouth.' He shook his head.

'Do it now, or you'll end up like Judy,' Maggie screamed.

But still he shook his head. 'Rather that, than—' he said before another tentacle fixed itself to his middle and took the air from him. But his meaning was clear; Jane had to take matters into her own hands.

'Hold his nose,' Jane said, and Maggie did as she was asked, although it was a furious struggle. Haruki was flailing his limbs about trying to resist the drag of the tentacle. Jane was bashed hard in the face. In the melee she knocked heads together with Maggie. Her face was pressed up close to hers. Jane felt her breath on her face as she breathed heavily with effort. It was warm and sweet, with an almost metallic tang. She remembered how Maggie had looked that day on the sheepskin up at Hilltops. Her white alabaster smoothness pressing down on Haruki's olive skin. Her fingers wandering over his chest.

An image flashed across Jane's mind: Maggie lying naked amidst white sheets, the sun streaming in through the sash windows of her London home…

She shook herself back to attention, angry that she'd allowed herself to become distracted. Haruki gasped, openmouthed, to grasp the air that Maggie had restricted by closing his nasal pathway. Jane fumbled for the jewellery box in her pocket. All the while the three of them were being pulled inch by inch towards the heap of furred mould. Then other tentacles shot out from the surrounding heaps. They reached from all directions, attaching themselves to him and pulling his hands, his feet, his head, until he was lifted up, tightly spread-eagled a foot off the ground. Jane was thrown off him onto the ground, but from there she found it easier to extract the piece from the box.

Maggie was already on top of him again, pinching his nose, and he was screaming enough to make this easy. Jane pushed the piece into Haruki's mouth. She held the flat of her hand against his face to ensure it didn't escape before he swallowed it down.

At first she thought she'd done irreparable harm. Haruki spasmed and she was thrown off him again. Then a hundred more tentacles shot out and encased him in white. She grabbed and pulled at the substance, but it didn't budge. She couldn't even get a grip of it. At her touch, it went smooth and hard, rejecting her attempts to get a purchase on it. Haruki was raised up into the air above her. Maggie was shouting as the last of Haruki's face disappeared behind the white encasement.

Jane screamed, although for her it was more in frustration. She had given Haruki the piece that she'd been saving for a special purpose. That was supposed to be her ace in the hole. She didn't quite have a plan as such, but she'd banked on having a surplus of the stuff. She thought it may have swung the tide in some way as yet unclear to her. But now she'd lost it. And she'd lost Haruki too, the fool. Why didn't he tell her? She understood he was scared. They all were.

Jane started to kick the mound of mould. She beat it with her hands. She screamed at it. She pulled at the tentacles that emanated from its furred surface. She laid her hands on it and tried to rock it back and forth, hoping to break it off from the ground it jutted out from. Maggie joined her. If they couldn't reach Haruki, they'd assail whatever they could.

But the mound remained undamaged. Until…

A scream behind them, Haruki's voice. 'Get it off me!' His face was uncovered. Then his shoulders appeared. Then his hands and feet. He was lowered to the ground as the white encasement subsided. It melted from him, reforming into ropy tentacles. Retreating back into the mound they had come from. Maggie got to him first, hugging him and kissing his face. Jane wanted to pull her off, but there was no need; she retreated as Jane approached. Haruki sat up.

'How could you?' His expression was that of a smacked child. 'I didn't want this inside me.'

'Better that, than you inside it,' Jane said, flushed with exertion, and something else. Was it anger? Was it guilt? Or was it jealousy?

THE ALIEN

The extra-terrestrial horror has been stalking me for years. That sounded completely crazy to him, but Haruki had to admit that it was true. He tried it out again in his own mind. *The alien has been controlling me for over twenty years.* He hadn't seen it because perhaps he hadn't allowed himself to see it. But now that he was forced to face facts, there was no denying it.

It had guided his hand ever since he'd picked up a paintbrush. It had even given him the paintbrush in the first place. In the guise of Frank, it had told him to go and paint, and that's what he had done. The feeling he got when painting was the feeling of channelling something deeper, something more than himself. So, was that the alien? His natural creativity, the skill he'd built up over years and years of schooling and practice, was that all given to him by forces outside of the Earth's natural physics?

Long ago, before he'd become a painter, he'd been with the Captain. He knew that much. Now that he'd swallowed more of that substance, those memories came back to him. He'd been part of this cult before. Before Barrowthwaite, the Captain had been up to the same thing long ago in Birmingham, and back then, Haruki was his muscle, his knifeman. He kept the other cultist in line. Others used charm and guile to drive the crowd, but ultimately it was Haruki who kept order. He was called upon to back up the Captain's word with cold steel if it came down to it.

Was that what Maggie had been to the Captain? Was she the coercion that kept the other villagers rallied to the Captain's call? Maggie was surely a large part of it all and had been for a long time. So, how much did she know? Was she just following orders blindly, or was she integral to the Captain's lie?

Then he decided not to torture himself with these questions; they didn't really matter. He had to forgive her for whatever complicity she'd been part of. No matter what her role in tangling them up in Barrowthwaite he would forgive her. With Judy, she had already paid a high price, but more than that, he would forgive her because he wanted to forgive her.

The alien, in the guise of Frank, had controlled Jane too. It had guided her own life and career in much the same way. So, they were all victims. Or, they were all complicit in this unholy cabal.

He was utterly convinced that the two adversaries, Frank and the Captain, were one and the same. They were part of the same entity; they were two sides of the same coin. Perhaps when it took a human's body the alien was influenced by its personality. Frank and the Captain were so different that perhaps it caused a fracture of some kind. They were opposites, but they were twins. Did they know they were two pieces of the same puzzle?

Jane loomed over him. He was sat on the cold ground looking up, the wet oozing into him through his jeans. Maggie was stood by her side, her delicate hand on her shoulder. 'I don't want this thing inside me,' he said. 'I had it once and I'm pretty sure I did terrible things. I don't want any part of that again.'

'You have to have it inside you, or you'll be eaten alive,' Jane said. 'And even if the mould failed to devour you, you'd be so spaced out by the time distortion that you'd be no use to us. Get a grip, Haruki. If you can't do this for me, then do it for Maggie.' Her tone was bitter, indicating that she resented Haruki's almost-relationship with the younger woman.

Damn, it was so confusing. It was clear to him how he felt about Maggie, but was that feeling based on something real, or was it just imagined? Was it anything more than a residual emotional connection to a dream long forgotten? And when he looked at Jane, he felt something just as strong. It felt different but with equal weight.

'Yes,' Maggie said, 'get a grip, Haruki.'

They helped him to his feet and they took a single track road up the hill that looked like it would skirt around the top of the village towards Maggie's house. He felt calmer out of the village's centre, trusting Maggie to know where she was going, and he saw that there were far fewer patches of mould higher up the valley.

But if the mould was frightening enough, sooner or later they would have to face the Captain again, or Frank. Or whatever that thing was that the girls had faced last time they were here.

'The Captain *is* the alien, and so is Frank,' he repeated distantly.

Maggie and Jane stopped in their tracks. They looked back at him. 'Very good, Haruki, kind of you to catch up,' Jane said. 'Now tell us something we don't know.'

'I was with the Captain, long ago.'

'We know, Haruki. He controlled you just as he's controlled all of us,' Maggie said, not unkindly, but it seemed to him that she were talking to him as if he were a confused child.

'No. Before all of this, long before. I worked for the Captain, I was his enforcer, or something.'

Jane peered through disbelieving eyes. 'You? An enforcer?'

'I wasn't always a painter, Jane. I know it's difficult to believe, but I was young. I was different.'

'And you've only just remembered this?' Maggie said.

'Yes, it's the substance, it jolts my memory. But I remember now that I've had the substance in me before. When I worked for the Captain, I was anointed then too. It was Frank who took it out of me. And I think he did something to me to make me forget. Jane, we've been manipulated all our lives. We are not who we think we are.'

'None of us are,' Maggie said. 'Don't worry about it, either of you. Everyone is in the same boat...' She paused, searching for her next words. '...whether or not they've been relentlessly manipulated by unstoppable aliens.'

Haruki stared at Jane because he saw a slight curl at the corner of her mouth. Then the smile broadened into a laugh. Before he knew it all three of them were laughing. They were laughing at the absurdity of their situation. They were laughing at the hopelessness of their cause. They were laughing at the disparity in power between three pathetic people and a timeless alien power. But they were laughing.

'We've been set up,' Jane said when the laugher had subsided. 'Our careers, our destiny. They've been handed to us from someone else. We've not had much choice in our own lives. Perhaps we've not had much choice in *who* we've spend our lives with? Look at us, Haruki, how can we be sure that we're even a real couple?'

'We're real,' Haruki said. 'We're real enough.' And to demonstrate his point he kicked Jane hard in the shin. This time, it was Maggie who laughed first.

THE OTHER

Maggie had never seen him laugh. He'd been charming in many ways and had this quality about him that was at once vulnerable and aloof. He had this stare that pierced through you and landed about a hundred yards behind, fixed on the landscape or some other detail to which his artist's eye was attracted. He wandered about the place in a dream, but when she demanded his attention he woke. During both his dreaming and wakeful states, Haruki was always kind, calm and gentle. Which made for a blessed change.

He was damaged, she knew. Ravaged by life and mauled by his estranged wife. But she knew how to fix him. She knew what he needed and she knew what he wanted. He was going to be her project, her do-up. Once anointed and free from temporal dissonance he would have been hers to shape.

But then Jane had arrived and thrown everything off-balance. Haruki had become even more confused. And to make matters worse, the Captain had let her down outrageously. He'd promised to chase Jane out, but instead he'd taken her for himself. She'd argued with him that it was cruel to keep Jane around. Cruel for Haruki, for Jane and also for Maggie, who had once been the Captain's favourite, not so long ago. But there was no changing his mind; he was a law unto himself.

In the end she'd relented because if the Captain was occupied with Jane, at least he'd finally leave Judy alone.

She remembered the day when he'd arrived in the village. Her father had allowed him to rent the old schoolhouse, although in those days it was just an old unused cottage at the foot of the village. At first, he'd been allowed to forego paying rent and instead he fixed the place up and made it into a valuable asset. Within a year of the Captain's arrival, both her father and her mother had died. Maggie had been twenty, Judy only twelve.

'Have you always lived in the village?' Jane asked but it took Maggie a while to respond. 'I asked if you'd lived here long,' Jane repeated.

'All my life, my father owned much of it and he passed it on to me…' *And Judy*, she was about to say.

'He was an influential man, then?'

'He kept to himself for the most part. He was always up on the fells, with his sheep.'

'A farmer?'

'We're an old family. For generations, we've looked over the land as best we can. But there aren't many of us now. After Dad died, his brothers moved away and we lost touch. I still have, or had, an uncle down in the village, but we don't speak. So, it was just me and Judy, for the most part. Judy ran the bakery, that was her thing. I made a living renting out our properties. Neither of us are good with livestock, so we rent out the land for grazing. I think the fells would miss the sheep if they weren't there. Sheep graze on all but Noonday Sun. We never let them graze there.'

'Why not?'

'Some sickened and died, so we had to keep the others well away from there. The Captain urged us to move them somewhere else. That's partly how he won our trust.' He'd tricked them, worming his way into the heart of the family.

But she couldn't blame herself; she was far too young to have known any better. Yet how it might have been different without the Captain: the village, her parents, Judy... 'What do you think has happened to her?' Maggie asked. 'What did that thing do to her body?'

'I don't know,' Jane said, 'but we'll find out together.' Jane's hand found hers and squeezed. That simple act made her want to cry. Jane could be harsh and uncompromising, yet she was also compassionate. They were both in love with the same man, but they were here, together, walking side by side, hand in hand. The world was a strange place. Perhaps in different circumstances...

But there were no other circumstances, and to prove it, Maggie's mind snapped back to think of Judy. A sharp image of her sister had inked itself onto the inside of her eyelids. When she blinked, she saw her with her mouth open and furry growths bubbling up from inside her. Glowing lights under her skin, pulsating and stretching it taut. She wanted to look away, but she couldn't. Every time she blinked she saw her.

'You think it's alive?' Haruki had caught up with them and was listening in.

'Of course it's alive, Haruki. It just attacked you, didn't it?' Jane said.

'That's not what I meant. I mean, does it think? Is it aware? Does it know what it's doing and does it know what we're thinking?'

Maggie thought she knew the answer to that, but she also thought that Haruki wouldn't want to hear it. 'We won't know the answer to that until—'

'Until it's too late,' Haruki said, probably catching the reservation in her voice.

Jane scowled at him. It wasn't an unkind gesture and it showed the closeness that these two had. Haruki was so obviously familiar with that look; it was part of their couple's language. It was intimate. It was a wife's gesture. It was the same intimacy Maggie had with Judy. Judy, stretched across the sofa, gently teasing her about men, or anything else she thought of. *You scare them off*, she'd once teased.

They had circled the village on a track that she knew. Now they had come out onto the main road near to the point where the dirt track lead up the hill to her house and, beyond that, to Hilltops. Down the hill was the Captain's house. 'Where shall we go first?' Haruki said. 'Which nameless horror shall we try to encounter next?'

Maggie didn't mind his repeated attempts at humour, if it helped him to get a grip. He was afraid, and she couldn't blame him for that. If it wasn't for Judy and the fact that this was her home, she wouldn't be here either. It was a wonder that both he and Jane had come back with her, except that it was easy to see that Jane was the strong one in their relationship. That much was obvious. And it was Jane who dragged him back to the village; it was her who seemed to know what she was doing.

'Jane, what's your plan?'

'My what?'

'Your plan,' Maggie repeated. 'I don't think you're the type of person to rush headlong into things. You like to think things through. So what's the plan?'

'We're all anointed now, so the Captain can't confuse us.'

'We're going to fight him.' This wasn't a question from Maggie; it was a realisation.

'Yes, and I think we'll find what we need at the Captain's house.'

'Great,' Haruki said, 'I would appreciate knowing I'm not facing certain death.'

More attempts at humour. She decided that this was for her benefit. At least she liked to think so. During their three months together he'd either been following her around like a bemused puppy or lounging like a cat on the big sheepskin rug up in Hilltops. That was before he'd spilled red wine on it and they'd had to replace it with an old Persian from the cellar. Funny that she thought about that now. One thought led to another, she supposed. It was only natural that the stress of the current situation led her to recall happier times.

'Jane, I need to ask you something.'

Jane winced and didn't even try to hide it. 'Is this is about Haruki?'

She was sharp and to the point, yet again her next words were not unkind. 'I think this is a conversation best left until we're safe. Let's wait until we've collected Judy.'

The mention of her sister was a sharp prod in the ribs. Jane had said *collect* and for a moment it gave Maggie a jolt of hope. But then she realised that she was applying the term to a dead body, not a live person. *Gather her remains*, was what Jane had meant. And to bring the conversation back to Judy was also a reprimand of sorts. It implied that she should not be thinking of another woman's husband when her own sister was lying dead and her body not yet recovered.

'Why *did* Frank kill the Captain?' Jane asked, and Maggie appreciated her emphasis that it was Frank, not Judy, who was responsible for the killing.

It was Haruki who offered an answer. 'The Captain and Frank were in competition. One was a natural brake to the ambition of the other.'

'So, when Frank won, the handbrake came off. All of this mould belongs to him, and it is free to grow unchecked,' Jane said.

'You're thinking all wrong about it,' Haruki said, coming close up behind her as it reluctant to stray too far behind. 'When I mix two paints, I take a green and a red and fold them into each other. I don't get parts of green and parts of red, I get one new solid colour. That's because whilst the colour is different, the paint material is made of the same basic composition. One paint is consistent with another, even if they are not from the same tube.'

She saw Jane gave him a withering look. 'What are you talking about, Haruki?'

He smiled ruefully, like a little child. Maggie liked how they interacted. They were comfortable accepting each other's chides. Perhaps that's what came with total acceptance and long-term trust? She could watch them all day, if it were not for the haunting sense of longing that she experienced when doing so.

Haruki turned to Maggie, piercing her with his intense stare. 'What I'm saying is, Frank and the Captain *were* different, but they were able to merge because they contained the same basic substance.'

'The anointment?' Maggie said, picking up his insight and running with it. 'They must have collected so much of that stuff over the years, and put it inside them, or it was there to begin with, I don't know. But by the end they were practically twins.'

'So, it was all about critical mass?' Jane asked. 'Whichever one of them collected enough of the alien substance, got to control what happened next?'

Maggie shrugged. 'Maybe, in his own way, the Captain *was* saving us from an alien incursion, after all?' Maggie said. 'It wasn't all a lie.'

'I think he was prolonging the party,' Haruki said. 'He was enjoying himself so much that he didn't want it to end. Or maybe he just loved digging?'

More jokes, but this time he looked like he regretted that one. He'd made light of a ritual that they had both participated in. A ritual that, as far as they could tell, had called more of the entity to Earth. And it was ultimately responsible for the infestation that had killed her sister and so many others by the looks of things.

Or had it?

From the final glimpse she had of her sister, Maggie remembered the flashing lights under her translucent skin, and the pulsating. Something had been going on inside her body. Something was inside her, growing and perhaps changing.

Decisively, Maggie turned uphill. 'Judy was in the Captain's house when we saw her last. But if any part of her has survived, she will have made her way back home.'

THE SISTER

From the way that the mould had not reached her cottage, Maggie had a feeling she knew what she'd find there. The white fur drifted in the air, its spores blown by the wind, and it lay in heaps across the path leading up to her house, but it stopped abruptly at the boundaries of her property. She stepped up to the threshold, and before she was even inside the porch, the front door swung open. Someone was inside, and she already knew it would be Judy behind the door.

There was no sign of distress on Judy's young face and her large, blue, innocent eyes stared out from behind neatly combed shoulder-length blonde hair. Her small nose, with its slight upturn, twitched at the sight of her sister, and a wry smile crept on to her face. Maggie already regretted the choice she'd made when she fled from the police, abandoning her, but seeing her whole and healthy like this made it much worse.

'It did the right thing,' Judy said as if reading her mind. There was a quality in Judy's voice that Maggie didn't recognise. She was more assertive, more confident, more knowing.

'Judy, I thought you were—'

'We have been waiting.' Judy peered over Maggie's shoulder and acknowledged the others. She gave Haruki an appraising look. 'It didn't scare this one off,' she said before coming closer to her and whispering, 'But it should try to scare off *the other.*' Judy's wry smile became a grin and then a laugh. She was so much like her baby sister and Maggie desperately wanted to believe that she still was.

She wanted to ask her what the alien mould had done to her, but all she could manage was, 'Have you been waiting long?' She hated the way she always skirted around the point. Jane would have just bulldozed in with a direct question. *So, what are you now? Human? Alien?* 'Are you hurt?' Maggie asked.

Judy shook her head.

'Can I have a hug?' She couldn't keep her at arm's length any longer. Whatever else she was now, she was Maggie's sister first and foremost, and it was the most natural thing in the world for her to extend her arms and fold Judy in them. Her sister felt warm and familiar, and her eyes began to water. 'I'm so sorry I left you. I won't do it again.'

Judy sniffed and soon Maggie felt warm tears soak her neck. She clung on to her sister as if that could make up for leaving her. But when Judy spoke again, once more it really didn't sound like her. 'We're cured. It took the tumour. We're free.'

When she was thirteen, Judy was diagnosed with the same thing that had killed their parents: aggressive and untreatable cancer. The doctors gave her weeks, but the Captain offered much longer. That was when he'd started the rituals and anointments. He offered salvation and healing, and not just for Judy but for the entire village.

'Judy, what did it do to you? What was the price?' Maggie was beginning to sound like Jane. The woman's directness was rubbing off on her.

'It's okay, we're fine.'

'*We're* fine? Who's *we,* Judy?'

Judy cocked her head. It was the action of a puppy seeking to understand its master. 'Anointment is only the first step,' she said. 'It tries to understand but it doesn't interfere. It opens the door, but it doesn't enter. It waits, until it is removed. Then it can enter.'

'The ritual on the hill? When the Captain took it from inside of you?'

'Yes, after that, we were open. He entered.'

'The Captain? Is he the one inside you?'

'He and the other.'

'Where is the Captain?' Jane interrupted. 'Are we in danger?'

Judy looked around the room. Her eyes opened wider and then her face showed signs of distress.

'It's okay, Judy. We can talk later if you would prefer?' Her sister was vulnerable and the sooner she took her away to safety, the better. 'Let's get out of here.'

'There is no *out of here*,' Judy said.

'We need to get away from here. Some place you will be safe.'

'*Place* is an illusion; there is no *place*, only the borders of a dream,' Judy said, snapping back her gaze to fix intently on Maggie.

'You killed the Captain. I saw it.' Jane again – did she have to be so abrupt?

'It was time for us to become one,' Judy said. 'We merged.'

'Merged?' Jane said. 'From what I saw, it looked more like a hostile takeover.'

'The Captain and Frank, they cancelled each other out, didn't they?' Haruki said.

Judy nodded. 'The Captain kept us away, but now we are here. With the merging, we are strong enough.'

'Strong enough for what?' Jane said. 'Do you intend to bring the entity here?'

Judy cocked her head again as if struggling to understand what Jane was asking.

She looked towards Maggie, but Haruki said, 'It's a fair question. Do we need to worry about you?'

'We won't harm it,' Judy said. 'It is safe from us.'

'I notice you haven't said that you won't turn us all into a patch of mould,' Haruki said.

'I saw that stuff all over you, Judy. Is that what happened to all of the other villagers too? Are they all dead?' Jane said.

'It should think of a chrysalis. It feels good. It shouldn't be afraid,' Judy said.

'I'm just glad it didn't hurt you,' Maggie said.

'We hurt, but we are good.'

Haruki stepped urgently forward. 'We've got company, outside.'

'We called and they answered,' Judy said.

Maggie flew to the window. 'Judy, what did you do?'

'We will help it. We will open it. When we enter, we will be the same. Then it will see. Then it will have no more questions.'

Outside the cottage stood a ring of villagers holding hands and she could hear them chanting. All of them turned to stare at her when she appeared in the window, and the chants turned to shouts and screams.

'What do we do now?' Haruki rushed to the window alongside her. 'Do we stay in here, or make a run for it?'

Maggie had already made up her mind that she'd never leave Judy again. No matter what happened. She was about to say so.

'We stay here for the time being,' Jane declared. 'We'll defend this position as long as we can. Or until we figure out what else to do.'

'And what if the Captain comes calling? What then?' Haruki said.

'Find some weapons, Haruki. I don't know. Look in the kitchen, get the knives out. We still have Judy. She has a foot in both worlds, so I think she can help us?'

'We're not using her as a weapon,' Maggie said. 'She's not going to take on the Captain.'

'We may not have a choice. Look.' Jane pointed to the window, and from beyond Maggie saw that more of the villagers had arrived. They surrounded the cottage, gathering in the little garden inside the low drystone boundary wall. They stood still, staring at the cottage, and those of them in front of the window gazed through it at them. But they were now silent. Whereas before they were braying and screaming, now they stood stock still in the utmost silence. It was worse than when they were making an unholy racket.

The reason for their silence soon became clear. Someone else had come amongst them, something else. From the silence a single drumbeat was struck. The crowd began to part. Another drumbeat, then another. Pushing through the crowd, moving them aside with the merest touch on the shoulder, was the Captain.

He didn't look like the monster who'd killed Matthews. He didn't look like the same man who'd terrified Jane and had caused all of this mayhem. His face was a picture of perfect calm and repose. He wore a conservative suit of dark blue, a white shirt buttoned to the top and a grey tie. In his lapel was a turquoise pocket handkerchief. His mannerisms were placid and he wore an innocent smile as he strode towards the front door. Maggie watched him through the window until she lost sight of him as he came close to the porch. They all waited in silence as the porch door creaked open, then closed with a dull thump.

She counted the seconds. They seemed to stretch. Far too much time had passed between them hearing the porch door close. Why hadn't he tried the inner front door yet? Maggie checked it was locked but didn't go too near it. She went back to the window to check he hadn't gone back outside the porch.

'He doesn't seem like the maniac you described,' Haruki said to Jane. 'Maybe he's now more like Judy? Perhaps he's calmed down?'

'Calmed down? You didn't see what I saw,' Jane said. 'You didn't have to witness him rip DC Matthews apart and drink her blood. No matter what he looks like or how he acts now, I know what he's capable of. I know what he's really like.'

'Maybe we should talk to him? We might be able to reason with him.'

'Reason with him?' Jane hissed. 'Come on, Maggie, help me out here. Tell Haruki what he was like.'

But something was bothering Maggie. Seeing the Captain again had triggered a thought. She had spent years with the man and all that time he hadn't seemed capable of harming her. In fact, quite the opposite. He seemed to genuinely care about her, Judy and the other villagers. 'Everything the Captain did was for a purpose. There was a reason for his behaviour. He was operating within a logical framework.'

'Yeah? Well, he's not the Captain anymore, is he? Not since Frank got the better of him. He's a monster now,' Jane said.

'I know what you saw, Jane. I'm not denying that. But if he's operating to some kind of plan until now, then he might still be doing so. I mean, why did he allow Judy to be changed by the mould? Why did he allow her to be influenced by Frank?'

'It was all Frank's doing. He was playing the long game. An elaborate plan executed over a long time,' Haruki said.

'What do we do now?' Jane sounded panicked and unsure.

A hammering at the door answered her. It received a pounding so hard that the frame rocked and the whole door threatened to cave inwards. A hoarse croak from outside put aside any doubt Maggie had that the thing outside could be reasoned with.

'Let us in, little piggies. Let us in.'

More hammering at the door.

'Let us in, little piggies. We are all Captains now. Let us in and we'll show you. We have something for you. We bring presents. Let us in and we'll show you.'

Maggie turned to Judy. 'What do we do?' she asked, but was horrified at the expression on her sister's face. It was one of placid amusement.

'Let us in,' Judy said.

'We don't want to?' Maggie said. 'Judy, how do we defend ourselves?'

'We will keep coming,' Judy said plainly. 'Unless it stops us.'

'Can we even stop you?'

'It did once.' Judy's face was neutral but not unkind.

'Electricity,' Jane said. 'It doesn't like electricity. We tasered it last time. So let's do it again. Judy, that's the answer, isn't it?'

'We know,' Judy said. 'We know what will happen, how and when. We see everything. It is all happening for us, past, future, present, all this is happening now. And we see it clearly, all of it.'

The door hammered again and the Captain taunted them. 'Listen to us, my lovelies. It can't do anything that hasn't already happened. And that we haven't already seen.'

More hammering, but the Captain stopped short of breaking the door down. Maybe he didn't intend to enter yet, or maybe he couldn't.

'I think that somehow, Judy is keeping him outside the house,' Maggie said.

Judy gave her a wry smile. It was that disturbing look again, of distant amusement. 'We are here,' she said. 'Within Noonday Sun, we wait, dreaming. Look for the blackened hand.'

'What's she talking about?' Jane said.

'The alien is there,' Maggie said, 'somewhere under the hill. That's why the sheep couldn't graze. But how do we find it? How do we destroy it?'

'Leave that to us,' Haruki said, looking at Jane. 'I know just where to look.'

Maggie knew what had to be done; she had come here to find Judy, or what was left of her, and to take her away, but now she needed her – they all did. 'Judy, side with us, don't let the Captain have us. Help us.'

Maggie tried to read her younger sister's face, but it had blanked over and was inscrutable. It seemed to her that Judy's eyes drilled through her, staring but unseeing. A long moment passed between them, during which even the Captain was quiet. Then Judy's face came back to life; she smiled, nodded and said, 'I will.'

I, Judy had said, not *we*.

THE BURNING

From where she was hiding behind the door, Maggie could hear the Captain's breathing and she could smell the sweet vanilla on his breath. Judy stood resolute in the doorway, her arms folded and barring his way. Her small chin jutted out in defiance.

'You cannot come in here,' Judy said. 'These are my people. Find your own.'

The Captain seethed with frustration, and his words became low and dark. 'All people are ours.'

Maggie became suddenly afraid that he would turn to her and see her through the thin crack between the door and the frame. When she played hide and seek as a child, she would never fail to check the other side of the door. That was the first rule in that game, wasn't it?

'It belongs to us, we created it. It is only alive because of us.' His words became louder, and they reverberated around the house, but they were meant more for the dozen or so villagers that were crowded behind him, jostling to follow him through the front porch and into the house. To do what? Rend her and Judy limb from limb?

'It's okay, I want to die,' Judy said, 'so there's no use in pressing your claim.'

'It wants to die? It rejects its host? It won't find another for a very long time. And never one that is so forgiving.'

If Judy so much as glanced in Maggie's direction, then the Captain would know where she was hiding. He would turn and find her with her bottle of barbecue lighting fluid in her hand. Then their plan and their lives would be over.

'The host is sympathetic,' Judy said, 'and that makes this bearable, but the essence is tainted. There is too much vanity here, and too much greed. That is something that *you* have brought to this. You've imposed the corruptions of your own host's personality.'

'Corruption?' the Captain sneered. 'We cannot be corrupted. We are a fundament. We are entropy. We are gravity.'

'We are a distortion,' Judy said, 'a corruption of time and space. In our greed and vanity we have lost sight of—'

'We do not distort time; we *are* time.' His voice grew quieter, then, 'The path is yet uncertain for it, but if it lives, it will see. All possibilities exist in unison.'

'All possibilities exist in unison, but only those that are observed are made real. I shall be my own observer. I alone shall make it real,' Judy said. 'I do not need the host. I do not want it. There is no *we*, just *I*.'

The Captain grew bad-tempered at that. Maggie felt him take another step forward. She could see his left shoulder now behind the door – another inch and she would see the side of his face. He could turn at any moment, see her through his peripheral vision. 'Without *we*, there is no possibility. Only *we* get to choose.'

Judy took a step forwards towards him and the Captain took a half step backwards. 'You may think that we are the higher power, but you don't understand that these people are the intersection between our notions of time and space. Our notions become theirs. Our power becomes theirs. Without them, we are timeless. Without them, we are lost.'

Maggie heard him breathing heavily from behind the door, as if he were pondering a deep and troubling idea. Judy continued, 'Our first attempt failed – there was no incursion. We broke into pieces. Our first host re-gathered much of what was lost, and so did our second. But one was vain and the other greedy: they kept us to themselves; they caused the corruption.'

'Greed? Vanity? What does it know about human traits?'

'Your host corrupted you, as mine did me. The Captain had too much love for his following, his rituals and his retinue. The other was a schemer; he spent years gathering and manipulating. Both loved the game too much, and both have diminished us.' Judy took another step forward, but this time the Captain did not retreat. 'Because of your greed and vanity, you refused to adapt. You did not allow a true union. You did not share. You wanted everything for yourself.'

'We have to take control.'

'No. Humans have lived with worse than us throughout their evolution. They evolve to adapt and accommodate. They are already host to millions of microbes and bacteria, so why should we be different for them? *We* have to adapt too. We have to accept our hosts and the rest of the flora that lives with them. Then the whole will be greater than the sum.'

The Captain sneered, 'It almost convinces us.'

Undaunted, Judy pressed on. 'I have been in this body for just a short while, but I can feel its beauty, and its innocence. It is working with me, not against. It is already something more precious to me than even my own essence.'

Even if she didn't know whether it was Judy speaking or an alien, Maggie felt very proud of her.

'Foolish thing, it is the one that has become corrupted by its host. And it is *we* who are precious, not these bodies.'

'They are not bodies; they are people,' Judy said. 'If you only think of them as bodies, then we should not be here at all.'

The Captain didn't reply to that. He was interested in something Judy had in her hands. She had pulled it out of her pocket and held it behind her as he tried to peer around her to see what it was. She brought it out in front of him. 'Oh, you want this, do you? You like these, don't you?' It was a chocolate bar, and even from her oblique angle, Maggie saw the Captain's tongue horribly extend a clear foot from his mouth, which gaped wide and low. Drool splashed the floor at his feet.

Judy looked directly at her now. She nodded and galvanised Maggie into action. The Captain realised then that someone was hiding behind the door and that the chocolate was a distraction. He turned to face her, his over-extended tongue slapping his own face like a wet rag.

Though it had provided her some comfort to think she was holding the means of the Captain's demise in her hands, she was suddenly struck with a loss of confidence. The plastic bottle of petroleum fluid seemed to diminish in size as she held it out. It no longer seemed large enough. And the little red disposable lighter in her other hand was too flimsy for such a task. Nevertheless, she squeezed.

A jet of gel erupted from the top of the bottle and caught the Captain even as he was still turning to face her. It splashed on his chin and as she squeezed harder the jet of liquid rose up to cover his cheek. Gouts of the substance flew past his ear to land somewhere on the floor behind him, so she adjusted her aim and redirected the flow directly into his face. Even as she did this she struck the cheap flint wheel and held the lighter to the base of the jet of liquid.

'Get back, leave this place. Or I'll burn you down.'

The Captain grinned, his eyes roving all over the place as if he were blind. 'It burns us, it burns all. It can't be contained. It will spread: the house, the rug, the curtains. Its home. It won't kill us.' He paused, sniffed the air like a dog and said,

'But where is its others?' He grinned. His mouth was too wide and it had too many teeth in it.

Maggie held the lighter as steady as she could, although her hands were shaking badly.

'It doesn't need to answer,' the Captain said. 'We know where its others are. It comes to kill us. It comes to Noonday Sun.'

'Leave here and I can call them back,' Maggie said, her thumb tightening on the flint wheel.

'We don't believe it. And we have already seen what happens. It has already happened. Others are already dead. Dead and buried.'

The brass wheel dug further into her thumb and turned the skin white with the pressure.

'They die together. They die in each other's arms. The painter of colours makes its choice.' The Captain's eyes flashed dangerously wide as Maggie struck the flint.

THE ORCHESTRATION

Jane crouched by the kitchen door. She was waiting for the pre-arranged signal, but she already knew the plan wasn't likely to succeed. They were taking a huge gamble with their lives, but it was one that needed to be taken. She and Haruki were to race out of the house and down the hill whilst Maggie and Judy would stay behind and distract the Captain and his followers. Haruki had insisted that he be the one tackle the Captain and had made good arguments centred around the fact that he'd known him the longest, and that the Captain had shown some renewed fascination with him of late. But then who wasn't this monster fascinated with?

Judy had insisted that it was Haruki who had to confront the alien under the hill, and no one was going to argue with her. Besides, Judy wouldn't leave the house and Maggie wouldn't leave Judy, so that pretty much settled it.

Crouched beside her, Haruki whispered, 'Are you sure this will work?'

'Electricity worked last time,' Jane said, 'so it should work again. And I have a feeling that we can also use fire. The alien is a thing of space and I think it is vulnerable against the physical things in this world.'

Her husband looked impressed. 'Makes sense, it needs a

human host to exist properly. Maggie said something once about gravity, waves and particles. It's more cosmic than earthly.'

'There's very little about Earth that the alien finds natural. This world is a hostile environment for it. I suspect that the electricity drove out some of it when Matthews tasered Judy. She's not as changed as the others.'

She heard raised voices from further inside the house. 'Now?' Haruki asked.

'Not yet.' She raised her hand. 'Wait for the signal.'

'What if she can't raise the signal? What if the Captain's got her already?'

The Captain screamed. It was a terrible, high-pitched shriek, but it was clear to her that the Captain hadn't *got* anyone; it was quite the reverse. 'Let's go,' she hissed. 'Keep low and fast, and don't stop for anything. And don't look back.' The last thing she wanted was for Haruki to get cold feet about leaving Maggie in the clutches of the Captain. She saw it in his face when Maggie had insisted to stay behind.

But Haruki needed little encouragement. He opened the back door a crack and slid out like an eel. Once outside he waited for Jane to follow, then he bolted through the garden. Keeping low and moving fast, just like she said. She saw him slip around the cherry tree as he headed for the low part of the drystone wall that surrounded the property.

She watched him vault it like an athlete, landing two-footed on the other side. He beckoned for her to follow, silently mouthing encouragement. No, not encouragement. He was cursing the scene behind her. She turned and saw a conflagration at the house. Almost half of it was on fire; from the porch through to the kitchen where they had been waiting was already engulfed in flames.

She turned back to Haruki, having the notion to physically restrain him from going back if needed. But her husband had something in his hands. A large rock. A piece of the drystone wall. He raised it high above and behind his head, and with two hands he launched it at her.

She ducked and behind her she heard a crack, which told her that he wasn't throwing rocks at her but at another target. A man cried out and the ground thumped as he fell to the ground close by. Jane rose and moved her feet. They had been noticed. Despite the diversion, the villagers had seen them and were giving chase.

Jane had almost reached the wall when the first of the grasping hands tripped her. Something knocked against her heel and although the contact was light, it was enough to disrupt her forward momentum and she stumbled. Immediately, hands grabbed her. They raked and grappled her ankles and feet. She tried to kick them away and tear free, but they pulled her to the ground. There were too many hands. They tore at her clothing, they ripped and gouged her, and their bodies were on her now, pressing down on her with their weight. She couldn't move. 'Haruki, run, do what you have to do.'

There was no use in struggling. Within seconds, more villagers would be upon her and if Haruki tried to intervene, they would only catch him too. From the centre of the melee, she saw Haruki's head disappear. He'd taken her at her word and he'd fled.

She struggled for a few seconds more, but as more villagers joined the fray, she gave up and became still. The villagers stopped fighting her, being content with holding her firm. She tried to count them. There was four of them, possibly five.

Then there was one fewer. A woman cried out and fell to the ground. She heard a thud, and then something snapped, like a dry twig breaking in a forest. More hands retracted. More of them stepped back away from her until finally there was only one villager left. Except it wasn't a villager; it was DC Matthews. She was fast and strong and leered at her with an inhuman expression. Perhaps she could be reasoned with? If Jane could talk to her...

Something heavy slammed against the policewoman's chest. It threw her backwards with the impact and she released her grip. Jane looked to see where the projectile had come from.

Haruki was behind the drystone wall throwing stones. He was throwing the wall itself. Hand-sized grey-blue slabs rocketed from over his side to pelt the villagers and keep them at bay. Then, when one man had edged close enough to reach her, Haruki lifted both arms back and hurled one of the larger stones. It narrowly missed, hitting the man's hand with what would have been finger-breaking force. Jane took the opportunity to stumble to her feet. As Haruki defended the space around her with rocks and shards of slate, she found a way over the wall to his side.

'Go ahead,' Haruki said, his breath short with exertion. 'Get a head start. I'll hold them back.' Wisdom indeed from her husband; she'd never been the fastest runner but Haruki was. He could probably run rings around these people. 'Meet you where we arranged,' she called over her shoulder as she broke into a faltering run.

Unchallenged for the rest of her journey, she made her way back to where her car was parked. A quick diagnostics check told her she still had over a hundred miles' charge left. Although where they were going was less that one mile away, she wondered if it was enough power. The passenger door flew open and Haruki slumped into the seat next to her. 'They're not following.' He grinned. 'I think they gave up at the wall.' But then his face dropped. 'No sign of Maggie?'

She shook her head. 'Let's just be quick about this, shall we?' Jane said, and pressed the accelerator. The car was silent and smooth as it picked up speed down the hill, and it handled well as she threw it into a tight turn. The steep decline levelled out as she burst onto the bottom road a little way past the post office.

This was the place where she'd seen Haruki arriving in the taxi. She had been running, heading out of the village and towards this same place. Haruki had slid by, with only a turn of the head to acknowledge her. That was the start of it, as far as she was concerned. That was the first in a long line of distortions and corruptions of time. As she slowed and pulled into the mechanics' yard, she saw that events had a way of repeating themselves, whether or not they were disrupted by a relentless time-shifting alien force.

She drove into one of the open workshops and put the car neatly onto one of the examination ramps. Haruki jumped out first and by the time she had followed his example, he was already over by the controls and preparing to raise the vehicle on the hydraulic lifts. She supposed all of the villagers were up at Hilltops with the Captain; there was certainly no one around to question what they were doing.

'Will this work?' Haruki asked.

'We have four hundred volts of electricity at our fingertips,' Jane said. 'We can't carry the entire assembly up to Noonday Sun, but I think we can isolate the individual battery packs. If we take the floor off, two of them are contained in the front housing, so those should be the easiest to get to. Now grab a wrench and give me a hand.'

Haruki tried to carry the batteries in his arms, but after a few steps that proved too much for him, so he tied ropes around them and dragged them behind him. The slabs of metal and glass were heavier than anticipated, but Haruki made a valiant effort to haul them the three miles up the hill. He didn't complain much either, even though by the time they were near the Captain's house, she could see that his hands were red raw with rope-burn.

She had questioned the wisdom of going back there, but there seemed no other choice. She had hoped that they could have found something in the garage that would have sufficed, but the battery cells needed to be overloaded and she couldn't think of a better way to do that than with what she hoped to find in the house.

The front porch was familiar to her in the same way that an old family home was. It triggered feelings of nostalgia inside her. It was only a day or two since she was here last, but it felt like years. And though she'd only spent one night here, it was as if she'd grown up here. In many ways, she had. If playing host to an alien parasite could constitute 'growing up'. It probably did, she decided, if only because her eyes had been opened to what was really going on.

There was no sign of the mould growing in the porch entrance, but when she kicked the door open and it swung silently back, it was everywhere. Heaps of the disgusting furry stuff lay all over the hallway and half-way up the stairs. It grew in six-foot lengths arranged randomly around the downstairs of the house. These were the bodies of the police, those who had been called by Matthews to the scene of the Captain's attack. They were still incubating. The mounds of blue-black mould pulsated gently.

Jane picked one and went closer. It didn't react to her like it had to Haruki when they'd arrived in the village. It remained inert. So, emboldened, she put her hand right against it and held it there.

'Do you want me to try?' Haruki offered, but Jane shook her head. This was her idea. She had orchestrated the plan that, for all she knew, Maggie and Judy had probably already died for. So, she should be the one to risk this.

She felt the tickle against her palms as the hairs brushed against the underside of her hands. She wanted to withdraw, but with Haruki breathing over her shoulder, she found the will to proceed. Locating the middle of the heap, she pressed her hand down into the mould.

It stank of vanilla, so rich and sweet that it caught at the back of her throat. She wanted to cough but managed to hold back. She held her breath, not knowing what particles or spores this thing had released into the air for her to take deep into her lungs with each breath. Her skin crawled at the thought.

Millions of fine grey cilia parted to accept her hand. She pressed it into the mould and watched it disappear. White translucent ropes snaked out of the mould heap and wound around her wrist, but they did not pull at her. It was like a handshake, a welcome.

Jane winced as she pressed both her hands into the filthy mould and tried not to think that she could be wrist-deep in the pupating body of one of the police officers. It was warm inside and felt like she was swishing her hands through thick custard. The smell added to that sensation.

Eventually, her hands caught on something harder, a lump of plastic. She pulled at it and it came free out from the middle of the body. The cilia parted to allow her hands to come out and the white tendrils uncoiled and snaked back into the pupa. Stinking of sweet vanilla and dripping with custard, Jane retched as she went into the kitchen to wash her hands. And to wipe clean the taser she had just acquired.

They wasted no further time in leaving the Captain's house and hiking up to Noonday Sun. Haruki couldn't be specific, but he told her that he'd know the exact location when he got closer. He hauled on the ropes dragging the Tesla batteries behind him, and she heard him frequently cursing when they regularly snagged on the rocky trail up to the top of the hill.

After a struggle, they stood tall on the flat top. Haruki pointed towards a lone tree growing out on its own in the middle. Its bare branches fanned wide outwards and up into the sky. From Jane's viewpoint she could see the sun shining behind it. It looked like it was trapped within the branches, or the tree was holding it in there.

'What's this one doing out on its own? Why isn't it with all of the others down the hill?' she said.

'It's a mother tree,' Haruki said, 'but all of its children have died. Maybe they were uprooted to clear the hillside.'

'Mother tree?' Jane asked.

'The largest tree in the forest looks after its daughters. It shares nutrients and water and some scientists think the network can actively communicate. But this one became isolated. Its daughters died and now it is dying too. It has no leaves.'

'How?'

'How what?' Haruki said.

'How do they communicate with each other, the trees?'

He shrugged. 'I don't know. I study form and character and how to paint them; I don't profess to know what goes on under the soil.'

'Anyway, they wouldn't be children, exactly,' Jane said. 'They would be copies of the same tree, duplicates.'

'So?'

'So, it's more like a single but distributed organism. That's all I'm saying.'

'Are we still talking about the tree?' Haruki asked. He didn't wait for an answer but instead pointed a rocky outcrop around the obscured side of the tree.

When they got closer to its base they discovered a hole in the ground that was flanked by two large stones. Or rather, one stone had split in two to reveal an entrance into the hillside, under the tree.

'Looks like we'll be finding out what goes on under the soil after all,' Haruki said before squeezing himself through, dragging, with some difficulty, the Tesla batteries behind him.

THE PAINTER

Haruki looked at what he had done and decided it was enough. He had wedged the batteries in the crack between the alien stone. It was an alien, but it was also an infection, and this was the source of the outbreak. This white stone jutting out of the floor of a tiny cavern under the hill. This was the thing that must have landed here ages ago. This was the thing that had used human hosts to spread its miasma of distortion and fear. They were going to blast out the infection using the unique properties of this world's iron core. They were going to scorch it with electricity.

The yellow taser felt heavy in his hands and they shook as he carefully prised open the outer plastic casing and retrieved the tiny hooks and coils of wire. Thankfully he hadn't set off the trigger mechanism, otherwise they would have shot out and discharged into his face. Instead, he managed to wire up one hook to the input connectors on each of the two batteries.

He had two chances at this. Then he doubted anything could prevent the infestation. The whole village was infected, and it had spread to the police station at Cragside and probably already into the neighbouring villages. He didn't know anything about disease control and spread. Pandemic, epidemic; they were all the same to him. He was only a painter, but he knew about paints and canvases, and he knew that if something didn't belong in a picture, he had to take out a scalpel and scrape it out.

'Time to get out, Jane. I'll handle it from here.' The effective range of the taser was around twelve feet. Two body lengths was precious little head start if the roof came tumbling in. The way back was a twenty-metre crawl over rough granite followed by a hard scramble up a six-foot wall of smooth granite. It had been difficult enough on their way down into the cave and it may even prove beyond them to get back to the surface at all. The entire way was dimly lit, although it helped that they would face the daylight instead of blocking it out as they had done on their way in.

'If you go on up, at least one of us will be safe,' he said, 'and if you get trapped down here, there's not much you can do for me, is there?'

'You should be the one who goes first,' Jane said. 'You're strong enough to haul me up.'

'I would feel a lot better knowing you're safe.'

'It's not all about you, Haruki. How do you think I might feel knowing I've left my husband down here to die? I should get a choice in the matter.'

'You'll be alive, you'd get to make all of the choices in the future...'

'And what?'

'Nothing.'

'There was more to that sentence, wasn't there? You were about to say, 'again'. You were going to say that I'd be able to make all of the choices *again*. Is that what this is about, Haruki? Has all of this been about you needing to have the choice?'

'No, it's just that it was me who got us into this mess. It's all my fault, so I should be the one to fix it.'

'And so it's up to you to save all of us because only you can do that.' Jane's sarcasm was plain; her claws were out. 'This makes you feel good, doesn't it? You get off on self-sacrifice, don't you? That's why you took the blame for the Captain's death. It wasn't about me; it was about you. But you didn't need to do that then and you don't need to be alone here now. Haven't you learned anything from that experience? You can't control anything, even if you think you can. You can't and you shouldn't try to control anyone. No one should.'

'So what are you saying, that you want to stay here with me? There's a good chance we'll both die. Should I just accept that?'

'Yes, you should.'

'Fine. That's what we'll do then. We'll die here, together, if that's what you want.'

Haruki raised the taser and outstretched his arm. Squinting, he closed one eye and lined up the target, even though he didn't need to do that; the wires were firmly connected to the right points in the battery to accept the overload.

'But why would you want to? Why die down here with me?' Haruki lowered the device.

He felt Jane's release of frustration before he heard it. She took in a large breath and let it out in a long explosion that was almost like a scream. 'You don't get it, do you? So, I'll explain it to you.' She sniffed, took another deep breath. 'We don't act like it and we haven't really been a couple for a long time, but I'm still married to you, Haruki. I always will be. I'll always feel that way. During the time we've been living apart, I've always felt married to you.'

'You are married to me.'

'But this is bigger that the facts. I *feel* married to you. I always have. I always will. Even when we're apart, I feel it. Even if we can't live together, it doesn't mean that I'm not your wife. Yes, I've left you. We're separated, but I've always been faithful.'

Haruki cleared his throat. 'Look, Jane, if this is about Maggie—'

'It isn't. Maggie couldn't be further outside this conversation. This is about us. This is about *our* future and it's about *this* moment. I think they are connected. I think that if I leave you now, then that's it. But if I stay with you now...'

'Then we'll both be blown to smithereens.'

'Or we'll survive, or something else will happen. Whatever happens, happens. Perhaps we can choose what happens, or perhaps we can't, but we *can* choose to be together when it does. And I think that right now, that is the most important thing of all. Don't you?'

Haruki stared at his wife's face. As the light streamed in from the opening and caught it from the side, it was the most beautiful thing in the entire world. He didn't want that moment to end, but when he blinked, the image was replaced with another picture. Smashed rocks and an earth-slide. Buried, asphyxiated, dead. A limp hand breaching the surface in a dark pocket between two slabs of stone. That was his prophecy about how all of this would end.

'It could be a suicide pact.'

Jane shook her head. 'You think you know how this ends? Look again. Paint another picture, Haruki.'

He shook the image from his mind and looked again at his wife's face. He traced the outline of her hair, her ears, her jaw. He suddenly wanted nothing more than to paint her, right there and then. He wanted to capture how she looked and what she meant to him in that moment. Then he blinked and another image came to mind. He was sat up in bed at his home. Sunlight and lace curtains streamed in with the soft breeze. Someone lay next to him. He reached over and put his hand on her thin white shoulder. Recoiling from the realisation that he wasn't thinking only about Jane, he said, 'Okay, we'll do it together.' He raised the taser, but he didn't pull the trigger just yet.

'I think that if we survive this, we should live together again,' Jane said.

'Jane, I don't know what to say—'

'I know that Maggie is a complication. I know how you feel. You feel as if you were, or will be, together. But I'm reminded of something the Captain said. Remember when I first arrived and telephoned the orchestra to check in? On their timeline, they hadn't heard from me for three months, but the Captain said I should try again later because things might have changed by then. I don't think that this time paradox is as stable as we think. Just because Maggie experienced sleeping with you doesn't mean that it has to happen. I think that's why I'm here. Something you did, or felt, triggered my appearance. You could say that I'm the universe's way of keeping you faithful. I believe that our deeds can change what *has* happened, as easily as they can change what *will* happen. I think somehow that the universe is defined by how we experience it. If we want to, we can write our own past and build a new future out of it.'

'Jane, we are not like the Captain, or Frank. We don't have that power.'

'We have the same substance inside us. We're part of it now. I think that's enough. But there's another way of looking at it. What if *we* had that power all along? What if that's what attracts the alien to us? It's feeding off us, and maybe that is what it is taking from us. Our power to define the world around us.'

'Why us?'

He watched her face screw up as she thought about this. 'It makes sense, if you think about it. We're both artists. We both have a certain way of seeing the world and making sense of it. You put colours and paints together. I do the same with sounds. We both create. It might be something to do with—'

Haruki's arm jumped. The taser had chosen that moment to deploy itself. A slight vibration told him that a torrent of electricity was discharging through the thin wires and into the battery inputs. But nothing happened. There was no overload, no explosion, no fire. The stone in the middle of the arrangement, the thing they had come to destroy, let out a small keening noise. It was like a puppy yawning. Then silence.

Haruki let his shoulders slump. 'It didn't work. Now we only have one more—'

A high-pitched whine. A pain at the back of his head. A rumble from deep underground. Ropes of electricity flew out from the stone in every direction. Lacerating the cavern walls and ceiling. Dark scorch marks appeared where they touched the sides. Haruki braced himself, expecting to be hit at any moment.

Then the stone shook. A great cracking sound erupted and the stone split. The resulting fissure was deep. As deep as the Earth. A wound that ran directly to the core. The world around him spun. Like he was on a roundabout, dizzy and nauseous but with excitement and energy. As the world turned faster and faster it tilted on its axis until it was turning him head over heels. He looked around for Jane. He reached out. But he could neither see nor feel her. He hoped that she'd found her own axis. He hoped that she would be spinning too. He hoped that when it stopped, wherever they both landed, whenever they both landed, they wouldn't be too far apart.

THE CONDUCTOR

Jane stopped spinning after what seemed like an eternity. She reached out to steady herself and her hand rested on the solid form of her husband. She leaned on his shoulder and he turned to wrap his arms around her. She looked into his eyes and saw them spin too. His pupils shook until he tilted his head, then they stabilised.

'What happened?' she said.

The cavern looked unchanged. There were no scorch marks on the walls and ceiling, no rupture in the centre. The alien was there too, untouched, untroubled by what they had tried to do.

Or what they were going to try and do.

Because whatever they had done, hadn't happened yet. That much was obvious. Haruki still had the taser connected to the Tesla battery.

'It reset the moment. It's protecting itself.'

'That's not good,' Haruki said. 'How do we destroy something that can hit the rewind button every time it is threatened?'

'No, it's a good sign. It means that at least we *are* a threat. Do it again,' Jane said. 'It might be different the next time, remember?'

Haruki didn't need more encouragement; he squeezed the trigger.

Jane shielded her eyes as the conflagration of electricity erupted for a second time. White and blue tentacles exploded outward. Spikes of power speared the walls and ceiling, leaving it blackened and burned. The Earth shook. It rumbled. The stone split. It was just as before, but this time the Earth didn't stop shaking. Soil and shards displaced from the ceiling and rained down on them. Larger stones came through the roof and landed with frightening force at their feet. Towards the cavern entrance, there was more disruption. The last thing Jane saw before the spinning started was the roof caving in shutting out the light and plunging them in darkness.

Vertigo inhabited her head. She couldn't see but knew she was spinning away. Far away. She lost touch with Haruki and thought she heard him screaming somewhere off in the distance. He was being thrown further and further away. The axis of Jane's spin changed and she felt like she was turning around feet over head, then she was falling head first through space. She landed on her feet, she thought. Now Haruki was beside her, moaning softly in the darkness. 'I'm hit,' he said. 'I think it's bad.' The plainest of statements frightened her. But she had her own problems: the spinning sensation hadn't stopped. She felt drunk, she was spinning out and at any moment she was going to pass out or throw up, or both.

She fumbled for the torch in her jacket pocket and thumbed the switch to turn it on. Light spiked the darkness and gave some respite to her dizziness. She found that focusing on something stabilised her vision and lessened the vortex in her mind. She focused on Haruki. 'Where are you hurt?'

When he winced at the light she'd shone in his face, she lowered the torch light and saw him clutching his right leg. She couldn't see too well with the little torch, but from what she did see, it looked very bad. He was clutching his shin and moaning. Blood was everywhere and pumping out of a wound where two jagged bones had ripped up his skin on their way through. The break was so bad that it brought her a fresh wave of nausea. 'Was it the electricity?'

'No.' Haruki grunted his words, but his voice was weak. 'I got hit, but I fell, I think.'

The panic rose up through her like electricity itself. She didn't have any medical training or equipment. She was fast losing him. And even if she could stabilise him, she'd never be able to move him. That was even supposing she could dig her way out of the tunnel.

She flicked the light onto the alien stone. She walked over to it and shone the torch down the fissure that had appeared down its centre. Was it dead? Had they destroyed it? Or had it reset the moment but at a different moment? One that was more advantageous to it? So, things could change. When time jumped, it didn't have to land exactly on the same two feet, or in exactly the same place.

'What's happened?' Haruki called from nearby in the dark, though it sounded like he was very far away.

'It looped again.'

'Is it dead?'

'No, but it's hurt.'

'Call it quits then. Jane...?' His voice tailed off into nothing. It was no more than a ghost of a whisper now. He was fading fast.

She rushed to his side and cradled his head against hers. 'It's okay, Haruki. I'm here. I'm not going anywhere.'

'But I think *I* might be.' Haruki's pain-filled words were so soft that she could hardly hear him.

'I'll hit it again,' she said. 'I'll find another way to hurt it. I'll go and get help. I'll come back. I'll force it to reset to another outcome.'

'No time,' Haruki said, and closed his eyes.

He died just like that. With a shrug and a simple phrase. With clean understatement. She didn't want to believe it at first. She wanted to pound on his chest, to claw at his clothes. She felt like shaking him awake, slapping his face until his eyes opened again and he'd come back to her. In the end, she did neither of those things. She just cradled his head in her hands and held him to her chest. He was gone; he'd bled out. She could do nothing to change that. She just had to give him up.

But that stung her. The ease of which she'd come to that conclusion didn't sit right with her. She wanted to rage, and shout and bemoan her loss in violent ways. She deserved that. Haruki deserved that.

Jane started to sob. She was alone in the dark with her dead husband and all she felt was the tears streaming down her face. Her chest heaved and her shallow breath came thick and wet. At last a response, one that was befitting her situation. But she knew only too well that she wasn't crying because she felt Haruki's death too keenly. She was crying because she felt it too little.

She stopped crying. It wasn't doing her any good. And the show of emotion wasn't for anyone else. There was no one else here. Another emotion slowly clawed its way into Jane's heart. A nagging voice that started on the periphery and then crept around behind her. Then it reached out to grab her. It was panic.

She was trapped underground. The entrance had collapsed and she had no means of escape short of digging herself out. She also felt that the air was getting thin. It wasn't just her crying that had rendered her breathing shallow. She was still panting in short breaths; the air was running out. Reluctantly, she put down her husband and laid him onto the ground as gently as she could. Then she took off her jacket and rolled up her sleeves.

Snatching up the torch from the ground where she'd set it down, she examined the damage to the entrance. It was a landslide. Rubble and stones had fallen in from the hill outside. There were roots and branches mixed in which told her that the disruption was significant. Not just a few stones separating her from the outside but several feet of dirt and soil. She'd have to clear away the bigger boulders by hand, then start digging like a dog.

She didn't have to lift the larger stones. All she had to do was dig with her hands underneath them. Once she undermined their foundations, she found she could pull them back down into the cavern. Where they'd roll and fall somewhere near Haruki, or the alien stone. She found that she didn't care where they fell, as long as they created space at the top of the landslide for her to make progress towards the outside. Her first priority was to open up a breathing hole. It didn't matter how small; she desperately needed to refresh the air in there. She could feel herself getting giddy and weak, and it wasn't just because of the sheer panic of the situation.

She was digging mostly in the dark because she couldn't hold the little torch for long between her teeth. The air became so thin that she needed her mouth wide open to suck it in. Her nails cracked, her fingers bled and she may have broken several of them as they got trapped between two rocks that she was trying to excavate at the same time. Her knees were raw too. And during her struggle, one was shattered by an errant boulder that dislodged itself before she was ready to pull it down. It fell on her patella and now she could feel the pain of the inflammation. It felt three times the size. But she kept digging.

After some time, she checked her progress, shining the little pocket torch onto the pile of rubble. She'd made it only three feet. But it was something. And if she could make it three feet, she could make it six. And six was a full-body length. And a full-body length was perhaps enough for her to break through to the outside. To open up the airway that she was now getting so desperate for.

Jane imagined what it would be like to have fresh air. To smell the open countryside, and feel the wind on her face. The moment when she broke through would be a glorious one. It would banish the musty smell of soil and earth. She would emerge like an earthworm from the hillside and wriggle clear to become a land dweller once again. Sheep would lick her face and…

She realised that she'd stopped digging. In fact, she'd been asleep. Her head was still against the damp earth, a stone at her head. Her gravestone.

She woke again. It was the lack of oxygen sending her to sleep. She knew that, but she could not fight it. She was just so very, very tired. She closed her eyes and felt her heart rate subside to a mere flutter. Soon it was a steady but light beat. She listened intently to it as it soothed her to sleep again.

THE PAINTER
OF COLOURS

Haruki felt the spike of electricity hit him in the chest. It pushed him backwards. He stumbled over a rock on the ground and fell. Trying to protect his head from the stony ground, he brought up his elbows and shielded himself. But as he fell, his right ankle became wedged in the rocky floor and his leg snapped.

The pain was like nothing he'd ever experienced. It was a shockingly forceful break. His whole leg exploded outwards at the shin. Bone shattered, and he felt, or imagined he felt, the spray of blood on his face as his artery was severed.

His mind reeled. His thoughts raced, but he couldn't catch any of them. He felt his lips move, but he couldn't hear what he was saying. He felt Maggie near. Or was it Jane? More wet on his face. It was blood, or tears. It was all the same to him as he closed his eyes. He felt himself being gently laid down. He heard sobbing as someone started to scrape and tear down the blockage at the entrance.

Haruki's mind was shutting down, but strangely he welcomed the same peace of mind that he'd experienced only in prison. Perhaps that's what death was, a prison. Nothing to think about, nothing to do, nothing to be, just peace.

His eyes snapped open. He could hear Jane's exertions a few metres away. He could feel the thump and rumble as she sent a large stone tumbling down towards him. He felt it land short. He saw it land short. He saw everything.

It was no longer dark but a cascade of colour and light. He imagined a blackened hand, as large as he was. It reached out to hold him, steady and still. Carefully, and almost tenderly. He looked down at what was left of his leg. In the dark he could still see, or imagine, black smoke-like tendrils curl and lap upwards and away. Where there was once unbearable pain, there was now simply a steady heat rising.

At the point it was getting too uncomfortable, the black smoky tendrils trailed away, leaving a refreshing icy coolness. Mindful of the fact that it should have been too dark to see, he watched, fascinated, as the bones receded beneath the skin. The artery stopped pumping his precious blood into the ground and his skin began to close over everything. It was like watching a film in rewind, like witnessing the chaos and destruction of a car crash resolve itself, restoring order with every backward creep of the frame.

Until he was as good as new. Better even.

The alien stone pulsated softly with a red glow. Then it intensified in brightness. It pulsated with light and movement; other colours rolled and slithered over each other underneath the red. It grew brighter still, a rich crimson red. The colour of Haruki's blood. It heaved and beat to the rhythm of Haruki's own heart.

It flooded the chamber with light and that light fell on Jane's body. She was no longer breathing. His newly keen senses detected that there was no pulse. No movement at her neck or in front of her ear, no rise and fall of the skin. He could not hear the thump of a heartbeat within her chest.

Haruki reached out to her, and with that, the ruby glow embraced her. It lifted her up and set her on her feet. It swaddled her with a warmth that Haruki could feel on his face. The red light now seemed to come from within her, not from the stone. Her skin became translucent, her organs showed through and her skeleton burned white inside her. The light grew until it threatened to push out the ceiling and walls and expand the boundaries of the cavern.

Then the light calmed and retracted. It grew dimmer, retreating into Jane's body. And when it finally flickered out, Jane was gone. It was now dark, but Haruki still saw everything.

From the direction of the alien stone, a sound came to him. A calming chime that felt like it connected with the baser parts of his hindbrain. The ancient parts that governed instinct, not reason. The parts that Haruki used to channel ideas and create.

White tendrils slithered out over the rocky floor towards him. They roped and bunched and knitted together like snakes, stopping just shy of his feet. He took a step backwards. They didn't encroach further but instead rolled back a little way towards the stone. They danced in the red light glow, weaving and bobbing together, slowly retreating towards the stone. They were not intent on seizing him, Haruki realised; they were not going to take him by force. If anything this was an invitation.

Haruki stepped forward. The translucent white ropes, now pink under the stone's glow, retracted with his movement. Then when he was near, they extended out behind his back and reached up behind him to cradle his body. He felt their touch at his knees and at the nape of his neck. They gently pulled at his shoulders and pushed out at his ankles. He didn't fight it but allowed himself to lean back until they bore him up and cradled him in the air.

The crack in the stone opened wider. It slid silently open to reveal bright pulsating light coming from deep underground. He knew that to be the thing itself. The real beating heart of the alien entity. Its body, and its soul.

In the caress of the tendrils, Haruki was lowered down into that well of light. It grew in intensity and he felt it bright and warm on his face and hands. It had all the properties of sunlight, but he knew it to be different. He understood that this glow had never seen the light of day. It had grown here, incubating and waiting. A seed had arrived long ago from a distant solar system and had taken root underground.

Bathed in the alien glow, he closed his eyes, and waited.

He waited for the end, but it didn't come. He waited for the pain, for the rending of his being. The alien parasite would engulf him and there was nothing he could do but to lie back and allow it to happen. Judy had said it would hurt, and just as Judy wasn't really Judy anymore, he wouldn't be Haruki. He'd die here in this cave and the alien would use his body for its own purposes. Whatever that purpose was wouldn't be his concern. He doubted that he'd be conscious of anything after this.

But the alien glow was warm. Like a comfortable bath. And the pain that he imagined never came. Instead, he was awash with positivity, with warmth and with hope. As the pain in his leg receded completely, he had the sense that whilst the alien was indeed a parasite, feeding off the people it caught in its snares, that wasn't the whole story. It healed, too. It gave something back to those it fed from. It shared.

And it was communicating with him. He felt it inside him. He could not read its thoughts, but he felt its essence. He felt what it was. And everything he previously thought he knew and understood about the alien was wrong.

It took what he didn't need or want. It fed on his pain. Pain and disease and loneliness and dislocation and everything else troubling and discomforting. It cleansed. It healed. It was beneficial.

And as it joined now with Haruki, he knew that it was using everything that was bad within him; it was using his negativity to heal itself. It was infected with the vanity and greed of men, and it needed him to cut that out of it. It allowed him to wield the knife and to sever the connection with the Captain, with Frank and with the village. Haruki was the surgeon. The knifeman.

But he was also the artist. He was a portrait painter. He'd practised this for thousands of hours and he'd studied hundreds of faces. His intense focus felt like he had a relationship with each. Something that drove him and his wife to distraction but that now felt like it was only the practice he needed for this moment. He felt that if he looked deep inside the alien lights pulsating below ground, then he may just be able to see the creature itself. And if he could see it, if he could study it, then he may be able to understand it. And if he was able to understand it, then he was capable of painting a new picture. He could create a new face, or a new landscape. He could create something new. He could try again.

Space, time and causation were all things that this entity had learned to master. But Haruki had the insight that the human mind could create all of these things too. *Intuition is different to objective reality. Art is transcendent.*

He understood now that art is the feeling that flows between all things. It is the universal connector. And if it is not subjugated to the frenzied ambitions of the few, then it can be something beautiful.

Haruki closed his eyes and hoped to God that he was right.

THE RESTORATION

Maggie shook him awake. He was in his own bedroom at the house in Barnes, and light streamed in from the window above the headboard. She kissed his forehead and nibbled his ear. He sat up, drawing the cotton bedsheets over his bare chest, proof against the morning breeze that streaming in from the open window. Finches and robins piped their morning jubilations from the bushes beyond. Maggie slid into bed beside him. She was naked, as he was, and he felt his body react to her skin. His mind reacted to her kisses.

The future is uncertain, but the end is always clear.

Did Maggie say this, or were they just his own thoughts?

We are all dead and dying, but we can find new ways to live in the past.

Maggie blinked at him. It was her voice he heard, but her lips were not moving.

'Enjoy this moment,' she said. 'Enjoy every moment.'

Light streamed in from the open window and folded around her. He tried to kiss her, but she weaved her head like a boxer avoiding a blow. Instead she reached back and handed him a piece of toast. 'Breakfast first.' She laughed and reached back again to fetch something from her bedside table; this time it was a mug of coffee and Haruki accepted it gratefully. 'Jane's in the paper again,' she said.

Haruki took the newspaper that Maggie now dumped on his lap. It was folded over to the arts section and there was a colour photograph of Jane. She was accepting an award from a minor royal. '*MBE for trail-blazing conductor*', ran the headline. She'd sorted out her ensemble in time for the Albert Hall. And she'd been rewarded for it. No, not rewarded, but honoured.

'She's practically royalty now,' Maggie said. 'We'll have to curtsey when she comes home.'

Haruki searched his mind for the relevant connections and he felt a momentary confusion before a warmth flowed through him, heating the back of his head and spreading out through his frontal lobes. It was strange to him at first, but he didn't panic. He had some early sense that this was how it was supposed to be. Then he imagined he felt a tearing in his mind, like a thin but opaque wall of tissue had ripped open to reveal a clear and colourful scene beyond.

This was his new reality. This was where the alien had set him down. At this point in time, and with this outcome. Maggie *and* Jane. He no longer had to make a choice.

Although he had tried to kill it, it had reached out in his final moments and made him whole again. It had restored all of them.

The future was his past, but would it present itself again? What about the Captain, Frank, the villagers? Was he yet to meet them? Would they know him if he did?

Would the outcome always be the same?

'Maggie, do you remember anything about Barrowthwaite?'

Maggie cupped his face in her slender hand. 'Of course,' she said.

Haruki said, 'I died in the cave under Noonday Sun.'

'You feel like you've been given a second chance?'

'What should I do with it?'

'Who knows?' Maggie sat up and drew back the white cotton sheets to reveal her smooth, youthful body. 'But you're the painter, Haruki. So why don't you paint us all a picture?'

EPILOGUE

Haruki stood in the field at the bottom of his garden. He looked down into the shallow pit. With a bit more hard work, it would be deep enough to lie there tonight. Skylarks fluttered and danced above their nests, warbling their liquid threats. The congregation shuffled and stamped uncomfortably in front of him. He'd already kept them waiting too long. Twelve disciples in all, and all of them eager to climb down and resume digging.

'What do I say to them?' he whispered to Maggie at his side.

'Whatever you feel. Just say what comes naturally. There's no magic formula. We just have to dig and lie down.'

'And that will bring it here?'

'Yes, that's enough to call it. You'll be fine, trust me. You'll make a great captain.'

Haruki cleared his throat and stepped forward. 'You have come because I called you,' he said. 'I called your names and you came.' He felt Maggie's supporting hand on his shoulder. A magpie streamed past, the sheen of its dark feathers glinting in the sunshine. The smell of willow herb and jasmine wafted through the air, and from the bottom of the pit came the smell of damp soil, and vanilla.

'I call you with my voice. Who will answer?'

'I will.' Judy stepped forward, smiling. She placed herself in front of him and took both his hands in hers.

'Why have you come?' Haruki said.

'I seek the truth,' Judy said, 'and to put an end to the lie.'

'Which lie?'

'The beautiful lie. The falsehood of living.'

'You want the painful truth? The sincerity of death?'

'Don't we all?' Judy said, and winked.

He turned to his disciples. 'Will you dig for me?'

'We will dig.'

Shovels appeared in Maggie's hands, and she and Judy distributed these amongst the twelve followers. Each climbed down into the shallow pit and resumed their excavation. Judy distributed herself amongst them, showing them where and how to dig, issuing praise and encouragement. She looked up at Haruki and smiled.

'Are we doing the right thing?' he whispered to Maggie.

'Of course, my love. It is almost exactly as the Captain did it.'

'But it didn't end well that time, did it? The entity was corrupted by him. Should we really be bringing it here to us?'

But Haruki didn't need Maggie to answer that question. He looked at Judy. She was so happy to be directing and supporting the congregation. She was so young and full of life. Healthy and vibrant.

And Maggie was so beautiful in the sunlight, with her tousled hair and her skin glowing fresh from their recent lovemaking.

He thought of Jane, happy in her world of music and royal openings and plaudits. She was free to return home at her discretion. She had her freedom, and she still had the stability of their marriage.

Maggie said, 'Things will be different, you'll see.'

He nodded, snatched up a spade and jumped into the pit with the others.

ACKNOWLEDGEMENTS

With love and gratitude to Vicki, Henry, Georgia and Luna. And to Heather, Simon, Paul, David Phillips, Sam, Andrew and all my friends in and of the Lakes.

I am in debt to many who have indulged my musings and given priceless and generous feedback, even though it is so hard to talk to writers about writing. Vicki, Barbara Turner-Vesselago, Marie-Elsa, Nic, Daragh, and the Hawkwood crowd to name a few. And special thanks to the novelist DJ Harrison who promised not to sue if I borrowed his name.

There are, of course, many people involved in the conception and development of Haruki, Jane and the others, and any resemblance to characters living or dead are entirely intentional. They know who they are, but you don't have to.

I could go on, but I don't have the time and space.

Not this time around.